CINNAMON SKY

THE CINNAMON FRY

CINNAMON SKY

Janet Woods

Severn House Large Print
London & New York

This first large print edition published in Great Britain 2007 by
SEVERN HOUSE LARGE PRINT BOOKS LTD of
9-15 High Street, Sutton, Surrey, SM1 1DF.
First world regular print edition published 2006 by
Severn House Publishers, London and New York.
This first large print edition published in the USA 2007 by
SEVERN HOUSE PUBLISHERS INC., of
595 Madison Avenue, New York, NY 10022.

British Library Cataloguing in Publication Data

Woods, Janet, 1939-
  Cinnamon sky. - Large print ed.
  1. Sisters - Fiction 2. Inheritance and succession -
  Fiction 3. Dorset (England) - History - 19th century -
  Fiction 4. Love stories 5. Large type books
  I. Title
  823.9'2[F]

  ISBN-13: 978-0-7278-7625-6

Printed and bound in Great Britain by
MPG Books Ltd, Bodmin, Cornwall.

For my brother Peter,
and his wife Helena, with love.

Janet may be contacted by email
through her website
http://members.iinet.net.au/~woods
or by mail:
PO Box 2099, Kardinya 6163, WA
Australia

One

The Honourable Alexis Patterson had the chicken's neck pinned down under a broom handle. Its beady eye gazed at her as it gave a doleful cluck or two.

'I'm so sorry,' she whispered, and closed her eyes as she jerked its body. She thrust the twitching carcass from her, and shuddered. 'Poor little hen.'

'You've got to stop being so squeamish if we're to survive, Lexi. It hurt you more than it did the hen.'

'But I always liked that hen. She was so sweet.'

Picking the bird up, her sister, Blythe, told her, 'We have five hungry mouths to feed, so we've got to be practical. Besides, the hen's old and has stopped laying.'

'We could have caught a fish instead. Or you could have shot a rabbit.'

'Sometimes it takes forever to catch a fish, and we can't eat rabbit all the time.'

Taking the chicken's carcass to the wood-shed, Blythe, who'd turned seventeen the day before, seated herself on a log, held the bird by its feet and began to energetically rip the feathers from the unfortunate victim. She stopped for a moment to gaze up at her elder sister, her blue eyes sparkling. 'Oh, do stop looking so tragic over it.'

Alexis wished she could be as sensible about matters as Blythe, who seemed to fear nothing.

Soon, Blythe's feet were surrounded by white feathers and the air was filled with bits of flying down.

'What about the insides?' Alexis muttered. 'The cook used to pull them out.'

Blythe grinned at her. 'Don't worry. I'll do it, Lexi. I just hope you know how to cook. Do we have vegetables?'

'I've sent Esmé and Daria to the vegetable garden to see what there is. Celeste is collecting the eggs. I picked some mushrooms this morning and there's half a cabbage. We can boil it all up together in a pan, I expect.'

'It was too bad of the cook to leave.'

Alexis shrugged. 'She was owed wages, so you can't blame her. Mr Hough said there was no money left in the estate to pay staff.'

'The earl squandered what he had. Wine, women and debauchery – whatever that is. He said we had to be careful of men like him, and we should find the fortune that our great grandfathers hid from the revenue men before they were hung, and use it to buy ourselves a decent husband apiece.'

Alexis frowned. 'The late earl was spinning one of his tales. We've looked everywhere, and there is no treasure. Besides I don't want to buy a husband, I want one who truly loves me.'

'The old earl had a good heart. What would have happened to us if he hadn't taken us in after the accident, I wonder? Do we have any relatives?'

'None that I know of. Father inherited debt, and the earl said he wasn't cut out to be a farmer. The earl and papa were the best of friends, I understand. I expect that's why the earl offered us a home, out of loyalty to that friendship.'

Alexis fell silent for a moment, wondering what was going to happen to them if it turned out that there did happen to be a damned Welsh heir. She and Blythe might be able to find employment, and perhaps Celeste, but Daria and Esmé were much too young.

Alexis had been nine when her parents had been buried under a cliff fall in the cove below the house, along with the son and heir. She'd been helping her four younger sisters collect shells at the water's edge, and was the only one who could remember that awful day.

Blythe paused in her task, the light in her

eyes dusted with sadness. 'The earl was such fun though. I do miss him, don't you?'

'Yes, I do, but you were his favourite. He said you had pluck.'

'He told me it was a pity we weren't boys, then we'd be able to defend the place against the damned Welsh. That's why he taught us to shoot and ride astride. He expects us to shoot them if they come sniffing around. He said the ghost ship will sneak into the cove one night and carry us girls off if we're not careful.'

Blythe imitated the gruff voice of the old earl. 'Keep a good watch out for them, you gels. There's plenty of ammunition in the folly, and you'll be able to pick them off one by one from the cliff top as they come up the path.'

Alexis giggled. 'How can we shoot ghosts, when the bullets would go right through them? Mr Hough said that if there were any living Welsh descendants left they certainly aren't living in Wales, since he's searched every nook and cranny. And why would they want to carry us off?'

'To ruin us, of course. Can you imagine what *that* would be like?'

Alexis often wondered what *that* would feel like, since she sometimes had urges she couldn't explain. Instinct told her they were related to becoming a woman. She blushed.

'That's why the earl taught us to shoot,'

Blythe said. 'So we don't get ruined. What does ruined actually mean, Lexi?'

Alexis grimaced. 'I'm not sure. I think it means that a woman loses her virgin state and has a baby out of wedlock. Everybody shuns her because her reputation is lost.'

'But how does the baby get inside the woman in the first place?'

'Do you remember when we saw those horses, and the stallion reared up on to the mare's back?'

'And I asked the earl what was happening and he laughed and said the stallion was just enjoying his oats...' Blythe stared at her. 'Surely it can't be like that for people. It's too awful.'

Alexis shrugged. 'We shouldn't be discussing such matters. It isn't polite.'

'But nobody else is listening, and how else will we find out about ... things?'

'We shall have to wait and see what happens if we ever marry. But I have no intention of shooting anyone. It's ridiculous to suppose the Welsh even know that the Patterson sisters exist, so why should they be making plans to carry us off? We have to remember that we're not related to the earl by blood, and this isn't our house. The manor is our family home. If Mr Hough can't find an heir to Longmore, the title and estate will revert to the crown, I believe.'

'But what if he does find a Welsh heir? He

11

might not want us living here. What will become of us, then?'

'I don't know. We'll have to go back to the manor and do the best we can.'

'But the floors are full of rot, and part of the roof has collapsed. If Mr Hough finds a Welsh heir, he might need a wife. As the eldest, you can marry him and we can stay here.'

'He might not want to marry me. Besides, he'll probably be old and already married.'

'Then I'll definitely shoot him,' Blythe said fiercely, then in the next breath, 'I wonder what a Welsh earl looks like.'

'I saw a drawing of a Welsh farmer in a book. He was big, fierce-eyed and hairy with a bushy beard, and with muscular legs ... from striding over the Welsh mountains, I expect. He carried a lute on his back. All the Welsh sing, I understand. It stops them from feeling lonely when they're in the hills. And he'll like sheep, too...'

'Damned sheep, I didn't realize they were so noisy,' Kynan Trent grumbled to himself, swinging his legs out of the bed.

He gazed through the window into a dimly lit morning, his waking eyes blearily absorbing the rustic scene of the bleating flock of woolly animals, the dog darting back and forth and the shepherd with his crook, as they passed by.

12

The sky was a blanket of dark grey. Only a trace of pale yellow on the horizon hinted that dawn intended to put in an appearance.

Country folk obviously rose at the crack of dawn, he thought, and that suited him today. Were he still in London he'd have slept for another hour, then exercised his mount in the park before eating a leisurely breakfast.

He stretched as he stood, his muscular, naked body relishing the movement after a night spent on an unyielding and lumpy mattress. His knuckles brushed against the inn ceiling as he reached full height.

As Kynan wondered if his valet had risen, for he wanted to make an early start on the second leg of his journey, a knock came at the door. 'Are you awake, my Lord?'

Kynan grinned. Even his man sounded self-conscious addressing him thus. But they must both get used to it, since he was no longer Mr Kynan Trent, head of a successful London import and wholesaling company. Recently he'd been informed that he'd inherited the title of earl, and the Dorset estate of the Earl of Longmore.

He shook his head, still surprised by it. He'd been unaware that the Trent family was related to a peer.

'Lack of communication was due to a feud between brothers,' the lawyer, Richard Hough had told him. 'We've traced the lines and you're the only surviving family member, though we didn't expect to find you living in London.'

Kynan had raised an eyebrow at that. Although he knew his paternal grandfather's family had originated in Wales, he'd never once set a foot on Welsh soil. 'I know nothing of any feud.'

'Oh, it dates back two hundred years or more. It was over a woman. She was about to marry the eldest brother when she was snatched from the altar by your ancestor and carried off to Wales, where he had inherited some property. The earl at the time swore that none of his brother's descendants would ever be acknowledged again. Each earl since has signed a paper to abide by his decision.'

Kynan had chuckled at that. 'You surely won't expect me to sign it before I inherit the title and estate.'

'Hardly, my Lord, since that would be to defeat the object of my visit.'

'Then I'm to take it that I'll have the dubious honour of being the first member of my side of the family to set foot on Longmore Estate in several generations?'

'Quite so,' the lawyer said in a sympathetic tone.

To which Kynan had offered a sharp look. 'Is there something wrong with the place?'

'Unfortunately, the late earl let the estate run down on account of the feud, since he had no heirs of his own. He wouldn't have wanted a Welsh heir to be handed a going concern, you understand. I will, of course, take care of the legal formalities.'

Kynan had found it hard to understand that someone would deliberately allow an estate to go to rack and ruin on account of an old quarrel. Not that money was a problem to him. The family business was an ongoing and lucrative concern, and he'd received a healthy legacy recently from the estate of his grandfather.

Nevertheless, Kynan now gazed in the direction of the county of Dorset with some trepidation, and the hint of an ironic smile. Of late he'd been bored with life. Although he worked hard, too many pleasures had jaded him.

Now life had thrown him a challenge, and he was glad of it.

He bade his man enter when the knock came for a second time.

James Mitchell was a man of average build. He didn't possess the servile nature expected of servants, an attitude which had lost him several positions in the past. But he wasn't intrusive. He suited Kynan, who found James to be quick-minded and good at his job, as well as being discreet and loyal. With James, Kynan could enjoy conversation on many topics. Kynan also discovered him to be a physical match for fencing. He paid

15

him well for his services.

Soon, the dark stubble on Kynan's chin was gone, and he was turned out impeccably for the ride.

While the stable lad saddled their mounts and their bags were being evenly distributed on the pack horse, the two men ate a hearty breakfast.

The serving maid bustled around them, slanting her brown eyes towards James and pressing her bosom against his shoulder as she set in front of them plates of sizzling bacon, eggs and pork sausages.

They made short work of it, wiping the grease from their plates with chunks of crusty bread spread with thick yellow butter. In its turn, that was washed down with a mug of sweet tea.

'I hope I made you comfortable, sir,' the maid said to James, giving him a smile when he slid her some coins.

James playfully slapped her arse. 'I'll pay you a visit again the next time I'm passing through Lyndhurst.'

Kynan grinned as the woman walked off, her hips twitching from side to side. 'Worth the hire?'

'She lacked finesse, but I managed,' James said modestly.

The two men rode out into an apricot-tinted dawn which progressed into a rather cool April day.

It was pretty country they were passing through. Tender green leaves filled with the rising of spring, flew like flags from the tree branches, while groups of daffodils clustered in pale and lambent yellows underneath their shade.

'Are birds usually this noisy in London, James?' Kynan asked.

His servant eyed a small blob of white on his thigh with a sigh of displeasure. 'No, my Lord. It appears to me that birds are more prolific here. And they appear to defecate more often.'

At midday they stopped at the Antelope Hotel in Dorchester for refreshment and to ask directions. The excellent pork pies they ate were served with a tankard of ale.

The ostler provided them with the information. He had a girl with him of about twelve years, who held the horses' reins and smiled.

'The village of Longmore be a half hour or so to the south east. Twenty minutes further'n that is Longmore House. You can't miss it. Leastwise, I hope not, since to do so will find yourself fallin' over the edge of the cliff and into the sea.'

The ostler cackled with laughter at his own joke. 'The village is but a short ride past the old manor. Used to be a thriving place, and all, but now 'tis almost abandoned since the estate hasn't been worked for some time.

17

The estate's agent used to live in the dower house just outside the village, though 'tis standing empty now. There be a couple of people who keeps an eye on the place.' His eyes went to the horses. 'I've given your mounts a good rub down, and though they be weary, I reckon they've got the pace left in them if you go nice and easy. 'Tis some fine beasts you have there. Be a shame to ruin them.'

'Thank you for the advice,' Kynan said politely, though not really needing it as he and James swung themselves up into their saddles.

The man's glance wandered from one to the other, an unspoken question in it. They settled on Kynan. 'The old earl passed on a little while back. You're not from these parts. Are you one of those lawyers come down from London who be helping old Hough look for an heir to the title?'

James said rather grandly, 'This gentleman is the heir, the Earl of Longmore, himself.'

The ostler turned to his daughter, saying sharply, 'Get yourself in to help your mother, Millie, and be quick about it. We don't want you noticed by the damned Welsh,' and he spat into the straw. 'The old earl was right worried it'd come to this one day.'

'Come to what?'

To which question the stablehand whipped his cap off to release a thatch of greasy hair, saying deferentially. 'Beggin' your pardon, my Lord. No disrespect was offered.'

'None was taken.' Kynan bestowed a faintly bemused smile on the man and dropped some coins into his palm before he turned his horse's head towards the coast with James following after.

After a few moments' thought, Kynan threw back his head and laughed. 'Good God, it's that damned stupid feud again. The ostler was worried I might carry off his daughter.'

'If she'd been older you'd probably have given him cause to worry,' James said irreverently.

'Nonsense. I'm very nearly a married man.'

'You've proposed then, sir?'

'I haven't got around to it yet, but I imagine I will, once I've decided what to do with my inheritance.'

'Mrs Spencer is an admirable woman in every way,' James said, though his words lacked conviction.

Julia most certainly was admirable. She was flawless – a graceful, grey-eyed beauty with a ready wit, who had put her widowhood behind her and was generous with her affections towards him. So why was he holding himself back from taking the final step to the altar?

'I value your opinion James. Be honest.

Can you find any fault with Mrs Spencer?'

'I have nothing against the lady herself, sir, just a mistrust of perfection. If I may be so bold, her wit can be a little ... sharp and narrowly focussed, and may prove incompatible with your own, which seems to find humour in every situation.'

'A small imperfection.'

'As you say, sir.'

Kynan's attention was drawn to what appeared to be the manor the ostler had spoken about. It dated back to Tudor times, would have been quite beautiful once, and still could be if the garden was rescued from the weeds and the hole in the roof was repaired. What a shame that it had been left to go to rack and ruin.

He had a sudden thought that Longmore Hall might have suffered the same fate, since the fields about them were overgrown with tall grass instead of the healthy young crops displayed elsewhere in the county.

Anger filled him because what seemed to have once been a thriving business, had been allowed to run down for the sake of a stupid feud. But obviously, old grudges died hard in these parts.

Behind a low stone wall, the former agent's house stood in a verdant garden carpeted with daffodils. The house was undoubtedly old, but of decent size and design, and built of mellowed stone. It was roofed in slate.

They stopped, and, finding the back door unlocked, went inside to inspect the place. Dust lay thickly over everything, but the house smelt dry and the furniture was solid.

'A pretty place, I wouldn't mind living here myself,' Kynan murmured.

Longmore village itself was a straggle of thatched cob cottages either side of a wide street. A picturesque church with a square Norman tower and an overgrown graveyard was half hidden by beech trees and a low stone wall. The place seemed to be almost uninhabited, though Kynan could almost feel eyes watching them from behind the windows. An old couple sat in the afternoon sun, a couple of children came running out of nowhere to take a look at them, and a black cat slunk off into the shadows at their approach.

Running down the estate would have put the villagers out of work. Where had they gone? Could he, a businessman with no knowledge of farming, put the Longmore Estate back on a sound, productive footing?

Much depended on the state of the house, of course. Kynan was not prepared to invest money into the estate if he couldn't count on it being returned if he sold the place.

His mind began to tick over, making a list of what he knew would be needed. He could live here while it was going on, he thought. He had a perfectly reliable manager in London to run the business there.

As they moved further towards the coast the land took on a slight downward incline. The breeze became stronger and carried with it the smell of salt.

Beyond a strand of trees they drew their horses to a halt and took in the breathtaking view. 'That must be Longmore Hall.'

Built of stone which had weathered to a dull grey, and surrounded on three sides by a thicket of trees, it left itself open to the view over the sea. The house seemed to be a solid and comfortable nest.

Behind the building they caught a glimpse of a stable block, a decent-sized house that was probably intended for the agent he didn't have, and some walled gardens. To the left and behind the trees barns and out-buildings stood. Perched near the cliff edge was a charming folly with castellated walls. Kynan imagined it might have been built by a knight for a lady to sit and dream in on a summer afternoon.

He smiled at the thought.

Accompanied by the sound of laughter, a dappled plough horse came out of a field with two girls seated astride its back. They were blue-eyed charmers of about eleven years, with light brown hair curling around their shoulders, and bare legs and feet. They offered him merry smiles as the horse plodded past. 'I'm Daria Patterson and she's

Esmé Patterson. Who are you? Are you coming to visit us?'

'I'm the new owner of Longmore.'

'It's the damned Welsh heir,' the one calling herself Daria whispered urgently. 'Hold tight, Es, we'd better tell Alexis and Blythe so they can be prepared.' She dug her heels into the horse's side and the beast picked up speed, the two girls clinging to its back as it lolloped in ungainly fashion towards the house.

Kynan raised an eyebrow, wondering how they were managing to stay on its back, and James grinned. 'At least there will be someone to greet you. Alexis must be the housekeeper.'

His own horse was too tired to do anything but walk. Dismounting, Kynan urged James to do the same and they ambled down towards the house, leading their horses, enjoying the change after such a long ride.

'Those girls are too young to be maids. They must belong to one of the servants. At least there will be a reception committee.'

But when they got to the house there was no sign of anyone. The front door was wide open. An old dog wandered out to bark crustily at them, but more in duty than with intent, since its tail flapped lazily back and forth.

'The damned Welsh heir is on his way?' somebody said in a startled voice from an open window above them. 'Oh, my good-ness! Where is he?'

There came a scuffle and a head was poked out of the window to stare in the direction of the sea. 'I can't see a ship. I can't see any-one.'

'Look down here,' Kynan said drily.

A pair of blue eyes in a perfect oval face framed by dark hair lowered to gaze straight into his. They widened. 'We were expecting you to come by sea. Are you really the Welsh heir? We thought you'd be older.'

He thought it judicious not to declare himself right at that moment. 'Actually, I'm from London and my name is Kynan. My companion is James Mitchell, who is my manservant.' He smiled at this vision peering at him out of the upper reaches of the house.

Her delicious mouth curved into a return-ing smile – one which quickly faded as she looked beyond him and shouted urgently, 'No, don't, Blythe.'

Turning, Kynan found himself peering down the barrel of a pistol.

'Stand very still,' the girl holding it said. 'State your business.'

'His name is Mr Kynan,' the one at the window said. 'Do put that down, Blythe. You can't go around shooting people, whatever the old earl said.'

'But the girls told me he was the damned Welsh heir, Lexi.'

'They must have been mistaken. But even if he was, he'd have a perfect right to be here, since this is his home.'

Kynan blessed her good sense. 'Have you shot many people?' he said in a friendly manner to the other one, wishing she'd point the weapon in another direction.

'Not yet. You'd be my first.'

The girl called Blythe resembled the one at the upper window except her hair was a lighter colour and she hadn't quite developed into a woman. 'I'm saving my first kill for the damned Welsh heir.'

From the upstairs came the sound of a muttered prayer, which wasn't very encouraging. 'Dear God save this poor sinner from Blythe.'

Behind him, James was nearly choking with repressed laughter. Kynan felt like laughing himself, and would have if the delicate hand holding the pistol hadn't been rock steady, and the trigger finger primed with just the right amount of tension. He'd have to divert the attention of this lunatic female, and fast.

He found his voice, loaded it with charm. 'I'm sure the damned Welsh heir is more worthy of your attention. Are you a good shot, my dear?'

Blythe smiled. 'The late earl himself taught me. He said I was better than anyone he'd ever known. See that post over there?' The wood splintered as she took aim and discharged the weapon.

'Thank you, God,' came the soft voice from upstairs.

Anger flooded through him and he hurled a dark look up at the one called Lexi. 'I want all the members of this household to assemble in the drawing room in half an hour. I have something to say to you.'

Her eyes widened and she uttered a soft, 'Oh!'

'You, with the pistol. Hand that gun to my manservant, at once. If you ever threaten me with it again, you'll be handed over to the authorities, I promise you.'

Relief surged through him when she did as she was told, but her bottom lip began to tremble and her eyes flooded with tears as her bravado collapsed. Without her weapon she was only a vulnerable young girl. He liked her better that way.

He handed her his handkerchief to dry her tears on, then bent to pat the dog as he moved towards the steps leading up to the main door. A low growl rumbled from the animal's throat. He swiftly removed his hand, despite his intuition telling him the dog was more menace than might.

Laughter floated down to him, but when he looked up Alexis was no longer there.

A little while later they were lined up in front of him, five females with similar looks ranging in age. Five pairs of eyes in various shades of blue gazed at him with frank curiosity.

'Let me introduce myself,' he said. 'I am the new owner of Longmore.'

The looks they exchanged were varied. 'He *is* the damned Welsh heir,' the middle one whispered almost to herself, her voice trembling with fright. 'What will become of us?'

'This is my estate. You may address me as Lord Trent, or my Lord. You may *not* address me or refer to me as the Welsh heir, the damned Welsh heir, or any other insulting variation you might think of. In fact, if anyone mentions Welsh to me again I'll send you to Wales on the next damned boat. Understood?'

The middle girl, who was about fourteen, gave a nervous hiccup then burst into tears.

Blythe handed his handkerchief over to the weeping child for a second soaking. 'You don't have to bully us.'

'I'm sorry.' Why was he apologizing? This was his house and these young women were employed by him. He was used to an ordered life, and didn't have to apologize. They did.

His glance went to the oldest one. Her smile told him she was enjoying his discomfort.

'Perhaps you'd like to explain to Miss

Blythe that it was she who was bullying me, earlier. After that, perhaps you'd care to enlighten me to the reason behind the extraordinary behaviour and rudeness I've been forced to endure since my arrival.'

She spread her hands. 'It's all to do with the feud, you see. My sisters were expecting you to arrive from the sea, if you arrived at all. The old earl has filled their heads with nonsense about – ' she quirked an eyebrow – 'the *unmentionable* branch of his family. I do hope you will forgive us.'

The little touch of irony was unexpected, but it was said so prettily that Kynan felt his insides melt. This girl was a force to be reckoned with. 'I imagine I'll stretch a point on this occasion. Where's the rest of the staff?'

'There is no staff. We, that is my sisters and I, live here as guests of the earl ... of the late earl.'

Matters were becoming clearer to him now. 'You'd better introduce yourselves and explain your circumstances to me.'

'I'm Alexis Patterson. These are my sisters, the Honourable—'

'I'll take the honourable part for granted.'

She smiled graciously at him. 'Thank you, my Lord, it is rather a mouthful. Blythe. Celeste—'

'I look after the chickens and collect the eggs,' Celeste interrupted, her eyes only slightly damp now, so his guilt over the accusation of bullying her lessened.

'Daria and Esmé are the youngest. They're a year apart in age.'

Alexis smiled when the pair made a graceful curtsy and said, 'Welcome to Longmore Hall, my Lord.'

All rehearsed to appease him, no doubt, since the Honourable Miss Patterson bestowed an affectionate and approving smile on them. She was all set to disarm him, but he wasn't about to allow himself to be handled.

'Why are you all living here, in my home, Miss Patterson?'

Imperceptibly, her eyes narrowed. 'The late earl took us in when our parents died. We have nowhere else to go except the manor, which is in a dangerous condition.'

'It can be repaired.'

'Financially, we're not in the position to undertake those repairs.'

Daria piped up, 'Unless we find the fortune our families hid from the revenue men, ouch—!' Esmé had kicked her on the ankle.

Blythe was sniffing the air like a hound.

'What on earth are you doing?' Alexis said to her.

'I can smell burning.'

The girls looked at each other in consternation then Alexis said, 'The chicken!' They scattered, heading off at a run.

Kynan turned to James. 'What d'you think?'

James chuckled. 'A spirited, but delightful pack of females. If I were you I'd beware, sir.'

'I am bewaring, but I feel as though I've walked into a lunatic asylum. I didn't expect to inherit five female guests. Hough should have warned me. Did I handle the situation adequately?'

'You could say that, since you're still alive and kicking, my Lord.'

'So I am,' Kynan said darkly. 'What on earth am I going to do with a pack of honourable young ladies, especially when two of them are old enough to be wed?'

James grinned.

'Definitely not!' Kynan said. 'Seduction is not on my agenda. They are to be treated with the utmost respect. Understand!'

'Yes, my Lord.'

The dog thrust its snout into Kynan's hand and huffed a steamy and sympathetic breath into it. He automatically fondled it and was snarled at.

'Be quiet, I'm in charge around here,' he snarled back, and to his surprise, the animal stopped growling at once.

Two

Dinner was a disaster, since Alexis had allowed the pan to boil dry. Although she removed the burnt bits and added more water to the pot, the lovely mushroom-flavoured sauce she'd envisioned had turned into a thin and tasteless brew.

Well, almost tasteless. As the damned Welsh heir had said, as he had given her a churning look from under his dark brows. 'I've never met anyone who could burn water before.'

And worse still, the hen she'd slaughtered had had the last laugh, since it proved to be as tough as leather. No wonder it had stopped laying, it had been ready to drop dead from old age. At least the cabbage and onions were soft, though.

When the earl shook his head and grinned at her, she thought rebelliously: Perhaps he'll choke on a bone and we'll be rid of him.

But he didn't oblige her. Instead, he stoically chewed his way through the small portion of meat he'd been allocated, then grimaced and set his knife and fork aside.

31

'Miss Patterson, perhaps you'd be kind enough to show me the quarters the former earl used to occupy before it gets dark. The rest of you can show James where the kitchen is, and help him clear the dishes away.'

He followed her up the wide staircase. Alexis took him to the front of the house and threw open the door to a corner chamber with its splendid views to the south and east over the cove and to the horizon beyond.

'The late earl used to sleep here. It's the best room in the house. It's been cleaned, and I've packed most of his clothes away.'

Lord Trent's glance went to the solid four-poster bed, as if expecting to see the late earl's body lying in state, there.

Her mouth quirked at one corner. 'He didn't die in his bed. He died in Longmore church, at the Sunday service. We thought he'd fallen asleep during Reverend Curruthers's sermon.' She smiled. 'The earl told the reverend he'd bore him to death with his sermons one day. And he did. The reverend is quite proud of that. He said God had given him the last laugh, which had served to strengthen his faith.'

Lord Trent chuckled. He was a handsome man, nothing like Alexis had expected one of the damned Welsh to look like. A lean, firm face featured high cheekbones, shadowed hollows underneath. His dark green eyes were flecked with brown and gold. His skin had an exotic hint of the foreign to it, as if it had been burnished with gold.

She realized he was looking back at her with a rather quizzical expression and started. 'I'm sorry the dinner was inedible. You see, the cook left to live with her sister in Dorchester two days ago, because she was owed a year's wages and it didn't look as though she was going to be paid it, so she thought she'd better look for another job. I've never cooked anything before. And I had to kill the hen first.'

'Then it was a laudable effort, and I'm sure we'll all survive it. Except for the fowl of course. It was a tough old bird.'

She shuddered. 'I hated killing her. She clucked at me and made me feel guilty.'

When he smiled, so warm did that firm and generous mouth of his become that her cheeks heated from the glow of it as he said, 'You're obviously soft-hearted. Had I known you were called to such trouble, I wouldn't have been so mean as to tease you about it. My sincerest apologies, Miss Patterson. Can you forgive me?'

Attacked by a sudden fluttering in the region of her heart, Alexis smoothed down the blue-checked skirt of her second best gown. She could not afford to upset this man, lest they be thrown out to fend for themselves. 'Oh yes, of course. Totally. I'm sure you'd never be deliberately mean to anyone, my Lord.'

His eyelids flickered slightly and she wondered if she'd gone too far. But he merely chuckled, then said smoothly, 'Where do you sleep?'

She stared at him and stammered, 'Me ... with my sisters. The earl gave us three rooms along the west side of the house. We're on the other side of the staircase. We also have a sitting room to use for ourselves, where we can sew or paint.' She smiled fondly. 'He used to send us there when he was tired of our chatter, or was entertaining, or when he just preferred his own company. We lock the doors at night,' she thought to tell him.

'In case the damned Welsh heir comes to carry you all off?'

She laughed. 'I hope you don't feel inclined to prove the legend, my Lord.'

'All I feel inclined to do at the moment is sleep.'

He moved closer and gazed reflectively at her, a faint aroma of spice about him reminding her of the faraway places the old earl had told her about.

Anxiously, she asked him, 'Have you decided on our fate?'

'I won't throw you out, if that's what's worrying you. But this is not an ideal situation for yourself and your sisters to be in. You must know that.'

'We've lived here since I was nine years old. Daria and Esmé practically grew up here and regard it as their home.'

'What happened to your parents?'

'They were looking for the hidden treasure; our father's business investments had gone sour and he was never much of a farmer. He'd previously found a passage in the cellar of the old manor, but it was blocked. He thought there might be a cave at the base of the cliff in the cove and drew a map of the likely course it would take. We were all digging there. My sisters were too young to be excited over such a task, so I took them to the water's edge to collect seashells. The cliff face collapsed on to our parents and buried them, along with our baby brother, who was with them.'

'I'm so sorry.'

'By the time we got here to ask the earl for help it was too late. That's when he took us in. He's been very kind to us. At first, he farmed our land along with his, to pay for our keep. Then he became unwell and lost interest. And when the agent was dismissed and refused to return the earl said he didn't have any strength left, and the estate could go to rack and ruin since he had no heirs that he knew of.'

The earl nodded. 'Thank you for telling me, Miss Patterson.'

'I'm the only one of us who remembers our

parents or the tragedy. To my sisters, the old earl was like family ... a revered grandfather perhaps.'

'I understand.' He took a step back, saying softly, 'Where's the bedding kept?'

'Oh, I'll fetch some, and I'll make your bed and find you some candles, as well.'

'Just bring the bedding and candles, if you would. I'm capable of making my own bed. James can sleep next door for tonight, in case Miss Blythe makes another attempt on my life.'

'She wouldn't ... Oh! You're teasing me again, my Lord.'

'Yes, I am, and you might have to get used to it.' He grinned and caressed her cheek with the tip of his finger.

That was something she *could* grow used to, she thought, and she hurried away before he saw the blush that rose to her cheeks.

After Kynan had organized the bed he seated himself in the chair by the window, his mind running through the seemingly endless tasks.

First up, James must be sent to Dorchester to hire some servants. He could discover the whereabouts of the cook and lure her back with the promise of the wages she was owed.

He would personally drop in on the solicitor, Mr Hough, and ask his advice about hiring a good manager for the estate.

He'd noticed a cart outside the stable, and they had a sturdy horse to pull it, so he would take that and make sure they, and the horses, had some provisions.

The sun had gone down now, the sea was a dull stretch of grey and the gloaming was filled with a purple light.

Kynan heard footsteps on the gravel below and a whispered, 'Jasper, where are you? It's bed time.' The soft whistle Alexis gave was answered by a husky bark.

He heard James's voice and the bolts being drawn across the front door.

Soon, there came a scrabbling at his bedroom door. It swung open and Jasper padded across the floor to where he sat. He placed a paw on his knee. His whole body was wagging along with his tail.

'Ah, we're to be friends then,' Kynan said, patting the creature. The dog licked his hand then settled at his feet with a sigh.

Lighting a candle from the lantern burning in the passage outside, Kynan wrote a letter to his mother, and another to his manager in London. He might be in time to get them on the mail coach in the morning. If not, they would go the next day, since there seemed to be less urgency to life here.

Peace stole over him. Longmore was a far cry from London with its theatres and parties. The air was fresh here. He could hear the soothing shush of the sea against the shore.

As it grew darker a tiny sliver of moon appeared like a smile amongst the stars. He smiled back at it. How peaceful it all was. When James knocked gently at his door, he said. 'Is all well, James?'

'All is well, sir.'

'Then close the door behind you and find yourself a bed next door, I can fend for myself tonight.'

After James bade him goodnight, Kynan sat there for a while, his ears taking in the alien sounds of the house. Then he blew out the candle, stripped naked and padded across the floor to climb into bed.

He sank into a mattress of feathers that smelled of sunshine, so he knew it had been washed recently, and certainly since the late earl had last slept here.

He'd already decided to get the estate on to a sound footing, but would he sell it? If he married and had a son it would be his duty to hold these lands for the next heir to have title over.

And his second son could inherit the merchandising business. And he'd have a couple of daughters to delight the eye.

Alexis Patterson came into his mind. What the hell was he to do with the Patterson girls?

He knew what he'd like to do with the eldest one, but to dwell on it would be detrimental to his own comfort. Forcing the thought from his mind, and with the sheets cool against his skin and a smile on his face, Kynan slipped almost immediately into a deep and untroubled sleep.

A shot woke Kynan. It was followed almost immediately by a second one.

A shout of jubilation reached his ears. 'I got both of them.'

He sat up, wide awake now and hurriedly reached for his clothes. Blythe Patterson was obviously at large with a gun. Who the hell had she shot?

Half-dressed, he took long strides to the window and gazed out. Nothing. He bounded down the stairs and along a corridor. Down another flight of stairs. To his left he could hear faint sounds of laughter. He followed the sound through a narrow corridor, to find himself standing in a doorway to the kitchen.

They all had their backs to him. Daria said, 'The cow tried to kick me when I milked her this morning and I only got a jug full.'

'That's because you don't grip her teats firmly enough and she gets sore. I'll finish her off. She can't be left unmilked else she'll be upset and carry on all day.'

He experienced relief when Blythe hung a pair of dead rabbits from a hook. 'Have we got a knife sharp enough to skin and gut these?'

'I sharpened one yesterday,' Alexis told her.

'You didn't do it very well, since it was still blunt.'

Alexis sighed. 'I'm not very good at such things and there's so much to think about, and so much to do. Celeste, have you checked the coop for eggs?'

'There were only seven eggs. Betty and Alice didn't lay any. They're sulking because we ate their sister last night.'

'Tell them they'll end up in the same pot if they don't produce eggs. We'd better give two eggs each to the earl and his man, since they're his chickens, and men have bigger appetites.'

Daria wailed, 'What will *we* eat for breakfast?'

'There will be an egg each for you three. Blythe and I will go without. We'll have to drink milk. There's some flour left, so I'll make some griddle cakes. And what about the mushrooms I picked this morning.'

'I'm sick of eating mushrooms.'

'I know, my love, but we've got to eat something. We can go into the village and buy some bread.'

'What with? We spent our last shilling on bacon last week, and it's such a long walk to Longmore when you're hungry.'

'I'll go to the manor and find something

we can exchange, a silver spoon perhaps.'

'You can't, Alexis. The place is too dangerous. The architect said the whole structure is weak. The building might collapse on top of you.'

Kynan's eyes narrowed. He must prevent Alexis from doing anything so foolish.

'Can't we ask the earl for some money? We could offer to be his maids and get paid for our work.'

'We're not competent enough to be maids, and he knows it. That dinner I cooked last night was no recommendation.'

Blythe laughed. 'Your face went all red when he said he'd never met anyone who could burn water before.'

'I like him,' Celeste said. 'He told me he was sorry he made me cry.'

Daria's head cocked to one side. 'He's got fierce eyebrows when he frowns.'

'But kind eyes,' Esmé offered.

'His horse is a fine beast. I wish it were mine.' Blythe gazed towards the outside door when the cow began to low. She heaved a sigh. 'She's complaining already. Pass over the bucket, would you, I'd better get her milked before she wakes up the damned Welsh heir.'

'You're not supposed to call him that, Blythe. Besides, he's no longer the heir.'

'I know, but we've called him that for such a long time that it's hard to stop, especially since half the district has called his branch of the family the damned Welsh for years. I wonder if he knows he's legendary in these parts.'

'I don't suppose it will be long before he finds out. Can you imagine how incensed the old earl's ghost would have been when he discovered Lord Trent snoring away in his bed,' Alexis said. 'It's a wonder he didn't cut off his head while he slept.'

Kynan grinned and backed silently away as they all began to giggle.

Betty and Alice must have responded to the threat, for everyone seemed to have an egg for breakfast.

'I'd like to see you in the study later, Miss Patterson,' he said.

She presented herself in the same patched gown she'd worn the day before. Her hair was neatly braided and tied with a blue ribbon. When she bobbed him a curtsy he was astounded, until he remembered the title.

'I want to thank you for looking after Longmore Hall so well, Miss Patterson. I request that you please accept this as a token of my thanks.' He pushed ten crowns across the desk.

As she stared at the money colour tinted her cheeks. Her eyes came up to his, blue and clear, slightly accusatory. 'You overheard us talking in the kitchen, didn't you?'

Kynan saw no reason to be less than honest. 'Yes. It's obvious you and your sisters are in need, and have been for some time. Are you going to be tedious and refuse it?'

'My first reaction is that I should, since you created a reason to offer the money to me.'

'That's pride talking, and totally untrue. Remember telling me that the earl farmed your land in return for giving you a home?'

'Yes.'

'I glanced through the estate books for the few years he farmed your land. The income he received from the produce far outstripped the cost of the care you and your sisters received. It was money he could have used to maintain your house. In other words, the late earl profited from having you living here.'

She smiled at that. 'I believe you are a clever man who is manipulating me to get his own way.'

He indicated a pile of account books. 'You may see the evidence for yourself if you like.'

She picked up one of the books, then placed it down again, her eyes all at once uncertain. 'But the debt is his, not yours.'

'The debt is owed by the estate, as it owes wages to the previous staff. Come, Lexi,' he said softly. 'This is only a small amount. Think of what you can do with it.'

'Daria and Esmé do need new boots.' She picked up the money, but there were tears pricking at her eyes. 'Thank you.'

'My pleasure,' he said, and meant it.

Three

They had written a list of essential items over breakfast. Even so, it was a long one, for the earl had been thorough.

Alexis went on ahead with the horse and cart, Daria and Esmé perched up beside her, chattering happily at the thought of owning a new pair of boots apiece. The rest of them would stay behind to go about their tasks. They were hardly on their way when they came across the cook. Red of face, she was seated on her bag panting for breath.

'Mrs Dawson,' Alexis cried out, overjoyed to see her. 'You've come back.'

'I heard the earl had arrived and thought he'd need a cook. I know I said I wouldn't work for the damned Welsh, but the fact is, I sorely need a position and beggars can't be choosers.'

'We're not allowed to call him damned Welsh any more,' Daria said to her.

To which Esmé added, 'He'll send us to Wales if we do.'

'Lord Trent is not Welsh. He's English, and comes from London.' Alexis changed the subject, since it didn't seem right to gossip about their benefactor. 'It's a long trudge from Dorchester, Mrs Dawson, you must be fatigued.'

'I thought I'd start out early since there's others coming after, miss. And I heard that Ada Brown, who worked under me before is after my job. But I'm that worn out from hurrying since before dawn, that I don't think I can take another step.'

'In that case, come up on to the cart and I'll take you down to the house.'

As she pulled the cart to a halt, the earl and his man were just coming out of the stable yard. Lord Trent was impeccably turned out in a donkey brown jacket and tall crowned hat, his legs encased in tan, calf-length leather boots over a pair of fawn trousers.

His horse danced prettily as he reined it in. The pair were a magnificent sight, Alexis thought, smiling at the sight of him.

James Mitchell dismounted and helped the cook down as Alexis informed them, 'This is Mrs Dawson, our former cook. She has heard that staff are needed and is here to offer her services.'

Mrs Dawson promptly curtseyed to the earl, who had a wicked smile on his face as his eyes flickered towards Alexis. 'Ah, that's good. I'm relieved you've turned up, since I'm in need of a decent meal.'

Mrs Dawson's smile had a smug edge to it. 'And you'll get one, my Lord, that I promise.'

'Good ... good. James, take Mrs Dawson's bag inside. No doubt she will show you where she's situated. You can catch up with us.'

'There are others on their way, my Lord,' Mrs Dawson said. 'Some who were in the service of the old earl, and they know better than to wait until the positions are advertised. The housekeeper, two of the maids and a stablehand are not far behind me. They're all honest, hardworking folk.' She sniffed. 'Ada Brown used to work under me in the kitchen before, though she tries to pass herself off as a cook.'

'Then she can work under you again if she wishes. We're on the way into town to purchase some urgently needed provisions at the moment, Mrs Dawson. I'll interview them when we return.'

'I'll personally provide reference for the housekeeper, my Lord,' Alexis told him. 'If you employ her straight away it will save you the task of interviewing the female house staff yourself.'

'Did you hear that, Mrs Dawson? Tell the housekeeper she can resume her former duties straight away if she wishes. Come along, Miss Patterson, turn that cart around and let's be on our way.'

A few moments later he brought his horse alongside the cart and smiled at her. 'Thank you for your advice. If you have any more, let me hear it, since I'm still in training for this new position of mine and you have the advantage.'

She laughed at that. 'The most important thing will be to hire yourself a competent agent to manage the estate. By the time the ploughing has been done it will be too late to plant a corn crop, but you should be able to grow some cabbage seedlings and transplant them in May. And there are also root vegetables that can be planted, such as carrots, turnips and potatoes. And if you buy a few sheep and cattle at the markets they can be fattened up for winter. Piglets too, for they can be smoked for bacon. I doubt if the estate will bring in any profit for a year or two though.'

Kynan had a bemused look in his eyes. 'I didn't realize farming was so complicated.'

'Oh, it isn't. You just have to learn what to plant each month, when it's time to harvest it, and how to sell it and where. As long as the rain comes when it's supposed to, and not when it shouldn't ... and as long as the sun shines when it's supposed to—'

'And not when it shouldn't,' he said.

'Then you will profit from the earth. Praying helps as well.'

'In other words, farming is as simple as

making a chicken stew without burning it, yes?'

He was grinning now, and she laughed. 'If you hadn't surprised us by turning up so unexpectedly, the stew might have turned out better.'

'Nothing would have made that chicken tender. You came as a surprise to me, too. A rather pleasant one now I've grown used to you. Where did the former agent go?'

'John Hardin left three years ago after an argument with the earl. He took a position in Wiltshire, I believe.'

'What was the argument about?'

'I'm not sure. The earl was upset about losing him, though. He ranted and raved and said it was our fault he'd left, but he wouldn't say why. He called us a pack of parasites. I was only seventeen then, and had never seen him in such a temper. It was quite frightening. I took my sisters to the manor and we hid there all night. It was winter, and we were cold and hungry. He came to find us the next morning. We had a lucky escape, because there was a storm the next night, and the roof caved in.'

'That was indeed lucky. Can you tell me where I would be able to find another agent?'

'It's a little late in the year to find a good one, but I do have a suggestion.'

'Let me hear it, then.'

'Mr Hardin had a son who remained in the district. Joshua his name was. He married a local girl. He knows the estate because he grew up here. He was good with numbers, so used to keep the estate books for his father. In fact he held the position of clerk. Mr Hardin was training him into the position, I believe. After the argument there was some talk about Joshua, which I believe was unjustified. But it prevented him from being employed elsewhere in the district. Joshua swore he'd never work for the late earl again.'

'But you think he might work for me?'

'It's possible, and I would certainly like to see Joshua offered the chance to better himself. He works as a farm labourer for his father-in-law, I believe. Although he hasn't had any actual experience in the position of agent, it might be worth taking him on for a trial period, to see what he makes of it.'

'A good idea. I'll go and see him if you tell me where I'm likely to find him. Thank you for the suggestion, Miss Patterson, you're a treasure.'

By the time James reached them, Lord Trent was ready to head off for the farm. 'Look after Miss Patterson and her sisters, James. I'll meet you all in Dorchester as soon as I've finished my business.'

When he cantered off, James caught her attention by asking, 'Would you like me to take the cart, Miss Patterson. We can tie my horse to the back.'

'That's kind of you.'

They were soon on their way again. It was a lovely morning with a slight breeze. Each time a shower came, the two young girls held a large umbrella over their heads until it was gone, then the sun came out and the landscape sparkled with light.

The horse seemed to go faster with James at the reins.

'Do you think Lord Trent will find it too quiet here after London?' Alexis asked him.

'I imagine he will. He led a very full life. Apart from his business interests, he often went to the theatre or to his club, and he belonged to a debating society and a fencing academy. He's a popular man amongst his peers in London. Mrs Trent complains that she rarely sees him.'

The sun disappeared behind a cloud. 'Lord Trent has a wife then?'

'I was referring to his mother. Lord Trent is unmarried.' Out came the sun again, until he added, 'The earl's heart is captured by a young widow of means, I believe.'

'Oh.'

There was a sudden shower and her sisters squealed with laughter as they struggled to hoist the unwieldy umbrella. Rain beat against Alexis's back, soaking coldly through the thin fabric of the gown, until her sisters managed to spread their little shelter above them.

'Is something amiss, Miss Patterson?'

'No, not at all. May I ask what the future countess is like?'

'Exquisite of feature and form, socially desirable and quite charming.'

A thousand emotions churned in Alexis's chest, like a nest of snakes, surprising her with their vehemence. Diminished in her own eyes, she told herself fiercely. Stop it this instant, you don't even know the woman.

But the future welfare of her family was uncertain and the revelation that the late earl had cheated them had rendered her heartsick. Even if their home had been sound enough to live in, they were unable to farm their land since there was no money to hire the labour required.

If Lord Trent married, surely his wife would not want five unrelated and dependant females cluttering up her home, she thought morosely.

Alexis would have been lying if she were to deny that the night before, while she lay in her bed, she'd secretly considered that marriage to the earl would be a most convenient solution for her family. But if his heart belonged to such a sophisticate of fortune, beauty and virtue, so be it. She could not compete.

To be constantly indebted to the charity of another, didn't sit easily with her, but she could see no way out.

They passed a group of people on a cart heading for Longmore Hall. One of them was the housekeeper. As they passed, Alexis informed her that she could resume her position. The woman's face lit up.

One or two doffed their caps at the sight of James, obviously mistaking him for the earl. He winked at one of the maids, leaving her giggling. The manservant had a way with women, she thought.

Kynan came across the man shovelling manure on to a field of turnips.

'I'm looking for Joshua Hardin.'

The man glanced up, smiled, and brushed the flies from his face. 'That's me.'

'I'm the new Earl of Longmore.'

Hardin's smile faded and his face closed up warily. 'Aye, I'd heard you'd arrived.'

'News travels fast.' Kynan came straight to the point. 'I urgently need an agent for the estate.'

'Ah, so you hope to turn the place into a paying proposition again, do you?'

'That's my intention. My trade is in import and merchandising, so I know something about running a business, but damned all about farming.'

Joshua grinned at that. 'Sound business

principles apply to both.'

'Miss Patterson suggested you might be interested in the position of agent.'

Despite his appearance, Hardin looked him straight in the eye and spoke like an educated man. 'I'd be interested, but something needs to be sorted out first, my Lord.'

'Which is?'

'Is the Patterson land to be worked with the estate land?'

'I've yet to consult with Miss Patterson about that. I've had a quick look at the books and it seems to me that the Patterson family received very little remuneration from the produce grown on their land. I intend to address that.'

'Aye, the old earl held those dues back from them. He believed that a roof over their heads, food in their stomach and a pair of shoes and a new frock every year was payment enough. My father argued about it with the earl, and the man set about him with his cane, as if my father was some cur he'd come across. Although the man was sorry, later, my father refused to return to the post. When I declined to take over the position, he flew into a rage, dismissed me and blackened my name in the district. I work for my father-in-law for bed and board now.'

'Thank you for telling me, Mr Hardin. I was already aware that an injustice had been done. The position will be on a trial basis, since I'll need to satisfy myself that you're competent and able to handle the responsibility.'

'I understand, my Lord. You won't find me lacking in skills, that I promise.'

'Then I'm to take it you'll accept.'

'I've got nothing to lose, sir. I'll tell my wife and father-in-law as soon as they come back from the market and I will be available to start work tomorrow. Please thank Miss Patterson for suggesting me, since it will give me the chance to better myself. It was good of her.'

'You can thank her yourself, tomorrow, when you move into the estate house.'

'My father used to use the old dower house this side of the village.'

'I know. I'd prefer you to occupy the estate house. I looked over it early this morning, and it's of adequate size, though will need a good clean.'

'As you wish, my Lord. My wife will be happy to clean the place, and she'll like being mistress of her own home.'

Kynan nodded, brought his horse's head around and moved off.

As always on market day, Dorchester was crowded. People jostled each other as they passed and there was a smell of livestock in the air. Geese honked, chickens squawked and the place was a swirl of colour as soldiers and ladies paraded. Children darted through the crowd and stocky farmers stood in groups, talking, laughing and making a raucous noise.

James had handed the shopping list to an assistant at the grocery store, and was seated on the cart and chewing on a straw as his glance roved idly over the crowd. Alexis saw him wink at a buxom-looking girl who was selling small tarts from a tray. The girl fluttered her eyelashes.

Alexis had purchased the boots, plus lengths of pretty, but cheap material to make gowns for Celeste and Blythe. Daria and Esmé kept looking down at their newly shod feet while Alexis gazed longingly at a straw-bonnet trimmed with flowers in a shop window.

'Ah, there you are, Miss Patterson. Are you thinking of buying the hat?'

'It is pretty, but not at the moment, my Lord.' She smiled at him. 'Did you find Joshua Hardin?'

'I did, and I hired him for the job. He impressed me with his honesty, and I think we will get on. I'm on my way to the tea garden at the moment. Will you and your sisters join me?'

The younger girls gave little cries of delight. 'Please may we, Lexi?'

She darted a glance towards the cart,

gazing at it perplexed. As if there had been a sleight of hand, there was now a boy in the place James had occupied. 'Where's James gone?'

'Oh, he had some business to attend to,' the earl said carelessly. 'The boy will look after the cart and the horses until we return.'

The tea garden, which was open on market days, conducted business in a marquee. It was filled mostly with women, since the men had gravitated to the inn. She was surprised that the earl hadn't gone there too. They seated themselves at a table. Their appearance attracted attention, and they were the subject of animated whispers and speculative glances.

'*Welsh heir ... damned heir ... Lord Trent.*' The word was passed rapidly around.

Her eyes brimming with laughter, Alexis whispered to him, 'Everyone seems to know you're in town. I'm acquainted with one or two people. Would you like to be introduced?'

'Not at the moment, Miss Patterson. I'm perfectly happy with the company I already have.'

But they were not to be left in peace. Before too long a woman dared to approach the table, obliging the earl to rise to his feet. Behind her was her husband, a rather unhappy looking man.

She said, her pointed nose quivering like a

hound on the scent, 'Ah, my dear Miss Patterson. How well you look? I was just saying to Harold, there are some of the Patterson family at that table over there. And a man with them ... a stranger.'

Alexis's eyes went to Kynan apologetically. 'May I introduce the Earl of Longmore. My Lord, this is Mr and Mrs Clark.'

Kynan was all charm as he gravely bowed over Mrs Clark's hand. He then shook the hand of Harold, who looked ill at ease.

'We do hope you've settled into the hall, my Lord,' Mrs Clark gushed. 'When you're receiving visitors do let us know, so we can call on you.'

The earl inclined his head.

'My husband is the chairman of the association of business owners.'

'Really. What business is it you're in, Mr Clark?'

'He's an attorney,' his wife said.

'A solicitor, actually, my dear.' Harold gave an apologetic, barking sort of laugh, then said in a defeated voice, 'As the late earl started the association, your position gives you the right to be its head. I will, of course, relinquish the position to you, my Lord.'

'There's certainly no need to, since I don't know the district well enough, yet. Besides, my time will be spent putting the estate back on a sound business footing. I also have business interests in London to keep me busy.'

Mrs Clark smiled. 'So you won't be staying here in Dorset?'

Alexis noted a slight irritation in the earl's voice as he said, 'I've only just arrived here. I haven't had time to decide that yet.'

'Ah yes, of course. Is the countess with you, my Lord?'

Kynan looked so taken aback by her forthright manner that Alexis cut in smoothly. 'Do be seated, Lord Trent. Your tea is getting cold. I'm sure Mrs Clark will excuse us.'

But Mrs Clark refused to take the hint. Her eyes became unfriendly and she looked Alexis up and down. 'You and your sisters are invited to attend Sibyl's ball at the assembly room in June, Miss Patterson. I'll send you an invitation. Oh, but I keep forgetting that you have no means, and no chaperone. How silly of me.'

'I'll be happy to escort the Patterson sisters, and my mother will, no doubt, be delighted to chaperone them. Good day Mrs Clark. Mr Clark.' The earl seated himself and turned his back on them.

After the Clarks departed, Daria and Esmé turned beaming smiles on the earl. 'How exciting. We've never been to a ball before.'

Because she didn't want their hopes built up, Alexis said, 'We have no ball gowns to wear. Mrs Clark was just reminding us of our poverty.'

59

'I hate her,' Daria said, clearly disappointed.

Esmé said, 'So do I.'

Alexis gazed severely at them. 'Our mother would be ashamed if she'd heard you say such a mean thing.' She gave the earl an apologetic glance. 'I'm so sorry. It was kind of you to come to our defence like that. Mrs Clark will not expect us to attend, of course.'

'Of course not. Socially you're above her. But pointing out your poverty insures Mrs Clark from being subjected to a snub by you turning down her invitation. But yes, Esmé, we shall go, even though she won't be expecting us.'

'But—'

'I insist, and will provide everything you need. Leave it to me.'

'I don't like to accept your charity.'

'It won't be charity. You can repay me in some way. I'll think of something, no doubt. Now, let's get on. I have things to do and we have very little time to spare.'

Daria and Esmé minded their manners because they were in public. They ate two cakes apiece and picked the crumbs from their plates with their finger tips. 'Shall we take a cake home to Blythe and Celeste? It was Blythe's birthday the day before yesterday, and she didn't even get a gift,' Esmé whispered to her.

The earl promptly arranged for a selection of cakes to be placed in a box. Alexis told her sisters, 'I thought we might buy her a bottle of lavender water from a stall today, a gift from us all.'

The earl thought to add a small amber brooch mounted in silver. There was a honey bee inside the golden orb, captured by the resin before it hardened. Alexis imagined the tree sap slowly and silently creeping towards the unwary bee, which had stopped to rest. How cruel nature could be at times, she thought.

Her thought must have shown in her face for he said apologetically, 'I thought Blythe might like it. Shall I return it and buy something more suitable?'

'Oh no ... I'm quite sure that Blythe will love it,' she hastened to say. 'I feel sorry for the poor bee, that's all.'

He smiled at that. 'It would have worn itself out collecting pollen and been dead by the end of that summer, anyway. Its beauty can now be admired, always.'

'Yes, I suppose you're right. Personally, I'd prefer to grow old and wrinkled.'

His glance swept over her face, dancing from mouth to nose to eyes like a green and gold butterfly as he murmured, 'I'm sure I'll admire your beauty, always.'

She avoided his eyes and blushed. 'You must not say such silly things, my Lord.'

To which he gave an odd sort of laugh. 'What a strange thing, to turn aside a compliment that any fashionable young lady in London would encourage.'

'I'm not a fashionable London lady. Please don't tease me, my Lord.'

'Would you condemn me for just thinking my thoughts, then?'

Which was something much safer for her, since she didn't want to fall in love with him, Alexis thought practically. There had been something disconcerting about his smile that told her his words hadn't been idle teasing.

'I've been given to understand that your heart is engaged by a lady in London, my Lord.'

'Good God, have you?' He looked startled for a moment, then he smiled, and shrugged. 'You're right to beware of me, then.'

There was still no sign of James when they reached the cart, but the earl didn't seem at all perturbed as he dropped some coins into the outstretched palm of the boy and took up the reins of the cart horse himself.

'James is not here yet, my Lord.'

'I'm sure he'll find his way home eventually,' he said, and gazed into her eyes. 'Could you bring yourself to call me Kynan when we're without company, d'you think?'

'You're unusual for a titled gentleman,' she said.

He leaned towards her to whisper in her ear, 'It must be the damned Welsh in me.'

Alexis giggled as he clicked his tongue at the horse and set it in motion.

Four

Her sisters fell asleep amongst the packages on the way back. Kynan seemed deep in thought, so Alexis didn't disturb him. Now and again he turned his glance her way and smiled.

Jasper's tail wagged enthusiastically on their arrival.

They returned to the services of a maid, her familiar face breaking into a smile as she took Alexis's parcels from the cart and was about to scurry towards the house with them.

'You've forgotten one,' the earl said to the maid as Alexis leaned towards her sisters to wake them.

The former stable hand appeared, nearly falling over himself as he came charging round the corner to take hold of the horse's head. Short and slim, but well-muscled, the groom had left his youth behind him, and was grey at the temples.

'How have you been, my lovely?' he whispered to the mare and she snickered and nuzzled her great whiskery nose against his palm, as if greeting an old friend.

Alexis shared a smile with the earl, who'd also noticed the exchange between man and beast. 'May I introduce the stable hand, my Lord?'

Kynan inclined his head. After the introduction, Jude shuffled from one foot to the other then moved to inspect Kynan's mount. ' 'Tis a fancy piece of horseflesh you have here, sir. Do he be a Welsh horse?'

To give him credit, Kynan said with remarkable patience, 'I bought him down from London.'

To which Jude gave a wise sounding, 'Ah, that accounts for it then.' Then he untied the mount and led him off towards the stable.

'Accounts for what?' Kynan asked her, looking puzzled.

'Best you don't ask,' Alexis said with a grin. 'Jude seems to have claimed his job back. When you've assessed his worth you might consider making him the head groom, and even allow him to act as coachman, since the last one has left the district. He's worked in the stables since he was a lad, and the horses like him.'

'Then I'll take your word they'd recommend Jude's services.'

Daria and Esmé had been sworn to secrecy about the birthday gifts, but they went scampering off in search of their sisters, to show off their boots.

Alexis entered a house that smelled of beeswax. The large table in the hall, around which the previous incumbents and their families had once feasted on captured Welsh marauders, if the late earl was to be believed, was in the process of having its patina revealed, due to some energetic rubbing from the housekeeper.

She gazed up when they came in, blew a strand of hair from her face and straightened to gaze nervously at Kynan.

Alexis said to Mrs Elliot, 'This is your new master, Lord Trent.'

The housekeeper curtsied. 'I'm happy to be in your service, my Lord.'

'Thank you, Mrs Elliot. The new agent will be here tomorrow. He's Joshua Hardin, who is known to you all, I believe. In the meantime I'll leave you in charge of affairs. Those staff who worked here previously and wish to do so again can resume employment immediately. The others can leave their names and can return and see Mr Hardin tomorrow afternoon.'

'Yes, my Lord.'

'Miss Patterson, I'd be grateful if you'd join me in the study at your earliest convenience. There's something I wish to discuss with you.'

How easily Kynan had assumed the role of master, as if he'd been brought up to the task of running an estate such as this, she thought, as she went upstairs to her room. Unlike his predecessor, Kynan was quiet-voiced, polite and considerate. Respect for him grew in her.

Washing the dust of the journey from her hands and face, she tidied herself up, brushed out her hair and secured it with a ribbon at the nape of her neck. It curled naturally, but in any case, she didn't know what the latest style was, or how to fashion it.

About to keep her appointment with Kynan, she noticed the bonnet on the hat stand. It was the one she'd been admiring in the shop window. Kynan must have bought it for her.

He was seated at his desk when she entered the study. He stood, came round to hold her chair while she seated herself, then resumed his own seat.

'Would you like me to send for some refreshment, Lexi?'

She shook her head. 'I'm curious. What do you wish to discuss with me? You were so quiet on the journey back I'm under the impression it must be something dreadfully serious.'

He laughed at that. 'I wanted to talk to you about your former home. If it cannot be restored at a reasonable cost, I do think it should be pulled down.'

She sighed. 'I know it sounds odd, but while the manor stands, I feel that my sisters and I still have a home of our own to go to.'

'I can imagine how you feel, my dear. But you have to be sensible. Better the house be safely pulled down than to allow it to tumble down, especially if you're inside it at the time looking for a silver teaspoon to sell.'

'You were eavesdropping on us in the kitchen longer than I thought.'

'It was unintentional, and because I was only half-dressed, I couldn't declare my presence.' He smiled. 'Shots woke me. I became disorientated finding my way downstairs.'

'Blythe was rabbit hunting. As for teaspoons, I've already uncovered them all and sold them. But I'm not the only one. Anything of worth had already been stolen from the house before I was old enough to think of doing it myself. I can't find it in my heart to blame the thieves, when they probably needed the money to buy food for their children.'

A pained expression appeared in his eyes.

'They were more likely to be people who seized on the opportunity to profit from your misfortune.'

'But the locals believe the legend of the hidden treasure, which draws them to the place. They're tempted by anything they find.'

'You make excuses for people who don't deserve it, and you trust too easily. You should sell the land.'

'To whom?'

'I'd be willing to buy it from you.'

He'd disappointed her, and Alexis didn't know quite what to say to him. The silence gathered around them.

'Lexi?' His words were spoken softly, like a sigh.

Unhurriedly, she rose to her feet. 'You're right ... perhaps I do trust too easily.'

Those dark brows lowered and his eyes filled with affront. 'Do you think I'm trying to cheat you?'

Gently, she told him, 'Not deliberately, but you seem to regard land in monetary terms. While it would be pleasant to have money to spare, once spent, we'd no longer have it, or the land. What would happen to my sisters, then? While we have the land it will ensure them an advantageous marriage in the future, for it can be divided into five farms which will provide an income.'

He reminded her, 'I don't understand your reasoning, since you haven't the means to work the land, or five suitors eager to take advantage of a match, come to that. Your affection hasn't been captured by some bucolic gentleman of means, has it?'

'No,' she said, giving a nervous laugh, because, despite her annoyance with him, she felt something close to affection for the gentleman seated opposite her. 'But the land will always be there. An asset, I believe it's called. While we have it, we'll always have something of value.'

'But can such an asset provide you with shelter and sustenance in the short term?'

'As you pointed out, it can if we're properly compensated from the profits provided by the previous working of it.'

'I see.' He curled a grin at her. 'You learn fast, and obviously you've been thinking about this. Please be seated again. Explain how that profit can be achieved in an amount that will enable you to comfortably house and support yourself and your sisters.' He moved round to perch himself on the edge of the desk, his attention entirely hers.

Sinking back into her seat Alexis gazed up at him, thinking; at least he was prepared to listen – as if she had something of value to say. Unfortunately, she hadn't thought about it hard enough. 'I cannot, since you brought the matter up without due warning, so the fine details of such an undertaking need more expertise than I possess.'

He chuckled. 'Feel free to regard this as the due warning. There's only one fine detail for you to consider. Your welfare and that of your sisters rely entirely upon my goodwill.'

Anxiety filled her to the brim. 'Which I mistakenly took for granted, and put down to goodness of heart. Your pardon, Lord Trent. Am I to take it that your goodwill will dissipate like a puff of dragon smoke if I don't agree to sell you our land?'

Her jibe didn't escape his notice, but he let it pass. Instead, he gave a long and heartfelt sigh. 'Why do you insist on jumping to conclusions? I'm not a dragon, and I do have an alternative plan to put before you.'

Cocking her head to one side she smiled at him. 'Then tell me of it.'

'I'm not ready to disclose it yet.'

'How annoying you are. There's something you should take into account, perhaps, Kynan.'

'Which is?'

She drew in a deep breath. 'To gain access to Longmore Estate you need to cross Patterson land, unless you come by sea.'

He leant forward to gaze at her, his eyes as sharp as those of a hawk. Silkily, he said, 'How can somebody so lethal appear to be so damned innocent? Is that a threat?'

'Not at all. It's *my* alternative plan. Oh, and I really must thank you for the bonnet, my Lord. The gift was unexpected. It's quite beautiful.'

She'd gauged his sense of humour correctly, for he laughed. But what she didn't expect was for her chin to be taken between his thumb and finger, for her face to be tilted up and for his mouth to touch against hers for one exquisitely tender moment.

It stunned her, his caress, leaving her with

71

eyes closed and her heart longing for another kiss just like it.

She opened her eyes to find laughter in the depths of his. 'You didn't think you were going to get away with what you said, did you?'

'Not for one moment.' She felt the colour rising to her cheeks. 'I didn't expect such a liberty to be taken, though, and I think you must apologize.'

'I certainly will not, since I'm not sorry ... and neither are you, I think.'

'That's entirely beside the point.' She stood, supporting herself on knees that threatened to collapse under her as she said stiffly, 'I feel I must show my displeasure by removing myself from your presence, at once. You're no gentleman.'

'I've never pretended to be.' He was laughing out loud now, and her cheeks were on fire. 'If you really must, leave then, Lexi. Perhaps we can continue this most interesting discussion another time.'

'Perhaps it would be better if the next one wasn't *quite* so interesting.'

With that parting shot she escaped. Closing the door on his laughter, she leaned against the panels for a moment. But when she heard his footsteps, she fled upstairs with a grin on her face.

There, the mirror begged her inspection. She looked exactly the same. But there was a strange, wicked awareness inside her like a hidden giggle, and her breasts nudged against her bodice, alive and tingling.

Picking up the spring bonnet Kynan had given her, she placed it on her head and danced around the room, her heels tapping on the floorboards, the green and white ribbons flying. Finally out of breath she flung herself on her bed and laughed with the sheer exhilaration of being alive.

The door opened and Daria poked her head around the door before advancing into the room, her eyes shining with the excitement of the day. 'Blythe's in the folly. We're going to surprise her. Where are her gifts?'

'On the dresser. I don't know where the cakes are.'

'Celeste has them. Esmé wants to give her the lavender water. I'll hand over the brooch and you can bring a jug of milk to wash the cakes down with. Should I tell her that Lord Trent bought her the brooch?'

'We must, for she'll need to thank him.'

'I do like the earl, don't you? He doesn't shout and rant like the old earl. He will let us stay here, won't he?'

Alexis, who wasn't sure of anything, because she found Kynan entirely unpredictable, told her young sister, 'I'm sure he won't throw us out if we behave ourselves.'

Her face solemn, Daria said, 'I'll be as quiet as a mouse, we all will, then he won't know we're here.'

In view of what the earl had said earlier, Alexis thought it might be wise to make themselves as inconspicuous as possible.

'From now on we'll have our meals in the schoolroom. After all, Lord Trent never invited us to dine with him. We just did. I'll tell the cook when I go down.'

Taking up a hair brush she tidied her sister's silky hair. 'I'm going to ask Mrs Curruthers if you and Esmé can attend her school.'

'But you've already taught us to read and write,' Daria wailed.

'But not well enough. You need to know more. I'll continue to teach you to play the piano, but I'll have to ask the earl's permission first. I'm sure he'll see reason when I tell him that girls have to grow up with grace, and be accomplished in all ways.'

'Blythe isn't graceful. All she wants to do is shoot animals, climb trees and have adventures, like boys.'

'Our mother would have wanted all her girls to be graceful and well-mannered. Blythe is growing up, so I expect she'll change into a lady soon.'

Daria giggled. 'I can't imagine Blythe being ladylike. What did our mother look like?'

Turning Daria towards the mirror, Alexis examined her sweet, heart-shaped face, petite nose and large, pale blue eyes. 'You're very much like her, my love. You have her dab of a nose, and the same shaped mouth.'

When that mouth curved into her mother's smile Alexis caught her breath as a dart of sorrow lodged in her. Life could be so unfair sometimes.

She placed her new bonnet on her head, picked up the small parcels from the dressing table and took her sister's hand. 'I'm ready, so let's go and find the others.'

Kynan watched from the drawing room window, a faint smile on his lips as the four girls walked down towards the folly in a line. Beyond the folly the sea was a stretch of sparkling light which cut into a horizon of the pale sky, across which clouds raced.

The breeze had come up. Lexi held her hat on her head with one hand and carried a jug in another. Her skirt whipped around her legs, sometimes exposing her slender ankles and shapely calves. Kynan's eyes narrowed. Naked, Alexis Patterson would be perfection itself.

He should have stayed with James, who by now would have found relief between the thighs of a willing woman. He would have envied his servant, except he knew that such relief never lasted. He had Julia Spencer waiting back in London for him. She was full-bodied, exquisite and available. He didn't need to stray when he had her within reach.

Only Julia wasn't within reach here, and he was ashamed that a pert and innocent young woman had stirred up his lust.

They'd disappeared into the folly now. He gazed down at the dog, which seemed to have attached itself to his ankle. It was an odd-looking creature. 'How would you like to take a walk to the beach, Jasper? I haven't been there yet.'

His companion huffed an assent and it wasn't long before he was strolling downhill along a well-beaten track. The fact that all this land ... the space around him, was his, awed him. His land wealth in London consisted of the small patch his home stood on, and his warehouses. Here he had riches indeed. But it was wealth that demanded the heart and soul of a man, since it needed labour for those riches to reach maturity.

He was almost pleased that his predecessor had ignored its bounty for the past few years, for that made it even more than a challenge. The dwelling itself was well appointed and strong and, although the wine cellar had been run down, that was something he could remedy.

'The Earl of Longmore,' he said out loud, the title surprising him once again. A little while ago he'd been an importer and wholesaler – albeit of a very superior business, which dealt in goods imported from around the world. His warehouses were stuffed to the roof with silks from China, carpets from Persia, teas from India.

Then there was the speciality of the Trent business, the expensive and sometimes rare spices from the Orient. His own favourite was the cinnamon they obtained from Malabar, and he took a small furl of the bark from his pocket to inhale its scent. But there was also cardamom from India, mace, nutmeg, juniper berries, ginger and cloves from the Mollucca Islands ... too many spices to remember.

Kynan didn't feel like an aristocrat, since he hadn't been brought up to it, not even a damned Welsh one. He doubted if his unassuming father had known he was heir to this place either. But Hough had traced him through the Welsh family tree, and there was no doubt. He was directly descended from the third earl, through his younger son.

As he neared the folly, which resembled a little turret with shutters to protect the windows, and a stout door to close against the storms, the sounds of female voices and laughter drifted towards him.

Kynan was tempted to stand and listen, but his sense of decency prevented him. Instead, he turned to the path that led down the slope to the beach – a path made safe by thick wooden planks forming steps, now grey and twisted by age and exposure to the weather. Several of the bottom steps clearly showed the high watermark, for they were slimy. A dinghy at the bottom, holed, and half buried in the sand, was tied by a long, seaweed-covered rope to the handrail.

He ambled along the damp sand at the water's edge, Jasper plodding after him. The cove was warm and sheltered, the breeze ruffled his hair and the gulls wheeled in the sky. He moved back, and, removing his jacket to use as a pillow, he lowered himself to the sand and rested his head on his tri-angled arms. Jasper subsided beside him with a grumbling sigh.

It wasn't often that Kynan had experienced the luxury of being entirely alone. The sky was as deep a blue as the colour of Lexi's eyes, the clouds raced across it like white horses. Feeling himself relax, he allowed his lids to drift shut and his thoughts to wander where they would.

The earl must have been asleep for a while, Alexis thought, for it had been two hours since she'd watched him descend the path.

She gazed down at him, at the dark sweep of his lashes and the even rise and fall of his chest. She must wake him soon, or the tide would. Jasper had long since returned to the house for his dinner, and the sand on him had given her the clue to Kynan's whereabouts.

The sea was molten gold from the sun, which would shortly begin to slide into its depths. A shame he should miss it.

She leaned forward, again inhaling a faint, but elusive fragrance of spice. 'Kynan, it's time to wake,' she whispered.

His mouth curved into a smile and his arm came round her, pulling her against his side. 'Why?'

'Because the tide's coming in, and your servant is looking for you. You must let me go before he thinks to look for you here.'

His eyes fluttered open, then widened. He stared at her for a moment with a quizzical frown on his face, then he chuckled. 'I think James would congratulate me for waking with such a beautiful woman in my arms.'

He released her, then rose to his feet, taking his jacket with him and holding out a slim, strong hand for her to steady herself as she also rose. 'The sky seems burnished with cinnamon,' he murmured as he donned his jacket. 'How pretty it is, here.'

'I don't know what cinnamon is.'

He brought a small curled stick from his jacket and handed it to her. 'It's a spice made from the bark of a laurel tree, which grows around the Malabar Coast.'

'Where's that?'

'Southern India. The smell comes from the oil, and it has many uses: perfume, medicine, and flavouring for food and drinks.'

Inhaling it, she smiled. 'I can smell this on you sometimes. I wondered what it was.'

'Now you know. Keep it,' he said as she went to hand it back. 'If you put it amongst your garments they'll pick up the perfume of it.'

As she slipped the cinnamon bark into her pocket, there came a sliding rush of water that nearly touched their feet, making them jump back.

'If you hadn't woke me, that would have, and with a vengeance. Quickly, let's run before the next one,' he said, taking her hand in his. They raced the tide along the curve of the beach to the path. He'd just pushed her up the step ahead of him when a surge of water covered the one he was standing on. It swirled around his ankles, then receded with a hiss.

The curse he gave was succinct. Eyes alight with laughter he instantly gazed up at her, 'My pardon.'

'I've heard worse. The old earl could out-cuss the devil himself. Quickly now, the next wave will cover the step I'm on.' She turned and began to scramble up the path, the earl hot on her heels.

They were out of breath when they reached the top. 'Let's watch the sun go down before we go back to the house,' he said.

It didn't take long for the fiery glow to slide

under the molten sea, which then turned the colour of pewter. But the horizon was still painted in yellow and red stripes and the air around them and the undersides of the clouds were tinted a delicate brown and gold. He turned to smile at her as the glory faded. 'I've never seen a sunset quite so beautiful.'

'Perhaps you've never had the time to notice it before. I imagine it would look just as pretty on the laurels of the Malabar Coast.'

'As if the air is tinted with cinnamon ... yes, I imagine it would.'

Alexis knew she'd remember the sunset too, for that moment the world faded around them and she was conscious only of him as they stood on the cliff top and gazed at each other in the cinnamon light.

'Exquisite,' he murmured, and she could not be sure whether he was being personal, or referring to the sunset.

When she found her voice it was a little husky. 'My sisters will wonder where I am.'

'Yes. And the wind has a chill to it.'

Alexis didn't feel any chill, just a glow of happiness, as if she were drowning in dreams. So this is what being in love is like, she thought, and a sudden agony ripped through her as she remembered the woman he loved in London.

At the sound of her name being called by

Celeste, she experienced relief. 'Excuse me, my Lord,' she murmured, and hurried away from that astute gaze of his before he saw what she felt.

Five

The table in the dining room was set for one. Light from the candlesticks gleamed on its polished surface and set the crystal twinkling. The monogrammed silver cutlery had been shone to perfection, and the maid was standing by the buffet, from which area appetizing smells drifted from several covered dishes carried in by the cook.

There was something missing, though, and Kynan frowned. 'Where are the Patterson girls, Mrs Dawson?'

'Miss Patterson told me they'd be having dinner in the schoolroom after we've served you, my Lord.'

'Did she, indeed? Perhaps you'd take a message to them for me. Remind them that they're my guests and, as such, I expect them to exercise good manners and join me at my table. Otherwise, they will go without.' He didn't notice Mrs Dawson's smile as he took out his watch and sprung open the lid. 'Tell them they have exactly five minutes in which to present themselves.'

He beckoned to the maid after Mrs Dawson scurried away. 'Lay another five table settings, please.'

'Yes, my Lord.' She had barely finished the job when there was a hesitant knock at the door.

'Come in, do.'

The girls were ushered in by Alexis, all pink-faced and flustered. Mrs Dawson followed them, then moved straight to the buffet. The girls arranged themselves around the table like a row of rather shabby flowers, their eyes firmly fixed on Alexis, who said calmly, 'I do hope we're not late, my Lord.'

Alexis Patterson rose in his estimation. She had a family depending on her, and was using her wits to survive without appearing to compromise. Momentarily he wondered how far she'd go to keep them fed and housed, then dismissed the thought as being unworthy of him.

All the same he was grinning as he responded to the challenge. 'On the contrary, you're exactly on time, as if your arrival had been timed to the split second.'

Esmé and Daria exchanged a glance, hard put not to giggle. Blythe grinned and Celeste smiled as she said artlessly, 'Lexi may have timed it.'

'Nonsense.' Alexis flicked innocent eyes his way. 'I'm quite sure the earl wasn't suggesting I had such a devious character trait.'

'Are you *quite* sure?'

'Yes.' Her smile and voice were as smooth as whipped cream. 'Let's not keep his lordship waiting any longer, Mrs Dawson. You may serve.'

Kynan chuckled, but left her with her small victory.

By the end of the week the house was staffed by a small, but efficient army. With two maids helping, who were far more proficient than herself with a needle and thread, Alexis presented Blythe and Celeste with their new gowns in time for church on Sunday.

They were as fashionable as she could make them, with puff sleeves and high waistlines. There had not been enough fabric for fancy frills and sashes, but Alexis had cut a white ribbon from her bonnet to make a bow to sew on the bodice of Celeste's gown.

Grinning happily, Blythe pinned the amber bee brooch to hers.

'Have you thanked the earl for his gift, yet?'

When Blythe shook her head, Alexis sighed. 'You must write him a note before we go to church.'

'Must I?'

'I insist. A lack of good manners from one of us reflects badly on the rest.'

'He might think we're clodhoppers instead of daughters of a baronet,' Celeste said worriedly.

'He's already aware of our background, Celeste. You may hand the note to his servant if you wish, Blythe.'

Blythe made a face. 'I haven't got any paper.'

'There's a sheet in the desk. You can write it while I'm dressing. Be careful you don't get ink on yourself.'

Wearing her new bonnet and her best gown, the colour as pale and delicate as the petals of primroses, Alexis led the way down the stairs a short while later.

It was a long walk to the church, but one they'd done on many Sundays when the weather allowed. The spring flowers would make the walk delightful.

The day was sunny and they didn't bother hurrying. Time to do that when the church bell began to peal fifteen minutes before the service started.

Naked from the waist up, Kynan watched them leave as James neatened his hair and brushed away the clippings.

'At dinner last night, Miss Patterson told me that the Earl of Longmore has his own pew at the front of the church. She said the parishioners will expect me to attend the service, and it's my duty to set a good example.'

'No doubt they'll be curious, my Lord.'

'Then I'd better not disappoint them. I'll

wear my brown jacket with the cream waistcoat and boots over fawn trousers. There's a fine carriage in the coach house. A pity we have no horses capable of pulling it. I'll have to try and get hold of some.'

'Yes, sir. I'll ask the groom to put the word out, shall I?'

'Do that James. I want a good, well-behaved four, and a coachman. They will also service the phaeton, whether poled or shafted.'

'Yes, sir. Would you prefer pleats, plain or ruffles?'

'A plain shirt with a cravat, I think.'

'As always, you're the epitome of good taste, sir.'

'Because you've trained me over the past few years. Tell me, what do you think of the Patterson girls?'

'They are delightful creatures, but if I may say so, sir, they could do with the guidance of an older woman ... Miss Blythe in particular seems to run wild, like a lad instead of a young woman.' He felt in his pocket and came out with a piece of badly creased paper. 'The young lady asked me to hand you this.'

Dear Lord Trent,
   Lexi said I must thank you for the brooch so you don't think we're all clodhoppers. It is pritty with the bee inside. If you'll let me

shoot your guns I will take you to the place where me and the old earl used to shoot deer for the larder if you want.
Blythe Patterson

Kynan winced at the badly formed writing and the blots. He also had no desire to shoot deer. 'You know, James, Miss Patterson does her best, but she has been trying to bring up her sisters since she was quite a young child herself.'

'Miss Patterson is a lovely young woman with natural grace.'

'Yes ... she is, indeed.' He watched as her trim figure disappeared over the rise and sighed. 'How old would you say she was?'

'The cook told me Miss Patterson celebrates her twenty-first birthday at the end of July, sir. It seems that the old earl had plans to wed her when she was of legal age. He wanted the land their house stands on, you see, and an heir for the estate, of course.'

Kynan shuddered at the thought of Lexi being pawed over and used to breed for the former earl. He'd seen a portrait of the man, which seemed to have been painted in late middle-age, for he was depicted as being white haired, rotund and paunched.

'I wonder if she knew.'

'Even if she did, I imagine she'd have been given very little choice, my Lord, since she and her sisters would have had nowhere else to go.'

'I feel responsible for them, you know.'

James raised an eyebrow.

'My predecessor kept what was rightfully theirs. I offered to buy their land, but Miss Patterson refused. She said it should be divided into five farms so they'd be provided with a dowry apiece.'

'A good plan for their future, sir.'

'For them, yes, if they wish to marry farmers. None of them strikes me as being practical enough to fill the role of a farmer's wife. Also, I have to rely on their goodwill for access, so would prefer to buy the land myself.'

'You could always wed Miss Patterson yourself, sir. Then her portion of the land would become yours.'

'That's an entirely despicable and mercenary plan, James. I'm surprised you'd imagine I'd sink as low as the former earl. Besides, Miss Patterson would see right through such a blatant approach, and I don't want her to think badly of me.'

James grinned as his master slid into his jacket and shrugged, so it snugged around his muscular shoulders. 'No, we wouldn't want that, sir.'

'What do you think of Cordelia Mortimer?'

James chuckled. 'I remember Mrs Mortimer as being a rather pleasant, but formidable lady, sir. Didn't she run a boarding school before she was widowed?'

'Exactly,' he purred. Cordelia Mortimer was his mother's cousin. 'She always expressed a desire to move to the country. I thought she might like to live in the dower house.'

'I see,' James said.

The church bell had begun to ring and the groom had brought his horse round from the stable. Taking his hat from James, Kynan smiled as he headed for the door, saying, 'I doubt it, but you soon will.'

Kynan entered the crowded church to restless coughs, rustles and talking. His servants were seated at the back.

He nodded to his agent. Joshua Hardin had taken charge of affairs without fuss. Beside him sat his wife, a handsome, capable looking woman. A small female with red curls and wide brown eyes was seated on Joshua's lap, and the woman's belly was swelling with another. Kynan experienced a moment of envy.

The noise gradually ceased as he progressed down the aisle, his footsteps loud on the flagged floor.

The Reverend Curruthers bestowed a grateful look on him as he settled himself into the empty front pew. Kynan realized that Lexi had probably told the reverend he'd be attending the service, and he'd committed the sin of being five minutes late.

'My apologies,' he said quietly to the reverend, and exchanged a smile with Lexi across the aisle. Immediately, there came a buzz of conversation from behind him, until the reverend gently coughed and said, 'Let us pray.'

The service was not a long one, and the sermon not as dull as Kynan had been led to expect.

People were inclined to linger and talk afterwards in the churchyard. Lexi introduced him to the reverend, who requested a private talk with him. She ushered her family together and they began to walk back towards the house.

'Miss Patterson is a good girl who cares for the welfare of her sisters,' the reverend remarked as they walked among the headstones.

'We are only of short acquaintance, but she's displayed many admirable qualities. They all have.'

'It's the Pattersons I wish to talk to you about.'

He sighed. 'I rather thought it was, Reverend. Rest assured, they'll not suffer while they're guests under my roof.'

'Which is exactly what they will do, since tongues are sure to start wagging.'

'For what reason?'

'I understand you're unwed.'

'Ah,' Kynan said, anger filling him. 'Would you condemn a young woman because of my unmarried state? The Patterson sisters came as a surprise to me, an inconvenient imposition at the time of inheritance. I could hardly throw them out to fend for themselves.'

'My Lord, there's no denying you've been good to them. I'm trying to make you aware that Miss Patterson could easily lose her reputation living within such an arrangement.'

'You needn't fear, Reverend, I'm entirely aware of the position she and her sisters are placed in. If you hear any gossip I'd be obliged if you'd instantly squash it, for I'm expecting my mother to arrive shortly. The Pattersons will be adequately chaperoned by her while I make more permanent arrangements.'

'May I ask what those arrangements will be?'

'I intend to offer the dower house to Mrs Mortimer, who is my mother's cousin. The Pattersons will be placed in her care, where the younger ones will learn some much needed social graces. I haven't discussed this with them yet, and neither will I until I hear from Mrs Mortimer that she's able to undertake such a responsibility. I will then negotiate terms for the rent of their land and the right of way.'

'I could arrange a marriage for Miss

Patterson. I know of a widower with two children who is looking for a wife. He has a good living in Hampshire.'

Kynan frowned at the thought of any woman being used as a convenience in a marriage to a total stranger, let alone Lexi, who already had her share of responsibility. As far as he could see, she'd never experienced a social life, something that most girls of her status would expect as normal to her upbringing.

Stiffly, he said, 'That's entirely up to Miss Patterson, of course.'

Curruthers sighed. 'She's disinclined to meet him. Perhaps you can persuade her.'

'Certainly not.' With some distaste, Kynan told him, 'There's nothing more to be said. I'm given to believe the former earl intended to make Miss Patterson his wife when she came of legal age.'

Curruthers nodded. 'I counselled him against it but he told me he didn't want to be the earl who went down in history as bringing the feud with the Welsh to an end. He was desperate for an heir for the estate. As it was, he died before his intentions bore fruit.'

'It was not necessary. He already had an heir. Me. The feud was all in his mind. As far as I'm concerned it takes two parties to argue. I didn't know the title existed, let alone that I was related to him. Neither did my father, I suspect.'

'It took Charles Hough a year to track you down, I believe. He couldn't find you in Wales and thought your branch of the family might have died out.'

'My family left Wales many decades ago. Several generations of Trents were born and raised in London. Hough told me that both family branches had sprung from the same loins. It would have made sense to prepare me for the responsibility of this estate instead of perpetuating some ancient myth and regarding me as a threat.'

'Quite so, my Lord,' the reverend stuttered.

'Only a stupid man would allow an estate such as Longmore to go to rack and ruin. Fortunately, I possess the means to put it back on a business footing, so eventually it will pay for itself. You'll have to excuse me now, Reverend, I have much to do. You must bring your good lady to dinner when I've perfected my living arrangements.'

From the corner of his eye he saw Mrs Clark heading his way with a determined look on her face. Hastily, he said, 'Good day, Reverend,' then jammed his hat on his head and strode off. He mounted his horse before he got any angrier and, ignoring the sound of his name being called, rode away.

Discussing Alexis Patterson in such a manner had left a nasty taste in his mouth. Such a delightful girl shouldn't be married off to an old man, he thought.

He caught up with the Pattersons, just in time to see them enter the grounds of their former home. The dry grass was almost as tall as Esmé, the carriageway overgrown with weeds, except for a set of wheel ruts where a cart seemed to have regularly visited. Leaving his horse outside he followed the girls on foot, in case they'd decided to do something foolhardy.

One of the manor windows had fallen out and the door had been taken from its frame, probably used for firewood.

'The earl wants to pull it down, and he wants to buy our land,' Alexis told her sisters. 'I've refused, because all we have is our land to share between us as a dowry. But I might offer him the use of it for rent.'

Blythe sighed. 'He can buy my portion if he likes. I can use the money as a dowry. I doubt if anyone will ever want to marry me, though.'

'Nor me,' said Daria and Esmé together, to which Esmé added, 'I'm going to live in the earl's house always. He's kind. I can look after him when he's old and fetch his brandy and slippers for him.'

Kynan found it hard not to laugh at that.

'He smells nice,' said Daria.

Alexis told them, 'It's the cinnamon he carries in his waistcoat pocket. He gets it from the bark of the laurel tree which grows in...'

'Malabar,' he prompted under his breath when she hesitated.

'...the southern coastal district of India.'

'Where's India?' Esmé asked.

'I'm not sure. We'll look for it on the globe when we get back. You know, we can't impose indefinitely on the earl's good nature. I think we should be prepared for changes before too long.'

There was silence for a moment; then Daria said, 'We can pay him for our accommodation when we find the treasure.'

'If treasure existed, our parents would have already found it, I expect,' the practical Alexis said.

Blythe said moodily, 'How could they have, when they died still trying to find it?'

A slate dislodged from the shattered roof and clattered down inside the house, making them jump.

'Somebody's pulled down the stable and most of the bricks are gone. Do you suppose somebody else is looking for treasure? They would have taken that too, I expect.'

'My dears,' Alexis said. 'I don't want to disappoint you, but I think the treasure was a tale our father and the old earl made up. So was the ship that anchored in the cove shrouded in mist and crewed by dead smugglers.'

Blythe grinned. 'I love that tale. The old earl told me it was the ghosts of the damned come to haunt him. He said if I saw it, I was to go to the folly and fire the cannon before the ship sailed away. Then the treasure would be revealed. He said the cannon would frighten them off and they'd never come back.'

'Don't you dare try and fire that cannon, Blythe. It's old and dangerous.'

Celeste smiled. 'She can't anyway, Lexi. There's no gunpowder. The earl had a servant remove it, along with the guns.'

Alexis's voice took on an impatient ring. 'Enough of this ghost nonsense. We're here to decide whether the house should be pulled down, or not. I think it might fall on someone sheltering from a storm, so we should err on the side of safety.'

Blythe had her say next. 'The only people being sheltered would be those who come to steal from us. They deserve to be buried under it. But I agree that it should be pulled down. We might be able to sell the bricks before they all disappear. Celeste, what do you think?'

'I hate the manor. It looks like a haunted house and reminds me that we're orphans.'

They jumped when one of the remaining roof beams cracked and a pair of birds flew in panic from a broken window pane. The two youngest girls moved closer to Alexis and she put her arms around them. 'You mustn't be frightened. This was once our

97

home, and the spirits of our mother and father will always watch over and protect us. And somehow, I'll always find a way to look after you.'

Alexis spoke with Kynan after dinner.

'We ... my sisters and I have decided it would be best for the manor to be pulled down, as you advised. We thought we might be able to sell the bricks.'

'I'll ask Hardin to arrange a sale of what can be salvaged. The slates, window frames, doors and fireplaces are of value. Is there anything in there you'd like to keep?'

'If anything is found intact I'd like to decide then. There was a portrait of our parents that I'd rather like to have if it hasn't been ruined. My sisters can't remember what they looked like.'

He nodded. 'I'll ask the workmen to keep a watch out for it. You and your sisters are making the right decision, you know, Lexi.'

'Are we, Kynan? The manor is the only link we have to our past. I'm desperately worried about what the future holds for my sisters.' Although she tried to keep back her tears her voice wobbled with defeat, and she dragged in a deep breath to steady it. 'I'd rather not sell our land, but you may rent it if you wish. I also feel the need to apologize for suggesting that the right of way would be withdrawn. What must you think of me?'

He couldn't leave her with such a melancholy thought to carry. 'I think you're a young woman who is at the end of her tether, and has no one to turn to for advice. My dear, Lexi, I've devised a plan which, although not quite finalized, I'd like to discuss with you now. Can I count on you to hear me out, for it might help to relieve any fears you might have.'

When she nodded, he indicated the chair on the other side of the fireplace and seated himself opposite.

'You're in a vulnerable position. It's obvious you cannot stay under my roof for much longer without being compromised. You know this. Your sisters are sweet-natured girls, and two of them are fast approaching womanhood. But they are uneducated and are lacking in most social graces. Blythe, in particular, needs the guidance of an older woman.'

Alexis nodded, her eyes large and blue as they engaged his. 'Before the service I asked Mrs Curruthers to educate the two youngest, but she has a waiting list so cannot take them until next year.'

He nodded. 'She might not need to. I have a widowed relative called Cordelia Mortimer. I've offered her the use of the dower house. It's of a comfortable size.'

'I've never been in it, but it looks comfortable, so I'm sure your relative will be happy living there.'

Straight away, he said, 'If she agrees to my terms, you and your sisters will move in with her.'

'Oh ... I see. What are those terms?'

'Mrs Mortimer used to run her own school for girls before her marriage. She's very accomplished. I've asked her to share with you the responsibility of teaching your sisters and turning them into presentable young ladies. In return, you can provide her with companionship.'

Relief filled her to the brim as he continued to outline his plan for them, explaining that they'd have a modest income of their own, paid from the debt owed to them by the estate.

'Well, what do you think?' he said finally.

Her smile couldn't have reached any further as she sprang to her feet. 'I think it's the best of plans. I must go and tell my sisters.'

He rose too. 'Until I've heard from Mrs Mortimer I'd ask you to keep this to yourself. She might prefer to stay in London.'

'Yes ... I will. What's the lady like?'

'She's an intelligent woman, rather straightforward in manner. She has no children of her own, though she has always wanted a family to care for. I'm sure you're mature enough to recognize her good qualities and cope with the day to day irritations that are bound to crop up.'

Her eyes sharpened. 'If you were sure, you wouldn't have needed to say it, Kynan.'

'You're too astute.' He moved a step forward, took her hands in his and engaged her eyes. 'Regard this as advice then. I know you want your sisters to grow into well-mannered young ladies who will marry well and lead useful lives. To do that they will need to learn some self-discipline. Mrs Mortimer will make sure they acquire that. There's a possibility you might find yourself in the position of having to take sides.'

'Yes ... it has already occurred to me,' she said slowly. 'But I'll discuss this matter with Mrs Mortimer first; decide if we will suit each other.'

'You don't understand, Lexi. It's not a matter of her suiting you, since she will not be hired. Rather, it's you who will have to learn to accommodate her.'

'Yes ... I see ... I misunderstood and forgot we're reliant on your good will. How silly of me.' Hurt choked her voice. She'd thought he was kind, now she realized he'd been hatching a plot to get rid of them all the time. And to make matters worse, she loved him. And that hurt too, for she knew he loved another.

She withdrew her hands, which had felt so warm and cherished in his. She had no other choice than to accept his offer to live with this Mrs Mortimer, since beggars didn't have the luxury of being choosers. 'I'll do my best to conform with her ways, of course.'

'Lexi, my dear. You're upset. It won't be as bad as you imagine. I promise.'

She couldn't bear to look at him in case he saw what was in her eyes. 'Don't, Kynan ... I'm sure everything will be all right ... I didn't mean to sound ungrateful. You've been so good to us, more than we deserve and I thank you a thousand times. It's just that it will be so hard to leave you ... to leave Longmore Hall, I mean.'

She gave a tiny hiccup as she tried to hold back her tears, then turned away from him and fled.

Six

The estate had become a hive of activity since Joshua Hardin had taken up his position. Somewhere, he'd found labourers to work the fields. The cart horse had been joined by a second. The pair plodded up and down creating furrows, their heads nodding wisely at each other.

The house was filled with servants busily going about their business, which made Alexis feel a little redundant, though the housekeeper still conferred with her and the cook requested her approval on the menu. Carts endlessly came and went, delivering goods.

When Alexis was summoned to Kynan's study she thought it was to be informed that Mrs Mortimer had replied to his letter about the dower house. But Kynan simply told her, 'The manor is being pulled down tomorrow. I thought you and your sisters would like to watch.'

They presented themselves the next morning. It was to be an exciting event, for the workmen intended to use gunpowder.

''Tis for the best, since the house is in a dangerous condition. The timbers have rotted over the years and the foundations have been sitting in water ever since your father diverted the stream to try and make a lake. He succeeded in doing the first, but not the second.'

Pointing to the roof, the foreman stated knowledgeably, 'Lord Patterson didn't take the lie of the land into account, you see. Yon house sits in a dell. See how she leans forward. Likely she'll fall that way, but you can never tell. We can't take her down brick by brick since she's too unstable and 'tis likely she'll fall down on us. So we're going to knock the legs out from under her, instead. We'll salvage all we can for the sale yard, but some of the slates and windows are bound to shatter. Best you young ladies move up the hill a ways and settle yourself there, lest you get hit by flying debris.'

Kynan joined them in the phaeton, on his way into town. The party seated themselves on the grass to watch proceedings as the men went about their business.

Finally, a series of shouts and whistles was followed by a moment when all was silent. Then came several muffled explosions. The house rocked and cracked with each bang. There was a moment when the walls and remains of the roof seemed to shudder, then the whole lot sank gracefully downwards into the trees that surrounded it. Clouds of dust billowed upwards.

The sound of cheers reached them and Blythe clapped her hands and gazed round at them wide-eyed. 'That was exciting.'

The other girls exchanged sober glances, then Esmé said in a tremulous voice, 'I feel sad.'

Alexis pulled her close and kissed the top of her head. 'It's for the best.'

'You could never have lived in it,' the earl said as the dust began to settle.

He became the recipient of a cool look. 'But it was our house and now we haven't got one. I feel as if we've lost another part of our family,' said Esmé with force.

'You mustn't be rude,' Alexis whispered, giving Kynan a nervous glance.

He said, 'I'd be upset if it was my home, too.'

'Oh, the manor has never been our home. Longmore Hall has,' Daria said cheerfully. 'I can't remember living in the manor and neither can you, Es, so stop being such a weepy mope. Come on, I'll race you back to the hall.'

'Me too,' said Celeste. The three of them took off in a skelter of skirts before Alexis could tell them it was unladylike to run.

'I'm going down to have a look at what's left of the house,' Blythe said, and strolled off.

'Don't get too dusty.'

'That leaves us,' said Kynan. 'Do you have plans?'

'No, but I thought you were on your way into town.'

'I am, but there's time to take a quick look around the dower house, if you'd like. You said you've never seen inside it. I'll deliver you safely back to the hall afterwards.'

'Have you heard from Mrs Mortimer yet?' she asked.

'I'll let you know when I have.' He helped her up into the phaeton and they were off, dashing through the lanes at a fast, though not reckless, pace. Even so she was forced to hold tightly to the rail, and laughed with the sheer excitement of it. As they neared the village, Kynan eased down the speed, his hands strong and sure on the reins as they came to a halt.

He was laughing too as he turned to her. 'I enjoyed the run. Having you up beside me inspired me to show off.'

She straightened her bonnet. 'Your skill with the reins impressed me. I've never travelled quite so fast.'

He jumped to the ground, and, coming round to her side of the phaeton lifted her down, his hands firmly planted either side of her waist.

The gate squeaked as he opened it and

they made their way up to the porch, where Kynan produced a key from under a stone. Inside, the house was dim and silent, for some of the downstairs windows were shuttered. It was as though the house were waiting for someone to bring it to life.

'There are four, good-sized reception rooms on the ground floor.' They wandered through them, Kynan looking under the dust sheets and murmuring unnecessarily. 'Dresser ... sofa ... table.'

'Oh look, this room has doors leading on to a patio.'

'The utility rooms are at the back.'

'This must be the music room.' There was dappled light patterned across the floor as it shone through dusty lace curtains. Kynan uncovered a piano, lifted the lid, played a ripple of notes and grimaced. 'It's out of tune.'

'Yes, I imagine it would be after all this time,' she said drily. 'Oh, look over there, this leads into the conservatory, which will catch the afternoon sun. Can you imagine how pretty it will be when it's cleaned up?'

'You like the house then?'

'Yes, it has a welcoming feel to it.'

'See the rest of it. I'll wait in the music room.'

She went upstairs where eight bedrooms of various sizes were situated. Her sisters could have a bedroom each if they desired, and

Mrs Mortimer could have the biggest one. Up the next set of stairs were situated four small rooms for servants, each window overlooking the weedy carriageway. There was a large attic to accommodate storage.

She thought she saw someone move at the far end of the garden, but the windows were grimy and when she took a second look she saw nothing.

She heard the sound of a Mozart minuet and went downstairs.

'Do you play?' he asked.

'A little. The old earl hired a tutor, who taught myself and Blythe. She left after two years, and was never replaced.'

'Then you'll know this simple duet.' He shifted up to make room for her and played the introduction.

She joined in, her hands small and pale when compared to his tanned ones. He had a deft touch, but laughed every time the piano hit a wrong note.

He went into another minuet, then another – andantine, giga and contradance. She began to laugh as he went faster, making a game of it.

'Enough, you win,' she finally cried, and placed her hands over his on the keys.

He turned his hands under hers, capturing them before she could escape, threading their fingers so their palms touched. When he turned, his eyes were amused. 'Is there a prize?'

Her heart, she thought, for it beat against her ribs so furiously he couldn't fail to hear the noise it made. She was too aware of him, of those hard palms against hers, as close as lovers, their fingers entwined like limbs.

His glance dropped to linger on her mouth, which then seemed to ripen against her skin like a succulent plum. He smiled, leaned forward and kissed her.

The kiss was so tender she couldn't bring herself to ruin the exquisiteness of it by pushing him away. Rather, she offered him a reward by emitting a small sigh of pleasure, so the kiss progressed a little further and she unfolded like the dewy petals of a flower to the sun.

She opened her eyes when the kiss ended, found herself gazing directly into his eyes, no longer amused, but dark, stormy and rather predatory, like a cat with a mouse. Only she didn't feel mouse-like, but splendidly feline, and wanted to stretch and purr so he'd be tempted to stroke her.

'Lexi,' he murmured, and she could hear the surprise in his voice as he let go of her hands. 'A thousand pardons. I don't know what came over me, and shouldn't have taken such a liberty.'

Had he been thinking of *her*, of the woman he loved in London? The reason for the caress came crashing down in ruins about her ears. Her hands came to her face as she said wretchedly, 'I shouldn't have allowed it. I'm mortified.'

They both stood at the same time and the piano stool went crashing over. By the time he reached down to straighten it Alexis was in the hall and out through the front door.

'Mrs Clark!' she exclaimed in horrified surprise, for the woman had her eyes cupped either side by her hands and was in the process of peering through the lace curtains of the music room. 'You gave me such a fright. What on earth are you doing here?'

Mrs Clark straightened, and although her eyes avoided contact her voice was strong, almost to the point of hectoring. 'More to the point, what are you doing here? I was about to visit Mrs Curruthers and heard music. I then heard a crash and wondered if there were thieves in the dower house.'

'You overheard me playing the piano from the street?' Kynan said, stepping out through the door behind her and locking it. 'I find your explanation hard to believe since my rig is plain to see. Miss Patterson caught you in the act of looking through the window so I can only conclude that you knew we were here and that curiosity got the better of you.'

Mrs Clark turned a bright shade of red and she began to splutter an abject apology.

Alexis felt sorry for her, but hoped she hadn't observed the intimate embrace she

110

and the earl had indulged in. 'I'm sure Mrs Clark's actions were as she said, my Lord. I beg you to offer her the benefit of the doubt.'

'Very well, Miss Patterson, as you request. In future, Mrs Clark, I'd be obliged if you'd rap at the door. I find your behaviour extraordinary.' He turned, his expression bland. 'Have you finished viewing the house, Miss Patterson?'

'Yes, my Lord. It will do very nicely for my family, and I do hope your relative will find us agreeable as co-tenants.'

'Good. Then I must deliver you back to the hall as I've got urgent business in town to attend to. After you, Mrs Clark, we don't want you to keep Mrs Curruthers waiting, and it's quite a walk to the other end of the village.'

On the way back to Longmore, Alexis said, 'What if Mrs Mortimer decides not to come?'

He flicked a glance her way. 'There's an alternative.'

'Tell me what it is.'

There was an air of remoteness to him, a cutting edge to his voice. 'You and your sisters can move into the dower house, since I'm sure you can fend for yourselves. Rent will be taken into account when the yields from your land are calculated.'

'I'll have to learn to cook.'

Her attempt to draw a smile from him fell

flat. 'Even I can boil an egg and make a stew. You do see now, why you can no longer have the run of Longmore Hall?'

She could indeed, and spelled it out for him, her voice as cutting as his. 'You're a man who cannot control his basic instincts.'

'Something like that. You're a temptation, and too much the innocent for me.'

Her face flamed at the unfairness of it. 'I didn't encourage you to kiss me.'

'Didn't you? Why didn't you resist? Slap my face ... show your displeasure in some way?'

'Because I was taken aback ... because I enjoyed being kissed by you ... Didn't you enjoy it?'

'Any man would enjoy kissing you, and would want to take it further. It would be easy to seduce you, Lexi, that's why I don't want you living under my roof. It will only encourage a desire to be together, which will cause speculation amongst the staff, and make it impossible for us to behave naturally with each other. What if it had been another man stealing a kiss from you?'

'It wasn't.' The thought of Kynan seducing her gave her a vicarious little thrill. Although angry with herself, she was more furious at him for suggesting she would allow any other man to kiss her. She snapped, 'Am I to be censured for something that took me so completely by surprise. Why are you so annoyed when you instigated the whole thing, and how dare you insinuate I'd allow other men to take such liberties? Please bring the rig to a halt this minute. I'm deeply insulted by your words, and would prefer to walk the rest of the way than spend another minute in your company.'

'I'll take you to Longmore.'

'You will not!' She stood precariously on the swaying carriage, clinging to the handrail, and shouted, 'If you won't stop, I shall jump.'

'Then jump, and to hell with you!'

She sat down again. This was not a man who would easily be told what to do. When he eventually slowed the rig and brought it to a halt, it was not to gaze upon her with anger, but with shame in his eyes and an apology forming on his lips. 'Lexi,' he said gently.

Trembling with rage, she knew she wasn't going to allow him to say he was sorry. She slapped him. The palm that had so recently snugged against his, flattened with a resounding crack against his closely shaven cheek.

His breath hissed through his teeth and he flinched. She'd never hit anyone before, and the instant gratification she felt was followed by a moment of trepidation, then panic. She jumped from the rig, stumbled, then strode off as fast as she could go.

After a while she had to stop and catch her breath. She gazed back at the rig, still where she'd left it, with Kynan still seated on it gazing after her. She wanted to go back and beg his forgiveness.

'Come back here, Lexi Patterson,' he said loudly, so she was startled into thinking he might have read her mind. But she could hear the undercurrent of laughter in his voice.

He would only tease her and make her smile. She shook her head. 'No! And I'm not going to say I'm sorry.'

They stared, challenging each other for a full minute, before Kynan mockingly blew her a kiss, turned the rig around and headed in the opposite direction.

'Damn you for a Welsh upstart!' she shouted after him, and stamped her foot.

Kynan's face stung. No woman had ever slapped him before. It had been a humbling act. He conceded that he'd asked for it ... deserved it even. His act of defiance had been a stupid and childish gesture.

She'd gone flouncing off as though there was a bee under her tail, her hips twitching indignantly with every step. 'Hah!' As he threw the laugh into the air he realized that if he'd gone after her he'd have kissed her senseless as punishment.

His control was slipping if a country girl

could make him react in such a way every time they met. He'd been too long without the ease a real woman gave – a woman like Julia who was generous with her affections as well as practised.

As he went back through Longmore village the curtains at the manse twitched. No doubt the two women were gossiping about himself and Alexis. He cursed Mrs Clark, and prayed she hadn't observed what had passed between them.

There was an old man weeding around the gravestones with a hardy looking lad. Kynan stopped and asked them if they had time to tidy up the garden of the dower house.

'Aye,' the old man said. 'I reckon me and the lad here can set about that for thee. What say you, Tim?'

The lad nodded. ''Tis a good garden for us to work in, Grandpa, with a tree to shade us when we need to rest, and good soils for raising plants.'

'I'll tell Joshua Hardin to see to your wage, then. What are you named?'

'Sam Hood. This here is my grandson. He's right good at growing things. You can safely leave the dower house in our hands, that you can.'

Kynan managed to get his business in town done. There was a letter from Mrs Mortimer expressing her delight in his elevation to the peerage, and saying she'd be down just as soon as she could find tenants for her own house.

He managed to hire two young maids of all work for the dower house, who would start work the following week. He'd provision the house and leave them to sort the place out. As soon as it was habitable the Patterson girls could move in. He bought Mrs Glasse's book, *The Art of Cooking made Plain and Easy* as a peace offering for Lexi. He also picked up John Farley's *The London Art of Cookery*, and toyed with the idea of buying that too, in case she preferred recipes more complicated. He remembered the burnt chicken, grinned and put it down.

The stage coach came rumbling in at noon, the horses lathered and snorting. Passengers disembarked, including his mother and her maid.

Kynan's face broke into a smile of relief and he hurried to greet her. 'I'm so pleased to see you. I thought you'd never get here.'

'Neither did I. What a tediously uncomfortable journey it was.'

Soon they were surrounded by luggage.

'You look as though you've brought most of your wardrobe with you, Mother.'

'My dear, I haven't brought a fraction of it. Besides, that large trunk was delivered from the warehouse and is addressed to you. Tell me, how is life treating you, my aristocratic son? You look as though you're thriving.'

He laughed. 'The fresh air took a while to get used to, and life is extremely interesting, if nothing else. I'll hire someone with a cart to bring the maid with the luggage. Will you ride in the phaeton with me?'

'I intend to. You can tell me all about those orphaned girls you found yourself responsible for. You sounded quite frantic in your letter. I'm dying to see the poor little mites.'

'Ah ... those girls,' he said vaguely, and smiled as he remembered Lexi calling him a damned Welsh upstart. He hadn't realized she was quite so fiery tempered.

Seven

At first glance, Florence Trent's son could have been moulded in her own image. Her dark hair was swept back with grey at the temples, her frame was tall and elegant, her olive-hued skin was stretched finely over high cheekbones.

Kynan's green eyes and astute business sense had been a gift from his father, though, as had been his more generously proportioned mouth and straight nose flaring perfectly at the nostrils.

Florence smiled as she observed his profile. Kynan was more like his father than he knew, and his father had been a man she had loved and respected while he'd lived.

He'd been staring into space while the horse and phaeton ambled along, his mind obviously on something else. She placed her hand on his arm to draw his attention. 'Tell me about your five orphans. What are their names?'

'Esmé and Daria are the two youngest. Then comes Celeste and Blythe.' He shook his head in despair. 'Blythe is more like a lad in her ways, and reckless. That pile of rubble we passed a while back used to be their home. It was dangerous so had to be demolished.'

'And the fifth child, the oldest. What's her name?'

His smile came as he softly said her name. 'The eldest of the Patterson girls is called Alexis. She's very protective of her sisters.'

The look on her son's face told her that the older girl was his favourite of the children. Florence had always wanted a daughter to bring up, but it was not to be. Now she looked forward to meeting this orphaned family of girls. 'What of the future of this family, Kynan?'

'They have means, but they're tied up in land. The plan is to work their land. The rent will provide them with the means to become independent, though their skills are woefully inadequate.'

She was surprised he'd go that far. 'Dearest Kynan, you are so like your father.'

'It's not a situation I feel able to handle adequately, but I've enlisted some help. Cordelia Mortimer has agreed to live in the dower house. She's always wanted to move back to the country. She's agreed to take the Patterson girls under her wing and teach them some feminine graces.'

'Ah, so you take this responsibility seriously.'

'They have nowhere else to go. Mrs Mortimer seemed an ideal candidate, and the dower house is not in uncomfortably close proximity to Longmore Hall.'

'Yes, of course. The children will be well supervised by Cordelia. At least they won't be able to run around your home making a nuisance of themselves.'

He gazed at her, apparently startled, and opened his mouth to say something. But just then the carriage crested the hill and she exclaimed with delight, 'Is that Longmore Hall?'

'Yes, it is.'

'How delightfully situated the place is, and how bracing the air, too. Is that the sea beyond?'

'Yes, Mother. There's a small, sandy cove, but the tide must be monitored because it quickly covers the beach when it's in flow. The path down to it is near the folly. Although it's roughly stepped and there's a handrail, you still have to take care. The Patterson family lost their parents and baby brother in the cove when part of the cliff fell.'

'Oh, how terribly tragic, and so sad for them.'

They fell silent for the rest of the journey.

Alexis was indulging in a moment of miserable solitude when she heard the phaeton.

She didn't think she could face Kynan after what she'd done to him, and wouldn't be at all surprised if he didn't march in and send her packing immediately.

She hadn't felt like remaining with her sisters in the folly. The house demolition and the whereabouts of the treasure had been the main topics of conversation.

Blythe had worn an air of secrecy about her. Her words had tumbled breathlessly, a sure sign of inner agitation. 'Mr Hardin has promised to keep a look out for the treasure. He's personally supervising the removal of the rubble and is making sure every brick and slate is counted and recorded before it leaves the estate. There are hundreds of them, and lots of broken glass everywhere.'

'Then you mustn't go there again. None of you must. You'll only get in the way.'

'I saw a rocking chair, but Mr Hardin said he'll make sure that anything of a domestic nature will be kept aside for us. I do hope he finds the treasure there.'

Because she was heartily sick of the subject, it was a sentiment affirmed silently by Alexis, herself, before she'd left them, but more noisily and hopefully by her sisters.

Alexis took the precaution of turning the key in the lock when she heard footsteps coming along the corridor.

It was Mrs Elliot, who knocked and said

against the panels, 'Lord Trent requests your presence in the drawing room, Miss Patterson.'

'Tell him I'm indisposed.'

'Lord Trent's mother has arrived.'

Alexis unlocked the door. 'Goodness! Then I must go down. Is her room ready?'

'Yes, Miss Patterson. Her luggage and her maid are both on their way.'

'I'll come and inspect the room.'

The room looked out over the sea and the walls were lined with watered pink taffeta. Mrs Elliot had found a rose-coloured counterpane in the linen cupboard, and some pretty lace hangings for the bed, which a good soaking had freshened.

'The room looks lovely, Mrs Elliot.'

'Thank you, miss.'

'Send the maid to ask the gardener to cut some apple blossom for her table. It will be a nice gesture to welcome the earl's mother with.'

Movement took Alexis's gaze towards the folly, and she saw her sisters running up towards the house. Blythe's hair was an untidy nest flying around her shoulders. She remembered the younger girls' faces had been dirty, like urchins.

The reason for their haste was clear to see, a cart with the luggage, and a young woman seated next to the driver.

'I didn't consider that Mrs Trent might

bring a maid. The girl can have the small room next door.'

'Yes, Miss Patterson.'

Alexis smoothed down her blue checked gown, which had been freshly laundered when she'd donned it that morning. 'I'd better tidy my hair. Would you send my sisters up so I can make sure they're clean. I don't want us creating a bad impression.'

'They're older than I expected,' Kynan's mother said, looking startled as the Patterson sisters smiled widely at her.

Daria had a hole in her hose, Esmé's face was streaked with dirt, and Blythe would have looked more at home running round a farmyard. Celeste, though, looked as dainty and as demure as an angel.

'Alice laid two eggs this morning, my Lord,' she said prettily.

'Tell her, well done. Where's your sister?'

Celeste gazed along the line, looking innocently back at him to say, 'Lexi isn't here yet.'

Daria giggled and Blythe grinned. 'I expect she's moping. She was in a ferment when she got home.'

'What's that supposed to mean?'

'Oh, you know. As snappy as a ratter, as if she wanted to bite someone's head off.'

Kynan wanted to laugh at the description, but knew it would be wrong to encourage

Blythe. 'You shouldn't talk about your sister that way.'

'Then you shouldn't have asked her to explain, my Lord.' Alexis swept into the room with a self-consciously determined look on her face. 'You girls look disgraceful. Blythe, go and tidy your hair this minute. Daria and Esmé, you can wash your hands and faces at the same time.' Apologetically, Alexis turned to Kynan's mother as her sisters scattered. 'You must be Mrs Trent. I do beg your pardon. My sisters certainly should know better than to present themselves so badly. What must you think?'

Celeste whispered, 'But it's not their fault, Lexi. We were on our way to our rooms when the maid told us the earl wanted to see us in the drawing room immediately.'

'Oh, I see.'

Both Lexi and his mother gazed at Kynan with the same questioning expression, obviously awaiting his explanation. They would be disappointed, for he hadn't one.

He sighed, letting them know he found females to be rather illogical when they were together. They seemed to have no problem at all in communicating with each other, often without speaking, as they did now, exchanging a faint smile of indulgence at his inability to understand them.

'Perhaps I ought to introduce you. Mother, this is Alexis Patterson.'

The smile Alexis aimed at his mother was so warm that Kynan found himself smiling too. 'I'm so pleased to meet you, Mrs Trent. You must be tired after your journey.'

'I am a little fatigued. It's lovely to meet you, too, though I expected someone younger, Miss Patterson.'

'Did you? How very odd.' Alexis turned her eyes his way. 'Have you ordered refreshment for your mother, my Lord?'

He hadn't had time to. It seemed that he'd barely finished shaking his head when she gently tut-tutted and reached for the bell pull. 'By the time you've refreshed yourself, your maid will have finished her tasks and will come down to show you to your room so you can rest.'

His mother seemed amused by the way Lexi was managing them all, Kynan thought. He imagined she'd have acted as mistress of the house when the old earl was alive, and he'd have encouraged her in that role if he'd intended to make a countess of her.

He was about to take her to task when he caught a glimpse of desperation haunting the depths of her eyes. She was breathless with nerves, probably because of what had occurred between them earlier.

His heart went out to her and he tried to put her at her ease. 'That's kind of you, Miss Patterson. Did your sisters find the treasure while I was in town?'

'I'm afraid not, so you'll be obliged to put up with our company a little longer, my Lord. I'm sorry we're the cause of such inconvenience to you.'

He felt the urge to take her in his arms and comfort her. 'I just want what's best for you and your sisters. You'll be pleased to know that I've heard from Mrs Mortimer and she's agreed to come down from London just as soon as she can.'

She nodded. 'That's good of her.'

'I've hired two maids to clean the dower house, and a man and his grandson to keep the garden tidy.'

'Sam Hood and Timothy? There's not much they don't know about gardens, and they're trustworthy.'

'Two maids should suffice and you should be able to move into the dower house within a week or two.' He unconsciously touched the cheek she'd slapped as he said with a faint smile, 'I'll see if I can find someone to tune the piano.'

She lowered her eyes. 'I'll ask Mr Fenning. He plays the organ at the church and tunes the one in the music room here.'

He picked the cookery book up from the table and handed it to her. 'Look what I found in Dorchester for you. I thought it might help you manage.'

Alexis glanced at the title and gave a

tremulous smile, as if she might cry at any moment.

Kynan moved closer in case he needed to offer her his handkerchief to weep into. 'Lexi, my dear, you know this is for the best. Will you tell your sisters, or would you rather I was there?'

His mother cleared her throat, reminding him she was present. He took a step back.

Alexis drew in a deep, shuddering breath, taking control of herself. 'It would be best if I informed my sisters of what lies ahead. Thank you for the gift, I'll invite you both to dinner when I've learned the craft of cookery.'

'As long as it's not chicken stew.'

This time her smile was more spontaneous as the humour of that first meal together was recognized and shared. 'It's really not polite to remind me of my shortcomings, my Lord.'

Outside the door, somebody whispered, 'Oh, good. Mrs Dawson has made our favourite cake.'

The maids who brought in the refreshment were followed by the Patterson girls, all clean and tidy now. They displayed their best manners and charmed his mother with their chatter, but Kynan could see she was tired, and was pleased when her maid came for her.

'Thank you all for making me so welcome.

I look forward to renewing our acquaintance at dinner,' she said to the girls.

After his mother had gone, Kynan rose. 'Your sister has something to say to you all. I'll leave you to it then, Miss Patterson. I'll be in the study if you need me.'

All heads swivelled towards Alexis when the door closed behind him. Her sisters' eyes were bright and filled with curiosity. Love for them almost overwhelmed her.

She said, 'We're to move into the dower house on the outskirts of Longmore.'

'Leave here,' Esmé whispered. 'This is our home.'

'No, it's not our home, Es. This is the earl's home.'

'Our home was pulled down this morning,' Blythe reminded them all.

'But who will look after us?' Daria wailed.

'We'll look after each other as we always have. There is also a Mrs Cordelia Mortimer coming to live with us. The earl thinks we need an older woman to teach us the things we need to know, and I'm inclined to agree with him. Mrs Mortimer is a cousin to Mrs Trent.'

Celeste scowled. 'I expect I shall hate her.'

'There's no reason why you should, Celeste. I'm given to understand that she's an educated and accomplished woman, who will be able to pass some of those skills on to us. The earl has been very generous, and we shall have two maids and a gardener to help us. I've seen inside the house. It's a good size and you shall have a room each if you wish. It will be such fun.'

'What about the cooking?'

Alexis shrugged and held out the book. 'Oh, we'll have to learn how to do that for ourselves. See, the earl brought me this book, which will tell us how to do it properly. How thoughtful of him.'

'It wasn't polite of him to remind you of your inadequacy,' Celeste said, and giggled at the thought. 'Can we take Betty and Alice with us?'

'They belong to the earl. But we'll have our own hens, and we can buy our bread and milk because we'll have rent from the land.'

'We'll start a vegetable garden, too,' Blythe said.

Esmé added excitedly, 'Can we have a cat and a dog?'

'We'll have to ask Mrs Mortimer.'

'I'll put a hedgehog in her bed if she says no.'

'You most certainly will not, Daria, else the house will be filled with fleas and we'll all itch,' Alexis told her. But when they all began to giggle at the thought, she laughed, for their reaction hadn't been as bad as she'd expected.

There was more excitement when they

went upstairs. A large trunk had been delivered to their sitting room.

'It must belong to Mrs Trent.'

'No, this has my name on it, so it must be for us.' Alexis took a scrawled note out from under one of the straps. It read simply, *This is my contribution to Miss Clark's birthday ball. Kynan.*

Her eyes widened as she whispered, 'I'd forgotten we'd been invited to the ball.'

Four pairs of eyes widened in excitement. 'All of us?'

'All of us. The earl said he'd escort us and his mother would chaperone us. But he was annoyed with Mrs Clark, who was intrusive and overbearing, and I thought it was just talk.'

'A pity it's Sibyl Clark's ball,' Celeste said gloomily. 'It will be a feather in her mother's cap to have the earl there.'

'Oh, Sibyl is quite pleasant, as I recall. And I should think Mrs Clark will mind her manners around the earl after what happened this morning.'

Everyone looked at her for an explanation.

Offhandedly, she said, 'Oh, the earl was showing me over the dower house and Mrs Clark was caught peering at us through the window. She was like a wasp when I caught her, and Lord Trent gave her a good dressing down. I don't think she'll cross him again in a hurry.'

Alexis's revelation was followed by various gasps, and a giggle from Blythe. 'No wonder you were in such a fury when you arrived home. You came bolting down the hill so fast I thought you'd fall flat on your face.'

Alexis didn't correct Blythe's assumption that Mrs Clark was the reason for it, but her face began to glow. Luckily, their attention had returned to the trunk.

They stared at it, breathless with the thought of what it might contain. Curiosity got the better of Celeste first. 'Shall we see what's in it?'

The top layer was a selection of silk wraps. Under those a tray containing accessories such as fans, ribbons, gloves and head-dresses was revealed, to many exclamations of delight. Reverently, Alexis handed them to Blythe, who laid them out on the bed. Then came evening dresses, high-waisted and gloriously soft. The two smallest were white over lace petticoats, with embroidered flowers of pink and blue at the hem, and broad satin sashes to match.

Daria and Esmé were enchanted by them.

Celeste's gown was the palest of pinks, Blythe's a soft, buttery yellow. Both were pretty and feminine.

Alexia's mouth was dry as she lifted out a dark blue gown. It was a drift of translucent fabric sprinkled with a spray of crystals that shimmered like stars down to the hem. The

131

gown had no other adornment, and was exquisitely beautiful in its simplicity.

'You can see through it,' Blythe whispered, in a scandalized tone. 'And the bodice is too ... *revealing*.'

Celeste picked up a shimmering chemise of silk, its more modest neckline pleated and studded with the same crystals. 'I think this is to be worn under it. And there's a feathered headband with a crystal decoration. Oh, Lexi, you'll look so grown up. All the men will fall desperately in love with you.'

'I'd prefer it if they didn't.'

'Let's try everything on,' Daria said. But the trunk hadn't finished revealing its secrets. 'Look, here's some blue satin dancing slippers to go with that gown. And here are some white ones for us, Es. And a corset with padding that pushes the bosom up. No ... there's two corsets, and some drawers. You don't think the earl chose them himself, do you?'

'How could he when he's been here every day?'

'One of the corsets must be for Blythe, because the rest of us aren't old enough to have grown-up bosoms.'

Daria and Esmé looked at each other and began to giggle.

Blythe scowled at them. 'I'm not going to wear a corset for anybody and I'm going to bind my chest. When is this ball?'

'In about five weeks' time.'

Celeste suddenly said. 'Does anyone know how to dance?'

The five girls exchanged glances of consternation.

'My dear Kynan,' Florence said to her son after breakfast the next day. 'No wonder you asked me to come and stay.'

'It's only until Mrs Mortimer arrives, then I'll be able to relax.'

'Cordelia is a good choice and will enjoy being useful. The Patterson girls are so lively and natural.'

'Too much so, at times. The younger pair threw their arms about my neck and hugged me this morning.'

'And the older girls?'

'Unsophisticated.' Kynan couldn't quite hide his grin though.

His mother laughed. 'She's lovely, isn't she?'

'Who is?'

'You know very well which one I'm talking about.'

'They're *all* lovely. Miss Patterson exquisitely so.'

'And they hang upon your every word. It's flattering for a man to be the centre of so much attention. It could turn his mind towards taking advantage of it. Take care, Kynan.'

He gave her a sideways look. 'You're reading too much into the situation. The Pattersons are reliant upon me for their very existence at the moment. Of course they're going to be nice to me, since they think they have to be.'

'Ah, so their motive is mercenary.'

'Not at all. I'm saying they've trained themselves to show gratitude to their benefactor, so it's second nature to them now. You have to remember they were permanent guests at Longmore Hall before it became my roof. They've been left to their own devices from what I can gather, and are uneducated except for what Alexis had been able to teach them. She's been in charge of them since she was nine. After their tutor left, you would have thought another would have been hired for them.'

'Many men regard an education as being wasted on women, especially those backward thinkers who wed for domestic and social convenience. Your predecessor was obviously one of them. I was lucky that my father was a teacher. He made sure Cordelia and I were given the means to support ourselves should the need arise. Your father employed me in one of the warehouses as a tally clerk.'

'He said he fell in love with you at first sight.'

She smiled gently at the thought. 'I think it

might have been the other way round. I wonder though, what will Julia make of this situation when she learns of it?'

He gazed at her. 'Why should Julia make anything of it? By the time she learns of it, the Pattersons will be residents in the dower house. Believe me, I'll heave a huge sigh of relief, then. Have you seen Julia?'

'I saw Mrs Spencer a month ago at the theatre.'

'Did you speak?'

'We were in opposite boxes and Mrs Spencer was part of Lord Haining's party.' His mother glanced down at her hands. 'They all seemed quite animated.'

The disapproving expression on her face made him smile and he suggested, 'Lord Haining is too old for Julia, you know. He must be forty, at least.'

'Her first husband was a far older man,' she pointed out, 'and Lord Haining has a reputation.'

He shrugged. 'Most unmarried men do. Peter Haining is steady enough, and good company. As for Julia's marriage, it was an arranged one. You might as well know, Mother, I'm considering making a proposal of marriage.'

'Yes, so I hear.'

'From whom?'

'I know you and Julia are ... *close*. There's been gossip. I hope you'll give the matter a little more thought, Kynan. You should invite her down here to observe how she fits into the district.'

His eyes narrowed. 'Has something happened in my absence I should know about?'

'Nothing specific. I feel uneasy about her need to constantly socialize and wonder whether the country life will suit her.'

'For business reasons I'll be spending each winter in town, so, if Julia and I wed she won't miss the London season.'

'And I've heard she doesn't want children?'

Her words took him by surprise. But how transparent his mother was. 'Ah, so that's what's worrying you. You're in a hurry to become a grandmamma.'

'I certainly am not! You're my only son ... I couldn't bear it if you married unwisely and spent a lifetime regretting it. Don't let Julia's looks and airs blind you to other qualities she may or may not possess. There ... now I sound like an interfering mother.'

It appeared to be sound advice to him. 'Not at all. I promise I'll be cautious. As for inviting Julia to stay, I've already done so, along with Philip Weatherby, Haining and Roxanne Dupré. That way, Julia won't become bored with her own company.'

'Exactly,' his mother said and her lips pursed slightly.

Eight

Finding herself attracted to the sound of laughter, Florence peeped around the door of what could only be a music room, for it contained a piano with decorated panels. Some music stands were huddled together in a corner like headless storks. Pairs of chairs, one upside down upon the other, lined up along the walls like tumblers grasping each other's ankles.

A space had been cleared. The Patterson girls were all in a row. Alexis was at the front with a paper held in her hand. She was wearing a patched blue gown, its hem stained beyond redemption. Over it, a limp white apron. 'This dance is an allemande and looks quite simple. I'll show you.'

She began to dance. 'Two steps forward and two steps backward – four times.'

The manoeuvre was successfully copied by her sisters.

'One step to the left and one to the right, then two steps forward and two back.'

They shuffled raggedly to her instruction.

'Good. Repeat the movements, then the

first steps again.'

They all ended up in different directions, colliding with each other and giggling.

'Ouch! You're on my foot, Blythe.'

'Sorry.'

Daria and Esmé went swirling off, laughing, until they got dizzy and fell over.

'Do behave yourselves,' Alexis said. 'How can we learn to dance if you don't take it seriously? We only have a short time to learn, otherwise we'll just have to sit and watch everyone else.'

'I don't want to dance anyway,' Blythe said. 'I feel stupid doing it.'

Celeste made a face. 'How embarrassing if we don't. Everyone will snigger behind their fans.'

'Let them. I wish we'd never been invited to Sibyl's ball,' Blythe said gloomily. 'Mrs Clark only wants us there to make fools of us.'

Florence advanced into the room, a smile on her face. 'No, my dear. She wants you there because your father was a baronet, and you will add some class to the affair. We shan't allow her to make fools of us, shall we, young ladies?'

There came an enthusiastic chorus of assent.

'Learning to dance isn't hard, you know, and you all have natural grace.'

The girls looked at each other with grins

on their faces at the thought.

'Would you allow me to teach you? You'll soon learn the dance steps for the most popular allemandes. By the time you've learnt those, you'll be ready for the quadrille and the contradance, which are similar except the former is danced in a square, and the latter in a line. Both are a little more complicated than the allemandes, but by then you'll know the basic steps, which will make matters much easier.'

'Thank you so much, Mrs Trent,' Alexis said. 'I'm sure we'll all enjoy the experience.'

Blythe gave a resigned little sigh.

Florence turned to one of the younger girls. 'Daria, isn't it? You seem fleet of foot. Perhaps you'd go and find my maid. Myra can play the piano and dance very well. She can also call the dances. If we practise every day for two hours, then you'll soon learn.'

The dancing lessons gave them something to do. Even Blythe seemed to enjoy the exercise it afforded her and, surprisingly, it soon became obvious she was the best dancer amongst them.

Florence mentioned casually to her son the following week, 'We need four couples so they can practice the quadrille properly. I'll expect you and your manservant to join us tomorrow for an hour or so.'

'But, Mother—'

'No excuses. I know both of you can dance

well. You and James can partner them one by one, so they can experience what it's like to be partnered by a man. All of them have done so well. I'm as proud of them as if I'd been their own mother.'

'Thank God you're not,' he said, and when a smile drifted across her son's face Florence knew exactly who he was thinking of. She just hoped that Julia Spencer didn't arrive to spoil her plans.

Blythe was in the folly, where she always spent a large proportion of each day. She was sprawled rather inelegantly over the barrel of the cannon, which pointed out to sea in case the damned Welsh came. All she need do was open the doors and fire straight through the window.

'Don't bother opening it,' the old earl had said. 'And make sure you don't stand behind the cannon, because the bugger will roll back, then leap forward again.' The cannon was secured to the back wall by a rusting chain, like a beast on a leash. 'It's never been fired as far as I know. It might knock down the wall and leap right over the cliff,' the old earl had said, roaring with laughter at the thought.

But the Welsh abduction of the Longmore bride had come by land. Blythe didn't mind the current earl at all, damned or not. The ship to shore battle she'd always created in her mind had never happened – neither would it. Unless...? There was always the ghost ship, she thought. Her face pressed against the cool surface of the barrel, as, with arms and legs dangling down either side, Blythe felt a thrill of dread as she imagined how the ghouls would look with their empty eye sockets and dripping mouths.

Lord Trent might have sent a servant to remove all the weapons and ammunition from the folly, but he couldn't move the cannon without taking down the wall. She grinned. And she now had the means to fire it for she'd filled her pockets up with gunpowder when she'd gone to look at the ruins of the manor. Let the miserable spirits in their pirate ship come, she thought. The cannon would blow them back to hell.

She heard her name being called and sighed, for she was loath to leave the place that had always been her home, and today they were to move into the dower house.

Oh, the earl meant well, but he didn't understand. She didn't want to grow into a sugary miss who sat at home and embroidered samplers, although she'd enjoyed learning to dance, she conceded – especially when the earl had danced with Lexi and he'd caught her eye and winked. She grinned. Lord, how Lexi had blushed.

Blythe didn't want any man to wink at her. And she didn't want to smile politely when she needed to laugh out loud. But it would happen, she knew. Lexi had told her that growing into a woman was inevitable, and it just happened gradually, without you even knowing it, so you woke up one morning and discovered you were one. The womanly curse was already a regular visitor.

'Nothing will make me wear that damned corset, though,' she said with a scowl, and scrambled from her comfortable perch when her name was called again.

Locking the door behind her, she pocketed the key and began to run towards where the cart waited, vowing to herself that she'd be back.

'Ouch. I can hardly breathe.'

'Oh, don't be silly, Blythe.' The yellow garment floated down over her sister's arms and head, slid over her chemise and settled around her ankles. 'You can put your arms down, now.' Alexis smiled when she did. 'You look so pretty with the curls. Lally is good at arranging hair.' Pinning some silk flowers to the nape of her sister's neck she turned Blythe around to face the mirror. 'There.'

'The flowers tickle my neck.' Blythe caught Alexis's eye and grinned. 'I look like a cabbage butterfly.'

'You look like the dear, sweet girl that you are.'

Blythe tried to flatten the gentle swell of her bosom the corset had pushed up. They sprang back into position when she removed her palms. She then hunched into her shoulders. 'I don't want to grow up.'

Alexis sighed. 'I know, Blythe. You have to accept that you nearly are grown up, and must act accordingly. Now, I want you to promise to be on your best behaviour tonight and set a good example to the others. Don't say or do anything outrageous.'

Blythe hugged her tight. 'I'll try not to. We won't all fit on the phaeton. Do you think the earl will bring the cart?'

The earl didn't. He arrived on the phaeton, looking devilishly handsome in his evening clothes of breeches and dark jacket. His elegance struck Alexis anew after a week of being apart from him. Behind him came the Longmore carriage, polished to perfection, the earl's coat of arms displayed on the door and a coachman in smart livery – a face they recognized – on his perch above. The carriage was drawn by a magnificent pair of dark bay geldings, ones they'd never seen before.

Blythe gave a whoop of delight. 'What wonderful horses. Hello, Jude. You look splendid.'

The new coachman grinned self-consciously. 'Thank you, Miss Blythe. So do you, even though I be out of turn saying it.'

'It's a pleasant evening, will you ride with me, Miss Patterson?' Kynan said with a smile. 'You'll be crushed if you all try to arrange yourselves in the carriage.'

'Daria and Esmé can be a little boisterous when they're excited.'

'I'm sure my mother won't mind, since we discussed the seating earlier. He leapt down from his seat with the intention of assisting her up. His proximity made her acutely aware of him. There was an inch of smooth skin between the points of his high collar and the dark sideburn. She closed her eyes for a second, imagining placing a kiss there.

'You look exquisite in that gown,' he murmured.

Her eyes flew open. 'And you look exceedingly handsome, Kynan.' She blushed. 'I meant, of course, that your manservant has turned you out well.'

'Oh, what a disappointment. I'd much rather be considered exceedingly handsome,' he teased.

Alexis rallied. 'Such a remark would only fill you with conceit.'

'And you with confusion for saying it.' He chuckled and leaned forward as if he was about to kiss her forehead.

Florence, who was gazing out of the carriage window at them, gently coughed. 'Celeste would prefer to ride with you, as well. Wouldn't you, dear?'

A wide smile was aimed her way. 'Yes, Mrs Trent.'

Blythe looked disappointed. 'Couldn't I ride on the phaeton, as well?'

'Blythe, my dear, we haven't spent much time together and I hardly know you. I've been looking forward to your company, so we can talk. You may ride with your sister and the earl on the way back.' Blythe had a resigned look on her face as she hitched her skirts up to her knees and climbed into the carriage.

'How pretty you look,' Mrs Trent said. 'Here, sit next to me. Daria and Esmé, do try not to wriggle, else you'll crease your skirts. I swear you resemble two little princesses.'

The carriage door was closed. Celeste joined them on the phaeton and Kynan seated himself and took up the reins. 'Hold on tight, ladies, I don't want to lose you.'

The smaller vehicle went on ahead – though not at too great a pace, so the carriage could keep them in sight. The weather was balmy, the air fragrant with the smell of lilac blossom.

'We should have the light from a full moon to guide us home,' Kynan said with satisfaction.

They arrived at the Clark's home a little late. Mrs Clark looked flustered when she saw them, but bustled forward to greet them, her husband in tow. He stood behind her, a rotund man with a long-suffering expression on his face. Bobbing a curtsy to Kynan, Mrs Clark gushed, 'How gracious of you to accept my invitation, my Lord.'

'Not at all. Miss Patterson and her sisters expressed a desire to attend.'

'Ah, yes.' Mrs Clark's eyes washed over them. 'How delightful you all look in your finery. Am I to take it you've discovered the whereabouts of the legendary treasure?'

'We're still looking for it,' Celeste said. 'We didn't buy the gowns, they were a gift from the earl for us to wear to the ball.'

Their hostess's lips flattened into a thin line; her expression scandalized.

'Not at all, Celeste, they were actually a gift from me,' said Florence, and laid her hand on Kynan's sleeve. 'My dear, are you not going to introduce us?'

Kynan smiled as he did so, but his eyes reflected the annoyance he felt. Harold Clark came forward to rescue Kynan. 'Allow me to introduce you to members of the Association of Business Owners, my Lord.'

'But, I intended to introduce him to the guests myself,' Mrs Clark cried out. 'Sibyl is so looking forward to meeting Lord Trent.'

Harold said with a deceptively vague determination, 'You can introduce the ladies instead. How pretty you all look. Let me provide you with a drink, my Lord.'

Talking business was obviously something

Kynan was prepared to do, and probably looked forward to, Alexis thought, as his smile encompassed them all. Living quietly in the country must be hard for someone used to city life. She felt sorry that she'd never experienced the London season her mother had told her about.

'Perhaps you'd introduce your daughter just before the first dance, and I can have the honour of escorting her on to the floor. As for you, young ladies, we mustn't let all that dancing practice go to waste,' Kynan said before allowing himself to be led away. 'I'll expect you to reserve me the first five dances after supper.'

'Your son has been teaching them to dance? What an odd thing for an earl to do,' Mrs Clark said, taking Mrs Trent's arm in a familiar manner.

'My dear Mrs Clark, you reach a conclusion rather too hastily. Lord Trent didn't teach my charges to dance. I did. I prevailed upon my son and his manservant to provide assistance, simply so we could make up two foursomes for the quadrille. My personal maid played the piano so we could have some music.' She managed to disentangle the grip Mrs Clark had taken on her arm without seeming to make any effort. 'What do you find so odd about it, pray?'

So gently did she say it that Mrs Clark couldn't possibly take offence at the reprimand.

'Oh, I merely assumed the former earl would have seen to their social skills.'

'As one would. When the former earl took these young women under his roof one would have expected him to take full parental authority. They should have been provided with the social skills their position in society demands from the daughters of a baron. Luckily, they're dear creatures who possess a natural grace that comes of good breeding. With guidance they'll soon learn.'

'I understand they're moving into the Longmore dower house soon.'

'Ah, yes ... my son told me you'd mistaken himself and Miss Patterson for felons and thought the place was being ransacked.'

Alexis was hard put not to grin when a flush appeared on Mrs Clark's neck and cheeks, but she felt sorry for the woman. 'Mrs Clark was brave to even consider tackling a felon,' she said.

'Or foolhardy. I'm sure I wouldn't have. Oh, is that your daughter, Sibyl, over there in the pink gown, Mrs Clark. How like you, she is.'

The girls exchanged grins, for it was Henrietta Palk, who was short and lumpy, and as garrulous as a goose.

Mrs Clark's mouth pursed. 'That's Sibyl's cousin, who is the child of Harold's sister. Sibyl is standing next to her.'

'My pardon. It must be the Clark resemblance I noticed.' Florence turned to them. 'Come, my dears, we'll occupy that vacant sofa by the window. No doubt, Mrs Clark will send a servant over with some punch so we can refresh ourselves. Afterwards, she may present her daughter to us.'

It was obvious that Mrs Clark had met her match in the earl's mother, for she retreated rapidly and went about her business.

'Sit either side of me, Alexis and Blythe. You younger ones must stand behind us. You may talk in low voices, but try to remember to look pleasant and laugh quietly, so you don't draw attention.'

Soon a music ensemble set up their stands and the first dance was called, a quadrille.

Two young officers quickly came to claim Alexis and Blythe as partners. Another young man was thwarted. Rather than turn back, he escorted a grinning Celeste on to the floor.

With innate courtesy, Kynan led Sibyl on to the floor for the first dance, and joined them to form a square for a quadrille.

Heart beating fast, Alexis hoped she'd remember the steps, but she needn't have worried, for there was a caller, and it all came back to her.

Florence smiled with satisfaction as she watched her pupils dance with barely a fault. 'Come and sit next to me,' she said to the youngest two, and she slid her arms around Daria and Esmé as they watched her sisters dancing. They were very much in demand, and were pink-flushed from their exertions by supper time.

After supper, the earl claimed them all, starting with the younger ones and working his way up. As he took Alexis on to the floor, Kynan whispered something to her. Florence saw Alexis laugh, and Kynan give a smile, similar to the smile Kynan's father used to bestow on herself. What she feels for him is written on her face, Florence thought. I do hope he doesn't break the girl's heart.

The drive home was made in bright moonlight, and the magic of their first ball stayed with them.

'Thank you for taking us, it was such fun,' Blythe said. 'I think I've got blisters on my feet from all the dancing. That soldier trod all over them.'

As the carriage came up behind them, Blythe jumped down from the phaeton without waiting to be helped. Alexis took the opportunity to thank him too. 'I enjoyed it, my Lord.'

'So did I.' He turned to help her down. His lips brushed lightly against her hair. 'Did I tell you you were the most beautiful girl there?'

'Twice.' She chuckled. 'I appreciate all you've done for my sisters and myself.'

'It's my pleasure. You were all very popular, even the youngest ones. I'll escort you and your sisters to the door and see you safely inside.'

Esmé and Daria were nearly asleep on their feet, and Blythe and Celeste took them straight up to their beds.

'Goodnight,' Kynan said, and touched her face with his fingertip. 'When I've got to know a few people I must have some social evenings at Longmore. You'll come, won't you?'

Alexis nodded. They gazed at each other without saying anything for a few moments, then he cleared his throat and his glance went to her mouth as he said softly, 'Goodnight, Lexi. Sweet dreams.'

'Goodnight, Kynan the evening—'

'Should end with a kiss.' His mouth was warm and tender against hers for a few blessed seconds.

'...was absolutely wonderful,' she whispered as he turned and walked away.

That night Alexis tossed and turned in her bed, yearning for the man she loved as she imagined the delights her body craved.

Just two miles away Kynan was also restless, and for a similar reason. He'd been a fool to have kissed Alexis, but her response had been delicious. What would be her response if he really kissed her?

He sighed, left his bed and gazed down over the moon-washed landscape to the rippling expanse of sea. June had covered the landscape in bluebells and a profusion of blood red poppies. Bright buttercups and pale daisies danced amongst the grasses and in the hedgerows.

Kynan experienced a sense of peace, of belonging. Talking with the businessmen of the area had grounded him, for they were every bit as astute and knowledgeable as his acquaintances in London were, and knew a damned lot more about the land.

He'd been too long without a woman, he thought, if a girl like Alexis could make him feel so rampant. And she was too susceptible. Men had been drawn to her at the ball, and to Blythe. He hoped Cordelia Mortimer would soon turn up to supervise them – especially the two older girls.

'Am I trying to keep other men at bay, or just keep her for myself?' he said to himself, perplexed, but couldn't provide an answer. His feelings were overwhelmingly physical when he was with Alexis Patterson. He knew he would have taken advantage of her, had she been less of an innocent. As it was, he felt protective of them all.

He told himself he'd experienced the same arousal in the company of other beautiful woman when the need was upon him. In London he had Julia to take care of his needs. Lexi merely attracted him because Julia was out of his sight. She wasn't really his type of woman.

Idly, he wondered if Julia was on her way.

Nine

Julia Spencer tossed her clothes over the bed and yelled at her maid, 'Where's my blue silk?'

'You told me not to pack it, ma'am.'

'Don't lie, girl. I distinctly remember telling you to pack it.'

Near to tears, the maid said, 'I can't remember that, Mrs Spencer.'

'Can't remember it? Your head must be filled with clay.' Julia hit her around the head with a bodice and flounced towards the door. 'Get the trunk packed.'

'At once, ma'am.'

Emily Talbot was a small woman in her early twenties. She would have walked out if she'd had somewhere else to go. But she had to be thankful for small mercies. At least Julia Spencer hadn't slapped her this time.

She gazed out of the window at the waiting carriage. Her mistress was standing there talking to Lord Haining and his cousin, Philip Weatherby, all smiles and airs and graces now. There was another female in the party, a languid creature called Roxanne

Dupré, who acted on the stage and was Mrs Spencer's friend. Emily was obliged to see to both of them. At least Miss Dupré didn't complain. Her mistress was never satisfied.

I'll take a pair of shears to her head if she's not careful, Emily thought mutinously, and turned to repack the trunk and refold the clothing, so it wouldn't be full of creases when they got to their destination.

At least Mr Trent was always kind to her. She'd understood he was an earl now, so he might think himself too far above her to pass the time of day, now. She couldn't understand why he would want to marry Mrs Spencer, though she knew the pair were intimate from time to time. But Emily wasn't daft. Although her mistress thought she was being discreet, Emily knew Mr Trent wasn't the only man who visited her bedchamber.

Emily had heard the two women talking, her mistress saying, 'Oh, I adore Peter Haining, but he doesn't approve of me, and is reserved. Now he's a peer I'll probably marry Kynan if he asks me. Being married will give me respectability, and I'd be a countess.'

Miss Dupré had given a light, tinkling laugh. 'Kynan might want to live in the country now he has an estate.'

'He can do as he pleases, but I have no

intention of exchanging my current life for one of rustic domesticity. I'm sure Kynan will understand that, since he has the same lust for living. I wonder he's remained faithful to me.'

'He strikes me as being that sort of man. Does he know you're unable to carry a child?'

'My dear Roxanne, it's not something you tell a man you intend to marry. Only you are privy to that little secret. If anyone else learns of it, I'll know exactly where it came from.'

Not exactly, Emily thought, with some satisfaction. You never knew when such information might come in handy. Her mistress had forgotten she'd been in attendance when her late husband had brought the doctor in to examine her. Emily slammed down the lid of the trunk and called down the stairs for the inn's man-of-all-work to take it, and the trunk belonging to Miss Dupré, down to the carriage.

'About time, too,' her mistress declared, scowling at her from the window of the carriage.

Emily clambered up to sit beside the coachman, who smiled sympathetically at her and said, 'Hold on, love, we're nearly there.'

Lord Haining and Philip Weatherby mounted their horses, the whip cracked and the carriage moved forward, scattering a family of honking geese.

It was one of those June days where the sky went on for ever, becoming bluer and bluer. It was one of those days when the wind sighed, when a song thrush in the hedge sang so sweetly that Alexis could have cried from the beauty of the sound. Seated just inside the French door at the little table, she closed her eyes. It was one of those times when the earth seemed to hush, when sounds faded into the distance and peace was renewed in the mind.

Her busy fingers had stilled on the stocking she was darning and she allowed her thoughts to wander. The smile she gave was tender as Kynan came into her mind.

'Oh, there you are.' Daria came racing through the door, scattering her thoughts. 'We've finished our letters. Can we take them to the earl ourselves?'

'Have you all finished the lesson I set you?'

Daria made a face. 'Yes, Lexi.'

'What about your tasks?'

'We've all tidied our rooms up.'

It was too good a day to stay indoors, so Alexis nodded. 'You may take my thank you note with you, as well. But you mustn't walk into the hall like we used to when we lived there. You must ring the bell and hand them to a servant. Then you must come straight back home.'

'Oh, we thought we might ask Lord Trent if he'd heard from Mrs Mortimer.'

'He'll either tell us, or bring her here when he has.'

'Can we ask Blythe to take us to look at the manor, afterwards, then?'

'You shouldn't go there while the men are working. You might suffer injury.'

'Everything is nearly gone now. Every day, more and more of our family home is carted away and the ground becomes boggier. I found a trunk the other day. I thought it was the treasure, but when I tried to lift it the bottom and the contents fell out. It only contained a few mouldy books.'

'I think we have all there was left of worth.' There was a silver snuff box and candlesticks, and a tray, all blackened by exposure. Alexis felt sad that their parents' portrait hadn't been found, and wondered who'd have wanted to steal it.

She picked up her stocking with a sigh. After the hole was darned she must go and prepare the vegetables. Their second maid would help her to cook the dinner. She'd even cook it if Lexi asked her. But Lexi knew she must learn these tasks for herself, for once Mrs Mortimer arrived there would be another person to feed, and she wanted to make a good impression on her.

Agnes enjoyed cooking, while Lally liked to

arrange hair, and was handy with a needle. Both maids were pleasant women, and hard workers. They seemed contented with their lot in life. Kynan had chosen them well, she thought.

'If Blythe's willing to take you, you can go and look at the manor again. Please don't go near the boggy part, else your frocks will stain, and be ruined.'

Daria kissed her on the cheek. 'Come with us, dearest Lexi. You work so hard looking after us, and have no time to just rest and do nothing.'

Alexis would have liked to, but they were a fairly large household, and running it seemed to consume all of her time. Besides, she enjoyed the peace and quiet when her sisters were out – the time to think and to dream ... especially about Kynan.

It was market day at Dorchester. Kynan had just managed to fit the large parcel he carried into the back seat of the phaeton, and had tied it securely with a length of rope.

The stage coach was running late. Kynan took a seat at the inn and sampled a pot of ale while he waited for it to arrive. A couple of people he'd met at the ball nodded, or came over to pass the time of day with him, but he invited none to join him.

Dorchester was busy, and it seemed as if

the two thousand-odd population were all milling about the town at once. The length of the high street was peppered with stalls, and throngs of people milled about them. Country women wore aprons and carried baskets over their arms. Ladies in silks and bright bonnets lifted their skirts above the litter of dung on the street and trod daintily around it.

The deep rumble of men in debate sometimes cut into the shrill cries of the stall women shouting their wares, or the high-pitched laughter of the children who dodged in and around the stalls, chasing after each other.

The horn sounded a warning. Into the soup of vegetable stalls, the people, and the clamouring livestock, came the coach, scattering all before it. The coats of the horses shone with sweat and were lathered from their efforts. Steam rose from their flanks.

Cordelia Mortimer descended. A woman of medium height in a sensible dark blue gown, she gazed around her with interest. Kynan rose to his feet and hurried outside.

'Cordelia, I'm so pleased you're here, at last.'

She gave him a serene look. 'In your letter you sounded quite desperate, Kynan. Or should I address you as my Lord now?'

He kissed her cheek. She was an attractive woman who had the same elegant bearing

160

and fine cheekbones as his mother, though she was a little shorter. They were of a similar age, too. 'I'm finding it difficult to adjust to such formality amongst people I know well and love. Only address me that way in public company if you please, since it's expected. Are you sure you're prepared to cope with the situation here?'

'I'm pleased to be of use to someone at long last, and I've always wanted to live in the country again. It's very pretty here. These girls of yours will present me no problem, you know. In fact, they sound to be quite delightful creatures.'

'They're not *my* girls, Cordelia.'

'Yes ... well, despite your protestations, you have made yourself responsible for them.'

'I could hardly have thrown them out.'

'Of course you couldn't. Now I'm here you don't have to feel threatened by them any more.'

'What makes you think I feel threatened by them?'

'The very fact that I'm standing here.'

Cordelia was probably right. He couldn't seem to control his thoughts in the presence of Alexis. Sometimes, he couldn't control his need to make the advances required to coax her along the path into his bed. A touch here, a kiss there ... the urge to twist the little lock of hair at the nape of her neck around his finger.

He sucked in a breath. Why should he feel threatened? Clearly, it was Alexis who should be feeling that particular emotion, since she was in danger of being seduced by him.

'After today I need only see her ... *them*, the Pattersons, I mean,' he amended, 'on formal occasions like the Sunday service.'

He felt uncomfortable when Cordelia gave him a probing look, then turned away with a knowing smile to say, 'Ah, here are my trunks.'

There were two trunks and two bags. Kynan called the ostler over and slipped him some coins. 'Can you arrange for these to be sent to the dower house as soon as possible?'

'It won't be no trouble. Young Jeffrey, he be helping shift the bricks from the manor, and will be over that way with the cart, later on. Will that do, thee, my Lord?'

'Very nicely.'

Cordelia placed a hand on his arm. 'I'll take the smaller bag with me now, Kynan.'

Picking up the leather bag, Kynan led the way to the phaeton and they were soon on their way.

Alexis was shelling peas when she heard Kynan say, 'You needn't announce me, Lally, just tell me where Miss Patterson is?'

'On the patio.'

Her heart jumped alarmingly. Dropping

the bowl to the table she scrambled to her feet, smoothing down her apron, then patted her hair as he strode through the door.

He was all in black, except for a gold brocade waistcoat. A ruby set in a gold pin secured his snowy cravat, and his hair was a cap of rioting dark curls.

I love him, she thought, inhaling the familiar scent of cinnamon that lingered about him. She smiled at the sight of him. 'Kynan, why are you here?'

'To see you, of course.' Eyes dancing with laughter engaged hers. 'Would you rather I stayed away.'

How dreadful the thought of never being able to see him again was. 'Of course not.'

'Good, because I have no intention of abandoning you all.' He helped himself to a handful of peas to eat and stood to one side. 'Come inside. Mrs Mortimer has arrived and I need to introduce you. Where are your sisters?'

'They've gone to the hall to deliver thank you notes for the ball.'

'It isn't necessary, Lexi.'

'It most certainly is. We enjoyed ourselves so much, and my sisters must learn their manners.'

'It was as much my pleasure as it was yours.' He took her hand in his and placed a kiss in the palm. 'I've missed you, you know. You looked exquisite in that gown. All the men fell in love with you.'

Except the one she wanted to fall in love with her. 'I'm sure you're exaggerating. We had better not keep Mrs Mortimer waiting,' she reminded him gently, and stilled his hand as he reached for more peas. 'Enough, Kynan, else there will be none for our dinner. Agnes will bring us some refreshments, and there's apple cake that Agnes helped me bake. I expect Mrs Mortimer will appreciate having something to revive her after her journey, too.'

She took the bowl of peas and handed it to Lally. 'Take this to the kitchen, please. Ask Agnes to bring us some tea and cake to the drawing room. Perhaps you'd make sure Mrs Mortimer's room is ready for her to occupy. Open the window a little, so it's aired, and place some fresh flowers on her table. Those poppies I picked for the music room will look pretty. I can always pick some more.'

The woman she was introduced to, slanted her head to one side and smiled. 'Miss Patterson, I've been looking forward to meeting you.'

'Thank you, Mrs Mortimer. I'm pleased to make your acquaintance at long last. I'm afraid my sisters are not at home at the moment. I've sent for some refreshment, and your room is being prepared.'

'I've just remembered, I have something in

the phaeton for you,' Kynan said, and headed for the door.

'The earl seems fond of you,' Mrs Mortimer said.

This brought the blood running to Alexis's cheeks. 'Lord Trent has been very kind to us.'

'He takes after his father in that regard.' She hesitated, then said, 'I understand you've been responsible for your sisters since you were quite young yourself.'

'Yes. They're good girls.'

'I'm sure they are, since you seem to have set them a fine example. I imagine you'll find it hard to relinquish your authority over them.'

'I love them dearly. They'll still be my sisters, and nothing will ever change that.'

'Of course not. I understand they need educating. To do that I'll have to supervise them every hour of their day. They're bound to resent it at first, especially the loss of their freedom to roam the countryside. They'll turn to you. Can I count on you to support me?'

'I know you'll need my support, Mrs Mortimer. You're the mistress of this house, which means I'm obliged to rely on your good will. I'd rather like to be involved in the education of my sisters in some way, if I may, since there have already been many changes in their lives of late. Perhaps I can learn something myself, just by helping.'

'I was hoping you'd offer to help. Lord Trent arranged this with the best motives in mind, you know.'

Alexis was beginning to warm to Mrs Mortimer. 'I'm well aware of the earl's virtues.'

'I've made sure of that.' Kynan advanced into the room, carrying a large, flat parcel wrapped in a piece of muslin. He set it down with an amused look on his face. 'I don't want to disillusion her, Cordelia, so please don't inform her of my faults.'

'The earl's here!' There was the patter of feet across the hall and Daria and Esmé burst into the room, breathless and dishevelled, laughing as they competed with each other to tell the earl the news.

'There's a coach and some grand ladies and gentlemen on horses...'

'...at Longmore Hall.'

The pair beamed at each other, then at Kynan.

Daria said unnecessarily, 'We saw the phaeton here. They're looking for you, my Lord. We came to tell Lexi.'

There was a slight rise of Kynan's eyebrow, an amused twitch to his lips. 'So I see.'

Disconcerted, Alexis rose to her feet. 'Daria, Esmé. Where are your manners? Look at you. Go and tidy yourselves. Where are your sisters?'

The pair looked at each other and giggled. 'Celeste is just behind us. Blythe fell in the boggy patch. She's covered in mud and Lally is trying to help her wash it off in the kitchen, before she tramps it indoors.'

'Oh dear.' Alexis wondered what impression all this was giving to Cordelia Mortimer. 'I'm so sorry, Mrs Mortimer. My sisters are not usually quite so...'

'Boisterous is the phrase you're looking for, I believe. I hesitate to describe them as bad-mannered this early in our acquaintance.'

Esmé and Daria suddenly noticed Mrs Mortimer. They gave her a wary look, then Daria said, 'I am Daria Patterson. I'm sorry if we seemed rude. We didn't see you.'

'And I'm Esmé. I'm sorry too, especially that we didn't see you. We've been looking forward to your arrival, really we have, even though we're scared, as well.'

'Thank you,' Mrs Mortimer said drily. 'I'd prefer your elder sister to introduce you properly. To that end, I intend to forget this unfortunate beginning. Perhaps you'd like to join your sister Blythe, with the intention of presenting yourself as the young ladies I'm assured that you are. When you and your sisters are ready, you may wait in the hall until you're called. In the meantime we shall finish our refreshment. You may leave.'

The two girls stared at Mrs Mortimer for a

rebellious moment, then they gazed at Alexis for confirmation of the request.

When Alexis nodded, her sisters turned and walked dejectedly away.

Kynan rose. 'It sounds as though my London guests have arrived, so I must cut my visit short and go and welcome them. I'll give you a day or two to settle in, Cordelia, then bring my mother over for a visit. She's looking forward to seeing you again.'

He turned. 'Miss Patterson, perhaps you'd care to walk to the gate with me. I won't keep you long.'

They left through the French windows and ambled through the trees.

'Cordelia's bark is worse than her bite, you know,' he said.

Alexis nodded. 'You needn't worry. I'm sure we shall get on, and I know my sisters' manners leave much to be desired, but they're usually not quite as bad as they seemed today.'

'Of course they're not.' A pair of laughing eyes were turned her way. 'I should have liked to have seen Blythe fall in the mud, though.'

Alexis gave a tiny giggle. 'So would I.' They reached the gate. 'Was there something you wished to say to me in private?'

He picked a white daisy from the hedge, tickling her face with it before handing it to her. 'I must change the name of this house.

Dower house sounds so ... dour? I wanted to reassure you that everything will turn out for the best.'

She smiled up at him. 'I'm sure it will. What about Florence House?'

'After my mother? Perfect. She'll like that. I'll have a name plate made for the gate.' They gazed at each other, saying nothing, and Alexis wondered if he could hear her thumping heartbeat. Then Kynan gently touched her hand and swung himself up on to the phaeton, saying, 'Until next time.'

He left, the horse stepping high between the shafts, leaving a cloud of dust behind him. Holding the daisy to her lips Alexis walked sedately back to the house, even though she felt like dancing.

Mrs Mortimer looked up when she appeared. 'I believe your sisters are assembled in the hall.'

Indeed, there was the sound of loud whispers and giggles going on. Alexis tried not to grin, but she couldn't help it as she pleaded, 'Mrs Mortimer, please don't be too hard on them. Remember, they were orphaned at an early age and have never known a mother's love.'

Mrs Mortimer gave a soft chuckle. 'Those words are a blatant attempt to manipulate my emotions. I'm aware of your background, my dear. Please call them in.'

Her sisters filed in after a bedraggled and

stained Blythe, who stood there with a resigned, but defiant look on her face, as if she expected a reprimand.

'May I present my sisters, Mrs Mortimer,' Alexis said.

'What lovely girls you are.'

'Thank you, Mrs Mortimer,' they all said together.

No mention was made of the state Blythe was in, and they all began to relax.

Alexis had forgotten about the parcel Kynan had brought in, until Celeste's exclaimed, 'Look! There's a big parcel. Is it for us?'

'The earl brought it.'

Immediately they were curious. 'Aren't you going to unwrap it, Lexi?'

The cloth wrapping was removed. They all gazed at the painting that emerged, Alexis with tears welling in her eyes.

'It's a man and woman,' said Daria.

Blythe whispered, 'That's *them* ... isn't it? That's our parents. I remember the painting. It hung on the wall in the drawing room, didn't it?'

Alexis nodded. 'Lord Trent must have found it and had it restored. How thoughtful he is. Can you remember them, Celeste?'

'I seem to remember a song our mother used to sing.'

Daria said quietly, 'I wish I could. Our mother was pretty, wasn't she? And our father is nearly as handsome as the earl. He has little crinkles around his eyes, so he must have laughed a lot.'

'Yes, as I recall, he did. He had a big, roaring laugh.'

Esmé snuggled her head against her side. 'Tell me about the day I was born and there was a storm raging around the house?'

'Ah, Esmé dearest child, you were such a sweet infant, and no trouble at all to look after...'

The door closed quietly behind Mrs Mortimer as she left the room.

She'd felt humbled by the spontaneous display of closeness and love the Patterson girls had displayed towards one another, and her own eyes were moist.

She followed the maid up to the airy room that had been prepared for her, pretty with a cream bed cover, and poppies in a jar on the dresser. She crossed to the open window and gazed out into a garden, which seemed to be emerging from a wilderness of weeds.

A young man was digging a garden bed, where a blackbird foraged for worms in the dark, moist soil he turned up. An old man was seated in the shade, wiping his face on a red handkerchief. Except for age, the two were alike.

The house was on a gentle rise with views of the field and copses in every direction.

Beyond the trees at the end of the garden the road wound lazily down into a village of cottages built mostly of whitewashed cob, their roofs thatched with reeds.

At the other end of the village, and set a little to the right, stood the pretty Norman church with its square tower. Further along was the manse. Built in similar style to the house she stood in, except slightly smaller, its garden was made glorious by a huge beech tree, the leaves so deep and rich a coppery red, that the colour stole her breath away.

She regained it, drawing in a deep breath of air that was perfumed with flowers. How fresh it was here and how peaceful. Having the Patterson girls to care for had given her life some new purpose.

They were extremely vulnerable, she thought, especially Alexis, who seemed to harbour tender feelings toward Kynan, if the look in her eyes was anything to go by.

Cordelia had never been blessed with children, and these girls had lost their mother – a woman who would have guided them into adulthood. As she taught them, so she must also cherish them, as if they were her very own, she thought.

Ten

Kynan had been anticipating his reunion with Julia.

'Oh there you are,' she drawled petulantly as he strode into the drawing room, a smile on his face. 'How tedious of you to hide yourself from us. We're miles from anywhere, here.'

Her peevishness put paid to his pleasure. He hoped she wasn't in one of her difficult moods. 'You must be tired after your long journey.'

'Of course I'm tired. The inn we stayed in last night was dreadful. Roxanne and I had to squash into one bed.'

Roxanne exchanged a faint grin with Philip Weatherby when he raised an eyebrow.

Peter Haining, brandy in one hand, swept a bow. 'You're a dark horse, we had no idea you were a peer of the realm until Julia told us. What's worse, as a mere Baron, I shall have to defer to you, *my Lord.*'

Kynan confirmed Haining's provocation with a nod of confirmation. 'No doubt you'll get used to it, as will I.'

'I admit I don't envy you the work involved in maintaining the ancestral heap, though. It will cost a fortune.'

'Longmore is a comfortable house, and the estate should be self-sufficient in eighteen months or so. All of you, welcome to my new home. How nice to see you again.'

'New home! You mean you intend to live here?' Julia cried out, quite clearly aghast at the thought. 'But Kynan, you told me you were coming down here with the intention of selling the estate.'

'I said I'd consider selling it. Now I've assessed its worth, I know the land will return a good income in the years to come. I do intend to spend the season in London though.'

'Thank goodness you're not going to desert us entirely, dear one. What say you, Julia?' Roxanne giggled and tripped daintily across the room to kiss his cheek. 'I like it here and will stay until you throw me out.'

'Or until the season starts, when you'll be in demand in every drawing room in London, and men everywhere will swoon at the very sight of you.'

Roxanne, whose eyes were the colour of honey, and a perfect match for her hair, gently fluttered her eyelashes at him. 'You're so gallant, Kynan.'

When Julia took possession of his other

arm he smiled down at her. 'I've missed you.'

Her grey eyes slanted lazily as she smiled. Julia lacked the dewy innocence of Alexis Patterson, but she was extremely seductive.

Peter Haining's eyes narrowed in on them. 'Leave the man alone, Julia. He has responsibilities, an estate to run. Beware, he'll be looking for a wife, so he can breed a house full of brats to pass it on to.'

Julia gave an uneasy laugh and shuddered. The good-natured Philip Weatherby laughed too. 'Now, what does a place such as this offer in the way of amusements? Any gaming houses in that quaint little town we came through. I swear none of the townsfolk spoke English well enough to understand.'

Roxanne picked up a dish from the table and offered it to him as she mimicked. 'Do ee want to boi moi cockles, good zur?'

'You usually give them away, my dear,' Haining said and chuckled into his glass.

Roxanne turned Kynan's way, her eyes full of glee. 'One of your maids asked, "Do it be troo that King Jarge be mad?"'

'When I said it was quite true her eyes nearly dropped out of their sockets. "Glory be," she said. "The cook will be fair mazed when I tell her. She'd better make another figgety pudden while she be at it, too, lest there be not enough to go around." I was quite alarmed. Pray tell me, your Lordship, what is a figgety pudden?'

The others burst into laughter and Kynan chuckled. Roxanne had an acute ear, and although her wit could verge on outrageous at times, a gathering was never dull when she was around. 'It happens to be plum pudding, and is quite tasty.'

Roxanne cocked her head to one side and lazily surveyed him, her eyes half-hooded as she murmured, 'You look quite tasty yourself, Kynan.'

She was being provocative. She winked at him when Julia broke in sharply, 'Oh, do be quiet Roxanne, you're not on stage now. Kynan, three shabby looking girls came and stared at us with their mouths hanging open, as if they'd never seen a human being before. They gave the maid some notes for you. Who are they?'

'Three of the late Lord Patterson's five daughters. They came to the dower ... Florence House, where they live, to inform me of your arrival. They grew up here, in this house.'

'They're related to you, then?'

'No. They were orphaned several years ago. The previous earl took them in.'

Haining nodded. 'Are they the daughters of Ralph Patterson? We knew each other at Cambridge and I attended his wedding. I heard that he and his wife died years ago. A cliff fall, wasn't it?'

'Yes. His son died with them, but his

daughters survived. They're impoverished, except for their land. The previous earl gave them a home here and they continued living here until I moved in.'

'It was quite right that you turned them out, my dear. It would be awful to have orphaned brats running around the place and getting under your feet.'

'I didn't turn them out. Florence House was standing empty, so I offered it to them rent free, and brought a relative down from London to care for them.'

'Oh, Kynan, you're a soft-hearted and generous person,' Julia said lightly, but there was a tightness to her mouth and a glint of annoyance in her eyes.

'Not at all. It's a business arrangement.' He disengaged himself from her clutches. 'Excuse me, ladies, you must be tired. I'll find my mother and see how your accommodations are progressing.'

His mother was comforting Julia's maid in the sitting room that had once been part of the Patterson's quarters. Emily, her name was, as he recalled. She had a red welt on her face. Her cheekbone was beginning to bruise and there were tears in her eyes.

'Has there been an accident?'

His mother took him aside and whispered, 'I found her crying, then she fainted dead away. I think she's been hit with a cane. There are raised welts on her arms.'

As he turned back to the maid, anger flared inside him at the thought that she'd been treated so cruelly. 'Is there a reason why you were birched, Emily?'

The girl hung her head. 'I'll get into trouble if I tell you, my Lord.'

'Then I won't insist on an answer.'

The girl burst into tears again. 'I'm sorry, my Lord ... Madam. With two of them to look after, I'm that tired from the journey. I hardly had time to sleep, let alone eat. I'll be all right in a minute.'

Kynan thought it might be his destiny to rescue maidens in distress as he handed over his handkerchief to the distressed girl to dry her eyes on. She looked exhausted and he was surprised Julia had driven her so hard.

'James can take Emily down to the kitchen,' he said to his mother. 'The servants can look after her and find her a room to sleep in. Take the rest of the day off, Emily.'

'But I'll get into trouble, my Lord. Mrs Spencer likes to have me at hand in case she needs me during the night.'

'I'll tell her you're unwell. Somebody else can unpack her things and she can fend for herself for the night.'

Julia appeared from around the corner. Her eyes darted sharply from one to the other. 'What going on here? Emily, get about your work.'

As the girl started to move, Kynan placed a detaining hand on her arm. 'Your maid is exhausted to the point of fainting. She needs to rest. Mother, kindly take the girl to James, would you please?'

When they moved out of sight, Julia shrugged. 'I'd prefer it if you didn't interfere with my staff, Kynan. The girl is just lazy.'

'She's exhausted, anyone can see that. You may have the services of another maid for tonight. How did she get that bruise on her face?'

'How do I know? She's clumsy, so I imagine she walked into a door.' Julia gave a light, tinkling laugh. 'You're being such a bore, Kynan. You invited me here, remember. Aren't you happy to see me?'

He pulled a smile to his face. 'Of course, I've been looking forward to it.' So why didn't he feel pleased? He did what was expected of him, pulled her into his arms and kissed her.

Her response seemed more calculated than spontaneous, and his own feelings towards her were lukewarm, for she stirred him not at all.

That night, Kynan slept alone in his own bed. He was up early the next morning, out and about the estate with his agent as they planned what would be done.

He got on well with Joshua Hardin, and

179

had learned a lot from the man in the short time he'd been at the estate.

'When's that baby of yours due, Joshua?'

'Any day now, sir. Jenny's as fat and as slow as her father's old sow.'

Kynan laughed. 'Your wife looks like a bonny girl to me. And your daughter is a pretty child.'

He chuckled. 'Young Kate tosses a right old tantrum when the mood takes her. She's as fiery as her hair. But I'm a contented man. I've got a good roof over my head, a woman to warm my bed and a daughter to keep me amused. What more could a man want?'

'A permanent position with a ten percent rise in salary, perhaps? Your skills are obvious, and I need a man I can trust on the occasions when I'm in London,' said Kynan. 'Do you need to think it over?'

Joshua grinned widely. 'I already have. A fifteen percent rise would be better, my Lord.'

'I daresay it would be, however...' Kynan gave a dry chuckle as he held out his hand. 'I imagine we can reach an agreement on twelve, don't you?'

Joshua Hardin took it. 'I reckon we could, at that. Thank you, my Lord. I won't let you down.'

A week later the earl and his mother disrupted the newly established routine of Florence House.

Alexis glanced up when she heard Kynan's voice and everything in her began to smile. Blythe had just come to the end of her reading and her voice trailed off. They all looked at one another and exchanged grins.

The girls were seated around the large, dining room table, and were about to abandon the lesson when the visitors were announced.

Cordelia held up her hand. 'Please remain seated. The earl has brought Mrs Trent to visit me, not you.'

The girls looked at each other rebelliously. Although they were trying their hardest, the sisters were finding it hard to settle to the loss of freedom that regular schooling brought.

Mrs Mortimer had obviously planned the schooling in advance, for the day after she arrived they'd been presented with a weekly roster of their lessons, and duties.

'What about the chickens?' Celeste had wailed. 'Who will look after them?'

'The servants. Young ladies of good birth do not look after chickens.'

The morning was divided into lessons. Two hours of writing, spelling and handwriting. Then one hour of arithmetic. In addition, they were to take turns to read out loud for fifteen minutes at a time, so they could expand their knowledge. They were reading about Marco Polo, the explorer. There was a globe, so they could discover where his journeys had taken him.

The early part of the afternoon was devoted to sewing. They were making linen aprons to wear over their gowns, with cross-stitch embroidery on the bib and hem. Painting and piano practice came after.

Then it would be time to prepare the dinner or undertake the other various household tasks that needed to be done. A certain amount of free time was afforded to them, in which they could do whatever they wished.

For two days every week they were free of lessons. On Thursdays the cart and driver from Longmore Hall took them into Dorchester so they could make necessary purchases. On Sundays they attended the morning and evening service, but could otherwise do as they wished.

Mrs Mortimer gazed at them now and said calmly, 'The lesson has not concluded. Supervise the reading practise if you would, Blythe.'

Blythe's eyes sprang open. 'Me? Lexi usually does it.'

'Miss Patterson will be joining me in the drawing room. I'm sure you'll perform the task ably. Your reading ability is good, considering your lack of formal education. I've noticed that the travels of Marco Polo interest you.'

A wistful smile lit Blythe's features. 'It must be wonderful to travel and have adventures.'

'If you think about it, my dear, you'll realize that you've found travel and adventure in that book. The lesson will end when the clock strikes the half hour. You can then practise your social skills with our guests. That's not too far away, is it? Please stay neat and tidy, in the meantime.' She smiled round at them all. 'I'm sure I can trust my young ladies to be on their best behaviour.'

'Yes, Mrs Mortimer,' they said together.

'Good.'

Alexis smiled wryly as they left the room. 'You've certainly won Blythe over.'

'Blythe has a good mind. She's a sensitive young lady whose feelings damage easily. The dear girl hides it behind a facade of bravado.'

'Blythe has always wanted to be a boy.'

'She needed to be loved. Knowing the former earl needed a son she adjusted her behaviour accordingly to obtain his approval. He was a great influence on her, you know. She needs to be given some responsibility so she can gain confidence in herself.'

Alexis thought that Cordelia Mortimer must be the wisest woman in the world, and she suddenly wanted to hug her. But by then they'd entered the drawing room. Basking in

Kynan's warm smile, Alexis decided she'd rather hug him instead.

While the two women greeted each other, Kynan murmured, 'Miss Patterson, how pleasant it is to see you again. You're looking well.'

Which served to make her acutely aware that she wore her oldest and shabbiest gown. But when she was about to instinctively tug at the skirt to straighten out the creases, Mrs Mortimer anticipated it and stilled her hand by patting it with her own, which reminded Alexis that she must not fidget.

'Where are the children?' Florence asked.

'They're still at their lesson, and will join us for refreshment. It's such a lovely day we might take tea in the conservatory. What do you think, Alexis?'

'That would be perfect. The gardener has cleaned the furniture, and we have some herbs and shrubs growing in pots.'

Cordelia said, 'Perhaps you'd inform Lally, Alexis. Then you can take the earl to the conservatory so he can see how pretty it is for himself, while I talk to Florence for a few moments.'

'Well, Lexi,' Kynan said as soon as they were alone, 'tell me, what you think of Cordelia.'

'I like Mrs Mortimer. Her presence has eased the burden of responsibility my sisters have always created for me. She's very learned, and, although she's firm with them, my sisters respond to her.'

She placed a hand on his sleeve, bringing him to a halt before her parents' portrait, which, at Mrs Mortimer's suggestion, had been hung on the music room wall for them by the gardener. 'Thank you for the portrait. I'm so pleased it was found. It was a wonderful surprise for us all to see it, and I appreciate the effort you went to in having it restored.'

'It was no trouble at all. The restorer was certainly an expert, for there was several rips in it where somebody had pulled it from the frame, and it had been affected by the damp. I can see the family likeness in you all.'

'Having it there reminds us all that we once had parents who loved us. It's especially good for the younger girls. They are fascinated by them. I believe it makes them feel they belonged to someone.'

'How sad it is that you lost them. I'm sure they'd be proud of the young woman you've become, though. Perhaps they're watching over you all.'

His quiet sincerity brought tears to her eyes. 'I like to think so.'

He pulled a face at her. 'You're not going to cry are you? I'm running out of handkerchiefs.'

She gave a cross between a sniff and a giggle. 'I'll try not to be melancholy. Have your London guests recovered from their journey?'

'They have, and they're looking for something to keep them amused. I'll expect your household for dinner at the end of next week.'

'As entertainment for your guests, my Lord?'

'Don't be so contrary,' he said with a light laugh. 'We'll dance, play cards or bagatelle, and each do a turn. I'll expect you to sing.'

Her mouth dried. 'No! I couldn't possibly, Kynan ... not in front of people I don't know. I wouldn't be able to get a word out.'

'Then, we'll play a Mozart duet together. I'll enjoy that.'

The colour rose under her skin and he grinned as his eyes met hers. 'I promise I won't kiss you during the performance.'

She'd rather he'd promised he would ... but Alexis suddenly remembered that the woman Kynan intended to wed was now his guest at Longmore. He'd save his kisses for her, no doubt.

Misery tore a wound in the fabric of her tender emotions. How painful it was to love a man whose heart belonged to another. Would she be able to stand seeing them together, watch them exchange looks of love and tender, seemingly accidental caresses? How could she sit there, a smile on her lips, pretending she was happy while her heart was breaking in pieces?

He was looking at her now, his head a little to one side, his expression pensive. 'Don't take my teasing to heart, Lexi.'

'I'm becoming used to it.' She dragged a smile from her depths and pressed her hands against her warm cheeks. 'I think, Kynan ... that it might be better if I sometimes ignored you completely.'

He said softly, 'You wouldn't be so cruel, my sweet Lexi. How could I survive without you?'

She took a deep breath to steady her trembling heart. He meant nothing by it. 'Come through to the conservatory. Tell me, did your mother enjoy having a house named after her?'

He followed as she showed him the plants, his body so close she could feel his warmth, smell that elusive fragrance of spice lingering about him. His breath stirred her hair, causing tendrils to brush against her neck and face. Her skin quivered. She was so aware of him she became breathless, and found herself exclaiming over the plants spearing through the moist dark earth of each pot, as if she'd made a discovery of utmost importance. 'See, this one is rosemary, and this one is lavender. If you warm the leaves between your hands it releases its scent.' She turned and held out her hands to him. 'Breathe in.'

'You rob me of breath.' He gazed directly into her eyes. He made her feel as though she was someone special to him. 'I can't believe we were at cross purposes when we first met.'

'You haven't listened to a word I've said,' she accused.

'I certainly have. My mother loved the renaming, and I've left a name plate with the gardener to fix to the pillar.' He took her hands, bringing her cupped palms up to his face, where he breathed in the scent of the lavender. His breath tickled against her palms and between her fingers as he exhaled. He placed a kiss there.

She murmured a half-hearted protest. 'Kynan, you mustn't.'

He brought her hands down to chest level, and held them there. 'I couldn't resist it. No,' he said, allowing only one of her hands to escape. 'I need this hand of yours for a moment.'

Drawing a piece of paper from his waistcoat pocket he laid it in her palm. 'This is the amount the sale of the bricks from the manor fetched.'

Her eyes widened when she saw the amount.

'I've placed the money in the bank, where it will gain some interest. I imagine you'd prefer me to handle it for the time being. I've asked Joshua Hardin to keep a separate account book for you, one you can inspect any time you wish, so you know where you stand.'

She nodded.

He placed a purse on top of the paper and closed her fingers around it. 'When next you're at Longmore I'll go through everything with you. In the meantime, here's the first half-yearly allowance for yourself and your sisters. I've been guided by my mother and have added an extra amount to start with, since she feels you will initially need some essentials such as clothes. She said you were sensible enough to manage your financial affairs for six months ahead, something I fully endorse.'

'Thank you, Kynan. I'll be careful to make it last. Mrs Mortimer will show me how to keep an account of what we spend. I should really like to learn to keep household accounts. It will make me feel more useful to her.'

'I'm sure you're already useful. Joshua Hardin's wife has presented him with a son, by the way. His hair's as red as that of his sister. He looks to be a robust child, and they're naming him Barnaby. I've agreed to be his godfather. Joshua wondered if you'd act as his godmother. I said I'd ask you.'

'Tell him I'd be honoured to become Barnaby's godmother.'

The clock struck the half hour and Alexis

sighed, for there came an instant clatter of feet as the lesson was abandoned. Giggles and whispers were heard on the other side of the music room door, then the quiet, but authoritative voice of Mrs Mortimer.

Kynan was still holding her hand. She quickly retrieved it and moved away from him, allowing some distance between them. He turned to inspect the nearest plant when there was a rap at the door.

Alexis fled to the opposite side of the conservatory when the door opened and everyone started to appear. First the maids came, carrying laden trays. They were followed by the cousins, who exchanged a glance and a smile when they found Kynan examining a small plant on one side of the conservatory, while a pink-faced Alexis examined a bigger one on the other side.

Alexis looked up, feigning surprise, her hand against her heart, and said, 'Oh! I didn't hear you come in.'

'Didn't you, dear? Watching plants grow must be an absorbing occupation, then, since we made quite a clatter,' Florence said drily.

'You look flushed, Alexis dear,' Mrs Mortimer said, her voice as sweet as sugar.

'It's warm in here,' she said vaguely, and placed the purse Kynan had given her amongst the leaves of the plant to be retrieved later.

190

Alexis warmed even more when Kynan gave a low chuckle and said, 'Behave yourself, ladies. This is a more tender flower than the ones you're used to in London. I don't want her feelings bruised.'

Florence exchanged a glance with Mrs Mortimer, and laughed.

'I'm fortunate to find myself in a company of so many lovely young ladies.' Kynan said to the Patterson girls. 'How are you all? Are you behaving yourselves?'

'Yes, my Lord.' Her sisters, who were grinning with delight at the sight of him, made a pretty curtsy as they each passed him.

Kynan arched a dark eyebrow and said, 'Do stop bobbing up and down like corks on a pond every time you see me. It's disconcerting.'

Daria grinned. 'I'm not sure what that means, but Lexi said we must treat you like a proper earl and not—'

'—like a damned Welsh one,' Esmé finished.

'Remind me to put Lexi over my knee sometime,' Kynan retorted.

'Needing to have the last word is an unfortunate trait for an earl to have,' Alexis couldn't help pointing out.

'You're right, so I'll allow you to have it,' he said, and his grin curled right into her heart. 'What is your last word?'

I adore you, she thought, as everyone stared at her with interest in their eyes. She'd been rude to him and could only murmur, 'I apologize for pointing out your unfortunate trait, my Lord.'

Mrs Mortimer's eyes widened in astonishment.

'*Touch*é,' Kynan said, his expression taking on a rueful edge.

Laughter trickled from Florence. 'I believe you've finally met your match, Kynan.'

'I wouldn't be at all surprised,' he said comfortably.

Alexis, whose accidental wit had surprised her, could only wish he had.

Eleven

It was Thursday.

'I've found the treasure!' Daria said to Esmé, waving the purse in the air. 'It was in a pot in the conservatory.'

'How can it be the treasure? The gardener has only just planted those pots.'

'It might have been buried in the earth he used.'

'Perhaps Mrs Mortimer put it there to find out if we were honest.'

'That would be a perfectly horrid thing for her to do, and she's not at all horrid. Do my buttons up, please, Daria. I can't reach.'

Daria did as she was asked, then picked up the brush and attacked the tangles in her sister's hair. After she'd neatly braided it, she said, 'We'd better take the purse to Lexi.'

They found their sister in her room on the window seat. She was staring dreamily out of the window, where a flower landscape to delight the eyes stretched into the line of trees that delineated the woods.

'We've found a purse, Lexi.'

She turned to smile at them. 'It's our allowance from the earl. I placed it in the plant pot yesterday, and forgot about it. How silly of me.'

'I expect you forgot it because we're not used to having any money.'

'Daria thought it was the treasure.'

'It is treasure, in a way.' Alexis took the purse and tipped the contents on the bed, thinking that their circumstances had taken a turn for the better since the demise of the old earl. There was more money on the bed than was adequate for their immediate needs for six months. She'd be able to buy them all a new garment each to add to their wardrobes, and pay their share of the household expenses.

She'd need to think about winter garments too. Not for herself, but for Blythe and Celeste, because they were growing rapidly.

'What do you think the treasure will look like? Will it be golden coins and precious jewels?'

'Esmé, I really do think the treasure is a tale the old earl made up.'

'But we did have ancestors who were put to death for smuggling, didn't we?'

'Yes, we did.'

'Well then, it could be true, couldn't it? There could really be treasure hidden somewhere.'

'Yes, I suppose it's possible.' She didn't have the heart to press her own doubts when Esmé looked so happy. 'Would you two like to come into town with me on the cart so I can buy us a new gown apiece?'

They didn't seem interested in new gowns. 'Must we? Blythe was going to take us to the cove for a picnic. Then we're going on an adventure to look for goblins in the woods. If we catch one we're going to put it in a cage, then take it to the summer fair. Blythe said people will pay a large amount of money to see a goblin.'

Another of her preposterous tales. Blythe's head was churning with such tales. So vivid was her imagination that she'd always been popular as a storyteller. Her young sisters looked so serious that Alexis was hard-pressed not to burst into laughter.

They'd been indoors for most of the week, and she could easily buy them something pretty and serviceable herself. 'What about Celeste. Is she going with you?'

'Oh, you know she doesn't like getting dishevelled. She can come with us if she wishes, but she'd rather go into Dorchester with you and Mrs Mortimer, I expect. She said she saw a goblin once and it spat some unpleasant green slime at her.'

Celeste would indeed rather go into Dorchester. The most feminine of her sisters presented herself in a clean gown, one that had been already extended to the limits of its hem and was now much too short for her. The bodice showed signs of strain at the seams. She must trim the gown Celeste was wearing and pass it down to Daria, Alexis thought.

The split in Celeste's straw bonnet was partly disguised by a posy of flowers picked from the garden.

When they were on their way, Mrs Mortimer said, 'I was thinking, my dear. Would you object if I bought your sisters a gown and a bonnet, and a few other garments that most young ladies need?'

'That's too generous of you, Mrs Mortimer. I couldn't accept such a gift.'

'My dear Alexis, don't allow pride to get in the way of your good sense.' She lowered her voice so the new stable lad, who was driving the cart, couldn't overhear. 'I have forty-thousand pounds in securities and a generous annuity for life. With no children of my own to spend it on, I beg ... no, *insist* that you allow me the pleasure of spending an extremely small portion of it on yourself and your sisters.'

Alexis gave a small gasp, for a sum so vast was entirely unimaginable.

'Before you decide I'd like you to consider the following. Although I fully understand your circumstances, I feel that having a family of shabbily turned out young females in my charge reflects badly on me personally. They will not thank you for refusing my offer.'

Nettled by such a notion, Alexis's eyes narrowed as she gazed at Mrs Mortimer. 'You're suggesting that my sisters will resent me for not accepting your charity. Allow me to correct that assumption.'

'Was that a reprimand, Miss Patterson?'

Alexis flushed, but held her ground. 'You wanted honest consultation between us. I must admit, I don't like being presented with a scheme you've already worked out in advance. Whether I, or they, like it or not, my sisters will grow up poor. They have to learn to economize. If that is a reprimand, so be it.'

'Could it be that you should learn to compromise, instead?' The woman chuckled when Alexis's eyes flared in astonishment. 'You're as astute as I thought you were, Alexis, but you're being too hard on me, and without justification. I'll put your feelings on this matter down to the uncertainty of your position. In my defence, I'll state right here and now that I had no ulterior motive in mind.'

Immediately, Alexis was filled with guilt. 'If I wronged you, I'm sorry.'

'Allow me to explain something to you. The bond of affection between yourself and your sisters is laudable, and is very much in evidence. I envy you, for nothing will ever break that bond between you. However, the time is not too far off when you'll feel the need to wed and have a family of your own.'

'While my sisters need me I'll never wed.'

'Then you'll do them a disservice, because a sacrifice like that will hold them hostage. Your sisters are vibrant young ladies of good breeding, who are bound to attract suitors before too long. Would you deny them the right to wed advantageously? The only experience you have to guide you is that which your own mother passed on to you, something which was withdrawn abruptly when you were young. They need to be prepared, and that means they must learn how to behave when mixing in society. Thus, they need to dress appropriately. That will help to give them the confidence they lack. You don't want them to become objects of derision, do you?'

As she remembered the pointed comment Mrs Clark had made, the thought of her sisters being laughed at became unbearable. 'You put forward a convincing argument, Mrs Mortimer.'

'May I make a comment?' Celeste said. She had been quiet up until this point.

Mrs Mortimer and Alexis nodded at the same time.

'Whatever the decision is we'll never love you any less, Lexi. And we won't like you any more than we do now, Mrs Mortimer. You might both think this is vanity, but I do so long to have something pretty to wear all the time. I feel ashamed of my appearance, even while I know we can't help being poor.'

A lump grew in Alexis's throat as she realized how selfish her thinking had been. 'Then Mrs Mortimer may make whatever purchases she deems necessary for you. I'm sorry I was so harsh in my opinion. It was formed without me thinking it carefully through.'

Mrs Mortimer placed a hand over hers. 'Entirely my fault. You were right in calling my attention to this. I should have consulted you earlier of my intentions.'

'I was too opinionated.'

'Alexis, dear, your opinion is important, and you have the right to question me. Differences between us must be aired if the relationship is to remain harmonious. You also need to think about your own future.'

Of late, the thoughts Alexis had on her future came wrapped in a misty white cloud which contained Kynan Trent. She lived for the next moment she saw him. Alone in her bed, her imagination conjured up sweetly tormenting lusts, and her body was wracked with such a compelling urgency that she tossed and turned in her bed and longed to have them satisfied. Unable to concentrate, she would fall into a reverie in the middle of a task, or her mind would wander off in the middle of a conversation, as if she was losing it.

Like now!

She sighed, for her imagination had become a lovely place to visit and she was loath to relinquish it. Straightening up she gazed at Mrs Mortimer, who smiled as though she could see right into her heart, and could see Kynan's name etched on each stroke it made.

'I cannot replace your mother, but you can confide in me if you ever feel the need,' she said. 'And perhaps if you address me as Cordelia it will help you to feel as though we are friends who are on an equal footing.'

Her hand curled around Mrs Mortimer's and she gave it a gentle squeeze, her mind already going back to her daydream. 'Thank you ... Cordelia.'

Cordelia had done wonders with the Patterson girls, Kynan thought, casting his eye over them in church the next day. The appearance of Alexis stole his breath away, arrayed as she was in a gown the colour of almonds and patterned in pink roses. She wore the bonnet he'd bought for her, he noted with some satisfaction.

His glance swept over her sisters. There was a subtle change in them all. Esmé's head rested against Cordelia's arm in a natural manner. They certainly seemed at ease with each other. Cordelia herself looked like a mother hen with her chicks around them.

He cast his glance over the congregation. There were more people than usual. Many smiled or nodded to him and he returned the pleasantries. He was becoming used to the attention his position drew, and found it pleasant to be able to stop and chat with an acquaintance in the street. Requests for his company arrived daily. Joshua Hardin advised him which to accept. His natural reserve had always served to prevent people from becoming too familiar. Now, it held him in good stead.

Next, he sought out the strangers. A man seated with the reverend's wife behind the Pattersons caught his eye. He was handsome in appearance, and appeared to be in his late thirties. Two children were seated next to him.

The man's glance was firmly fixed on Alexis. But then, so were the glances of one or two other men – men he recognized from Mrs Clark's ball.

He nodded to the Clark family. Sibyl's eyes widened. She was a shy, polite young woman. Well trained, and attractive, ready to marry and settle down as a perfect helpmeet for some man of means – but that man would not be himself. He had Julia. He just needed to propose to her.

Kynan frowned. He must warn Cordelia to keep an eye on Alexis. He didn't want her head turned by someone unworthy of her.

She chose that moment to look up and her eyes met his. The smile they exchanged was spontaneous.

For the space of several moments it was as if the world had faded from around him. Then Julia tugged at his sleeve, saying peevishly, 'Who is that woman you're staring at?'

At Julia's instigation, Kynan had recently resumed his earlier relationship with her. He'd had very little choice because she'd crept into his bed and aroused him so blatantly from his sleep that even a man with one foot in the grave would have found what she was offering irresistible – and somewhat questionable, too. He'd wondered where she'd learned such tricks.

Kynan chose to misunderstand Julia. 'That's Mrs Mortimer, who is my mother's cousin. She's with her wards, the Patterson sisters. You met three of them on the day you arrived. I'll introduce them to you after the service if you wish.'

'Oh, they're those ragamuffin orphan girls who used to live at Longmore Hall.' Julia sounded bored all at once. 'Must I meet them?'

'It's not imperative, since they'll be among my guests for dinner next week,' he said shortly.

'Where is your mother, Kynan?'

'She's suffering from a headache and has

decided to rest. She intends to attend the evening service with me.'

'How boring it must be to be obliged to conform in such a manner.'

'My life here is never boring. The responsibility of this estate is challenging, and running it takes up much of my time. The church service allows me to set a good example, and gives me the chance to meet people I otherwise wouldn't.'

She pouted. 'I wouldn't have visited if I'd known I'd see so little of you.'

'I'll try and think of something to keep you amused, Julia. There's a country fair soon, with a troupe of travelling players, sideshows and a shooting contest.'

'You'd keep me amused if you moved back to London permanently.'

'That won't happen. I have responsibilities here at Longmore.'

There was a clatter as Lord Haining and Philip Weatherby came strolling down the aisle. Necks craned. Philip stopped to stare through his eyeglass at the women, an affectation he'd recently adopted, by all accounts. He stopped to gaze at Alexis and Blythe, an inane smile on his face.

Alexis looked at him warily, then ignored him. But when Blythe gave him an intimidating glare he poked his tongue out at her. She obliged him by doing likewise. Weatherby backed off, joining Haining at the other end of the pew and grinning from ear to ear.

Kynan chuckled. Thank goodness Cordelia had turned aside to attend to something Celeste was saying, so hadn't observed the incident.

Weatherby's humour was questionable at times, but playing the fool was a front. He was an astute businessman, who owned sporting clubs in several major cities. At the age of twenty-two, he was an expert swordsman, and the best pistol shot Kynan had ever seen – at least, until he'd moved here. His gaze slid to Blythe and he grinned. Her shot could have simply been an accident, he supposed.

Roxanne appeared, timing her entrance for maximum effect, for the church bell had stopped pealing and the Reverend Curruthers had just mounted the pulpit.

She swept down the aisle in queenly fashion, the fashionable train of her blue gown gathering balls of fluff from the floor while she bestowed smiles on the congregation.

Alexis smiled at Blythe, clearly amused by the spectacle the earl's friends were affording her.

'I do hope I haven't held up the service,' Roxanne cried out, and apologized prettily to the reverend. The smile he allowed her earned him a frown from his wife.

Kynan was wondering how Roxanne had managed to get to the church when he saw

James slip into the shadows at the back.

'Shall we pray?' said the long-suffering Reverend Curruthers.

'By all means,' Weatherby said, and Roxanne gave a small, husky laugh.

As was usual after the service, Kynan was held up by people wanting to talk to him. Giving an exaggerated yawn, Julia wandered off.

Alexis and her sisters were passing the time of day with Sibyl, while the stranger with the two children was holding a conversation with Mrs Mortimer.

'Who's that man talking to Mrs Mortimer, Reverend?' Kynan asked.

'He is Reverend David Hill, and those are his two children.'

'The man who is interested in a match with Miss Patterson.'

Curruthers nodded. 'He's a widower with means of his own, so is willing to take her without dowry.'

'A man of his age will be too set in his ways.'

'Hill is a decent, God-fearing family man. If she accepts him she will not lack for anything.'

'What of her sisters?'

'My understanding is that Mrs Mortimer has provided them all with a good home. Is that not so?'

'Yes, it's so. I won't allow Miss Patterson to

wed him, you know. It's out of the question.'

Curruthers's mouth pursed. 'With respect, my Lord, I rather think that's a decision Miss Patterson might like to make, don't you?'

'No, I don't. Miss Patterson is too unworldly to marry.'

The look Kynan received was bland. 'All the better, for an older husband will be able to mould her to his will.'

Seething, Kynan watched the man approach Alexis. The smile she gave him faded when he began to talk, then she looked down at the two small children and he could almost see the doors in her heart opening as she bent to speak to them.

She looked over at him. Their eyes met, hers full of uncertainty. But there was some sort of yearning that caused his gut to tighten.

No, please don't, he willed, and almost felt her waver. A feeling of relief hit him, leaving him feeling weak, as the man bowed slightly and moved away.

Alexis came to where he stood. 'I didn't see your mother in church, my Lord. Is she well?'

'A slight headache, that's all. She hopes to be at the evening service. That man who approached you, the Reverend David Hill.'

'What of him?'

'Damn it, Lexi, you know exactly what I'm

saying. You can't marry him. He's too old for you.'

'He didn't propose, just asked if I'd give him permission to call on me. I refused, since to give him false hope would be wrong.'

'There are bound to be others.'

'I'll judge each one on their merits.'

'Good. How are you keeping?'

She laughed. 'As well as when you saw me yesterday.'

'It seems longer than that.'

'Does it?'

Julia hooked her hand around his arm, her nails digging into his flesh through his jacket. 'Kynan, dearest, you're neglecting me terribly. Must I drag you away from these people physically?'

'Miss Patterson, this is one of my guests, Mrs Julia Spencer from London.'

'Mrs Spencer, I'm pleased to meet you.'

From the corner of his eye Kynan saw Blythe detach herself from her family group and head towards them. James was helping Cordelia and the rest of the Patterson sisters on to the cart he'd brought Roxanne to church on. They headed off.

'Ah ... yes, I've met some of your sisters,' Julia drawled and turned to Kynan. 'I take it that this is one of your clodhopper charity cases, Kynan? How sweet, but I thought the parish dealt with that sort of thing.'

Alexis seemed to flinch. The light in her eyes faded, to be replaced by anguish. Alexis had never seemed so vulnerable to him and Kynan longed to comfort her when she choked out, 'Excuse me, my Lord, I must set off home.'

She turned towards Blythe, who by the fierce expression on her face had overheard. Blythe's arm slid around Alexis's waist and she was hugged against her body as they walked away together.

Kynan disentangled his arm. 'That was unnecessarily cruel and unforgivably rude, Julia.'

'Oh, don't let's quarrel, Kynan. How was I to know the girl had no sense of humour? If our relationship means anything to you, of course you'll forgive me. I'll apologize to her, I promise.'

'Then make sure you do.' How much did his relationship with Julia mean to him, he wondered? No doubt, the carnal nature of it was satisfying to them both. But each day brought fresh doubts crowding into his mind.

In this different environment Julia seemed like another woman to the one he'd known before. Every day his illusions peeled from his eyes like the layers of an onion, as if he were a blind man gradually regaining his vision. One thing was becoming obvious to him, Julia Spencer didn't belong here in the

country. If he wanted to take their relationship a step further, it was clear he'd have to
abandon his plans of living on the estate, and
return to London.

The coach was crowded with five of them
in it. Julia had seated herself half on his lap
and half on Peter Haining's. She was animated, and talked incessantly, her voice at a
strident pitch, about the last social gathering
she'd attended. But the air was fraught with
tension.

Jude drove the horses sedately as befitted
the sabbath. Outside the carriage, the day
had a Sunday reverence to it, a tranquillity
that reached into Kynan's soul. The sky was
misty, the air slightly humid. He'd rather be
part of it than cramped inside the carriage.

The narrow road was flanked either side by
tall hedges, so they seemed to be in an
emerald green tunnel. The land here belonged to the Pattersons. They only had to block
the road to deny him access.

Hardin had said, 'Patterson land produces
good feed for sheep and cattle, but you'd
know all about that, coming from good
Welsh stock yourself, my Lord.'

He'd given a faint smile. 'Damned Welsh
stock, you mean, don't you?'

'No, my Lord. I reckon you might have
changed a few opinions on that since you
arrived.'

When the carriage passed Alexis and

Blythe they flattened against the hedge to allow the vehicle passage. Two young ladies as innocent and as fresh as flowers. Kynan waited until the carriage had rounded the bend, then called out to Jude to bring it to a halt.

'I feel like walking,' he said to his guests. 'I'll see you back at the hall in a little while.'

Alexis was astonished to see Kynan leaning casually against the trunk of an oak tree just where the road curved.

Her face flamed and she came to a halt. She was heartsick, still, from the cutting remark made by the woman he intended to marry.

Blythe took her hand and threatened, 'I swear, Lexi. If that man upsets you I'll take him by the neck with my bare hands and squeeze his wizzen shut.'

A reluctant giggle forced its way from Alexis's mouth. 'The earl hasn't been in Dorset long enough to know what a wizzen is.'

'He'd soon learn when the air stops going in and out of his windpipe.'

Misery was coiled inside Alexis like a spring. She ached with it. 'It really wasn't his fault, Blythe.'

'He could have said something to that ... that fancy *goocoo* he had on his arm. If that's an example of London manners, I don't want to learn them.'

Alexis was quite sure Blythe could be more than a match for Julia Spencer if she put her mind to it. 'Mrs Spencer isn't a cuckoo. In fact, she's quite lovely, as well as grand. And James told me she has a fortune. You can't blame the earl for being in love with her. And stop using such vulgar expressions.'

'The earl would display more sense if he fell in love with you.'

Alexis's heart stood still at the thought. 'Do you think so?'

Blythe peered at her. 'You look as if your wits have fled. You're not in love with the earl yourself, are you?'

She coloured. 'Certainly not. How could I be? What a silly thing to say.'

'Why is it silly? He's such a handsome man that we're all in love with him. Your heart won't break when he marries that Julia Spencer woman then?'

Her heart was already threatening to crack. 'I'm not the slightest bit interested in knowing who marries him,' she lied.

Blythe sighed. 'You know, Lexi, we can't stand here all day. Either we move forward, or we leap over the hedge. Which would you prefer?'

'Neither.' She gazed nervously at Kynan, trying to gauge his mood. He wasn't smiling, but then, neither did he look annoyed. He just leaned against the tree trunk, waiting.

She took in a deep breath and moved forward, dragging Blythe with her. He came upright as they approached him, and said, 'Ah ... I was waiting for you.'

'Really, my Lord. For what reason?'

He fell into step beside her. 'I wondered if Mrs Spencer's remark had upset you.'

'It's kind of you to enquire, but really, it was of so little consequence I'd already forgotten it.'

The scornful sound Blythe made was hastily converted into a coughing fit.

Kynan took a small tin from his waistcoat pocket and handed it to her. 'It sounds as though you've swallowed a fly, Miss Blythe. Would you like a peppermint lozenge?'

He moved closer to Alexis so their hands touched, and his little finger hooked around hers. 'You're not annoyed with me, I hope, Lexi.'

She unhooked her finger. 'Why should I be?'

He smiled. 'Why indeed!'

Blythe handed him back his lozenge tin and slanted him a glance. 'Would you allow me to borrow the old earl's pistols, my Lord?'

The earl looked as surprised as Alexis, and spluttered, 'Do you intend to finish the job you started when we first met, and shoot me?'

In all seriousness, Blythe stated, 'I want to

enter the shooting contest at the summer fair. There's a purse of fifty guineas.'

He shook his head. 'I'm sorry, Blythe. I know how good a shot you are, but young women do not compete against men in public shooting contests.'

'Why is that? The old earl—'

'—is dead. No, I will not allow you to use the pistols. I can't be clearer than that, and have no intention of discussing the matter further. Let that be an end to it.'

When Blythe sent her a look of appeal, Alexis shrugged. 'They are not my weapons, and Lord Trent has given you his answer.'

'Oh, you would side with him.' Blythe strode on ahead as fast as her legs could carry her.

'Do you think I was wrong?' Kynan asked her.

'You acted as your mind dictated, and should not expect me to endorse your decision.'

He gave a mirthless grin. 'I've upset her.'

'Blythe must learn to hide her feelings, and she must accept that our lives have changed. She'll get over her disappointment in a little while.'

'With your permission I could arrange a shooting match at the hall for next week. We'll surprise Blythe with it. Weatherby, who is one of my guests, happens to be a crack shot, so don't expect her to win. You've

213

already encountered him in church.'

She chuckled. 'Not that strange young man with the eyeglass, surely?'

'Don't let that incident throw you off. Philip Weatherby isn't as foolish as his manner suggests. I'm sure you'll like him once you get to know him. There are bound to be bets on the outcome, too, and money in the pot for the winner.'

'Then it might teach Blythe a lesson when she loses. I must ask Cordelia how she feels about it.'

'Oh I daresay Cordelia will enter it herself, since she's not a bad shot. What about you, Lexi? Will you enter?'

'I'm afraid I don't like the thought of what guns are used for. Besides, I'm a terrible shot and the noise when it fires makes me jump.'

He stopped and took her hands in his. 'My dear, sweet, Lexi, don't you ever lose your soft heart.'

When he pulled her close and kissed her forehead she felt as though she was in heaven.

Neither of them noticed Blythe, who'd seated herself on a stile in the hedge to wait for them, and reacted to this intimate act with total astonishment.

Twelve

They had been discussing it all week.

'Honestly, I swear the earl was kissing her!' Blythe whispered.

Eyes round, her sisters exchanged glances, then Celeste said, 'Perhaps we should tell Mrs Mortimer?'

Horrified by the suggestion, Daria uttered a little cry. 'We daren't. She might cast Alexis from her home and hearth!'

'Lord Trent must like her if he was kissing her. And Alexis must be in love with him if she allowed him to kiss her. Imagine allowing a man to kiss you. It would cause a scandal if it got out.'

'We've got to do something to get rid of that awful woman the earl intends to marry.' A smile slid across Blythe's face as various ways and means of doing so filled her mind.

The talk stopped abruptly when Alexis drifted into the room. The pale yellow gown she wore was partnered by silk rosebuds woven into her long, dark braid.

'You're all very quiet,' she said.

The two youngest girls had gone back to

each painting a watercolour of a bowl of roses on the table. The eldest two were stitching a sampler; Blythe, a little reluctantly. Outside the conservatory a bright day teased her and the garden beds were gaudy with butterflies.

Alexis ran her fingers over the piano keys, then smiled at them all. 'Mrs Mortimer is entertaining Mrs Trent, Mrs Curruthers and Mrs Clark.'

'Oh, the poor thing,' Blythe said. 'Except for Mrs Trent, of course.' She grinned. 'She's lovely. The earl takes after her, don't you think so, Lexi?'

'You shouldn't really describe a man as lovely, but yes, I suppose the earl is lovely when thought of as a whole person rather than applying the word to just his looks – which nevertheless, are exceedingly handsome.'

When Alexis finished her rambling explanation with a sigh, and a soft and dreamy expression in her eyes, her sisters exchanged glances, grins and nods of confirmation.

As Blythe was to say later: 'It was as plain as the nose on Reverend Curruthers's face.' Their eldest sister was indeed in love with the Earl of Longmore.

Alexis seemed suddenly to gather her thoughts together. 'To reward you for the fine essays you presented yesterday, Mrs Mortimer has given me permission to take you to the woods so we can have a picnic. I've asked Lally to pack a basket. I'll put in some of those cheese scones I made.'

'What about our reading? I'm supposed to practise.'

'You can practise there, Blythe. But we must wear our bonnets and stay in the shade so our complexions don't become ruined. We don't want to attend Lord Trent's social gathering tomorrow with our skin burnt to a crisp by the sun.'

Needles and paint brushes were hurriedly set aside and they quietly made their way upstairs to fetch their bonnets.

Kynan was out riding with Haining and Weatherby. They'd left the women behind at the hall, which was a relief, otherwise they would have been slowed down considerably.

They'd gone along the coast to Weymouth, spent an hour or two in an inn sampling some fine ale, and another hour watching the progress of the ladies along the promenade.

The men were good-humoured in their companionship, and drew the eye.

As they waited by their horses for Weatherby, who'd become involved in a card game, Haining said, 'I'm enjoying the countryside round here, Kynan. You keep a fine table and cellar. But I must be back in London by the second week in August. Why don't you come with us?'

'There's too much I must do here.'

'You have an agent.'

'I know. And I have a good manager for the import–export business in London. For my own satisfaction, if nothing else, I need to know every aspect of estate management from the ground up.'

'You never did anything in a half-hearted manner, and you seem suited to this life. Don't you miss the bustle of London?'

Kynan patted Haining on the back. 'I miss the companionship of my friends most. But like I said, I'll be in London every season.'

'I'd be surprised if Julia settled here. May I ask what your intentions are towards her?'

'I'm still undecided.'

'From an older, but not necessarily wiser head, may I offer you a piece of advice?'

Kynan nodded.

'Don't do it.'

'May I ask the reason?'

Haining shrugged. 'Instinct. You've gained something special here, Kynan. Something that will enrich your life in many ways. I envy you that. Julia's exquisite, I grant you. Just tread carefully. A companion is one thing, a wife, another proposition altogether.' He shrugged. 'Choose with your head and heart, not with your balls, else the result will bring you nothing but misery, as I found out to my cost before I was widowed. I was lucky to have gained a son from my union. That's all I intend to say.'

It was rare for Haining to offer unsolicited advice, which was a trait Kynan respected in the man. He nodded. 'I'll be careful.'

Weatherby came sauntering along, jingling coins in pocket. He began to laugh as he neared them. 'The locals nearly cleaned me out. I'd better win that shooting contest of yours, Kynan, though I'll have to beg you for a loan so I can place a bet on myself. I take it that James will be running a book, as usual.'

He nodded. 'You won't have to beg, Weatherby, since I know you're good for it. As for the contest, I think you'll have some real competition tomorrow.'

Weatherby laughed as he mounted his horse. 'That will make a change.'

The three rode companionably back towards Longmore, chatting, laughing and trying to outdo each other with bawdy jokes. As a result they took the wrong road at the fork and lost their way, ending up on the other side of the woods.

They reined in their horses and Kynan surveyed the fields. There were two labourers hoeing along a row of what appeared to be carrots. They were his fields, for in the adjoining one he recognized one of the farm horses ploughing a furrow. His brow wrinkled as he tried to remember the calendar

Hardin had given him, one that would tell him what was planted when, and when it was harvested.

Turnips, he thought, and soon they would harvest the hay. Only hay wasn't harvested, he recalled. That was the corn crops, such as wheat and barley and rye, of which none had been sown this year. Hay was long grass. There was plenty, due to the neglect of the former earl. Hay was cut with a long handled scythe and gathered. Corn was cut with a hand sickle, and harvested. He must try to remember the difference.

'I think these woods come out on the near side of Longmore village. That track over there seems well used. We'll follow it.'

Weatherby chuckled. 'After you, my friend, we're counting on your nose for direction since we appear to be on your land.'

A fact which hit Kynan with considerable force from time to time. But could he ever really claim the land as his own? He could touch it and crumble the dark, fertile earth through his fingers. But wouldn't that same land still be here in years to come?

One day another man would enter this stretch of woodland, someone who carried Trent blood in his veins, too. The man would feel the same sense of pride and, yes, the same sense of belonging that now flooded through him – and would probably be his son.

An uneasy notion came into his mind. Julia had been seventeen years of age when she'd wed, and had not produced a child during the five years of that marriage, though her husband's mistress had borne him three daughters. His own two-year relationship with Julia had never caused her a moment's worry that an infant might result from their coupling.

Peter Haining's advice took on a new meaning for him. There was bound to be some basis of fact behind his remark. But Kynan wouldn't push him any further because he knew it was something he must deal with himself.

The woods provided a welcome shade. There was a sense of quietness pressing in on them as the growth closed about them. Light slanted down in dusty shafts to play upon the leaves, changing the colour of the bracken from light to dark and back again, as the breezes stirred through them.

After their eyes adjusted to the light they picked their way carefully, avoiding the moss-covered roots. The path was well-defined, though narrow. The trees were dense and there wasn't room for a cart between them, only a horse or a man on foot. Around them, the air was a cool kiss.

Nobody spoke. There was just the sound of the breeze, the creaking of leathers and the muted thud of the horse's hooves as they picked their way through the damp leaf underfoot.

A bird flew across in front of them, its wings making a whirring sound. Kynan's horse side-stepped, then whinnied as he got it under control.

'Did you hear that?' Esmé said. 'It sounded like a horse.'

They were seated in the glade they usually used. Here, a stand of ancient oaks had been felled to provide ships for the Royal Navy fifty years previously.

The old earl had been a young boy then, and had watched the desecration with great excitement. He'd told them he'd wanted to become a sea captain when he'd set eyes on the splendid uniforms of the officers his father had entertained at dinner. But his dream had never been realized because he'd been the only one left to run the estate.

Now, some beech trees and pines had filled the gaps left by the mighty oaks, some of which still sailed the oceans disguised as ships, Alexis imagined. Standing in a tall group were several slender silver birches, their leaves rustling loudly when the wind rushed through them.

The dog Cordelia had bought – a companion to the cat, which had walked in off the street and made himself at home – was making small rushes at the hedgehog Blythe had unearthed. It was curled in a defensive ball.

Alexis told her, 'You're not taking that home, they're full of fleas.'

'I was thinking of putting it in Julia Spencer's bed,' she whispered.

Alexis chuckled at the thought, then sighed, for it was a glorious afternoon, but she had the feeling it was getting late, and it would soon be time to go home.

'We'll stay for just a few minutes more,' she said.

They were seated on a carpet of soft grass sprinkled with daisies. Beyond was a fallen pine, decaying in a gay shroud of bright, prettily shaped, fungus and lichen. It guarded a stream, which trickled so slowly it hardly seemed to move.

They'd dug into the wet earth, making a bowl of stones to collect water to drink. From the artificial bowl the water made its quiet way to a boggy patch, where it seeped into the earth. They'd finished their reading. Blythe had read a story she'd written. It had been an exciting one and her sister had read it well, Alexis thought.

The sound of riders came more clearly now. Men's rumbling voices, laughter, and snickering horses.

Alexis recognized Kynan's voice and her hand flew into her throat when he and two other riders emerged into the clearing.

'My Lord,' they all said in chorus, and, as usual, bobbed curtsies.

Alexis grinned when Kynan gave them a relieved look and said, 'Thank goodness. I thought we'd be wandering around in here for the rest of the week.'

'The lane into Longmore is about half a mile ahead. We were just going home, ourselves,' Alexis told him.

'Then allow us to walk with you. You haven't officially met my gentlemen guests yet, have you? This is Lord Haining and his cousin, Philip Weatherby. Gentlemen, this is Miss Patterson and her sisters. The Misses Blythe, Celeste, Daria and Esmé Patterson.'

The two men dismounted and Haining kissed Alexis's hand. 'I knew your father at Cambridge, Miss Patterson. I was so sorry to learn of his demise. And your mother and brother, of course. It must have been hard on you.'

'You're most kind,' she said. 'Yes, it was hard. Luckily, good friends came to our aid.' Alexis smiled at Kynan, who'd just lifted Daria and Esmé on to his horse. Lord Haining did the same for Celeste, and the two began to converse.

The dog went on ahead, sniffing at every tree.

Meanwhile, Blythe had engaged the fascinating Mr Weatherby in conversation. 'I hope you're not going to look through that silly eyeglass at us again. Your eye looked as big as a dumpling.'

'How exceedingly unpleasant a description. I shall give up the eyeglass immediately. Just don't stick your tongue out at me again,' he grumbled. 'I nearly expired from fright and fell down dead in the aisle.'

Blythe giggled. 'You stuck your tongue out first. It almost reached to your waistcoat button. You were very rude, Mr Weatherby. You should know better at your age.'

'So should you, you pert creature. How old are you?'

'I'm seventeen.'

'What a coincidence. So am I.'

'Hah!' she said.

He took the basket from her. 'Allow me to carry that. What was it I saw you roll into it with your foot?'

'A hedgehog,' she whispered. 'Don't tell anyone, and be careful you don't catch its fleas.'

'Ah, yes, m'dear ... a hedgehog is an essential accessory for any young lady to carry in her basket.'

He laughed, and so did she.

When they reached Florence House he handed her the basket and said quietly, 'Here's your pet prickly, my dear. I'll look forward to seeing you again the day after tomorrow.'

'I like you, Mr Weatherby. You're funny,'

she said.

'Thank you, Miss Blythe, I like you too. We shall be friends, I think.'

Later that evening, Blythe managed to escape her sisters and hurry to Longmore Hall.

The servants were busy with serving dinner. Undetected, except by Jasper, who wagged his tail as he waited for a pat, she went in through the terrace doors and headed for the stairs.

She was wondering where Julia Spencer slept when she caught a glimpse of the maid who'd arrived with her. She watched from the shadows as the girl went into the room Blythe had once shared with Alexis.

A little while later the girl came out and walked past her as she went down the stairs towards the servant's hall. Blythe thought she looked sad.

Slipping up the corridor, Blythe entered the room and gently tipped the contents of the picnic basket on the floor.

That would teach that Julia Spencer woman to upset Alexis, she thought, and closed the door behind her. Grinning, Blythe made her escape.

Thirteen

Her visit wasn't going as Julia had planned. In London she'd been used to Kynan's full attention when he hadn't been running his business.

Here, she had to compete with a thousand interruptions and irritations for his time. Idly, she scratched at her arm as she watched Emily lay out her clothing. 'Not that gown. I distinctly remember telling you I wanted to wear the red one.'

The maid's lips tightened a fraction. 'I'm sorry, Mrs Spencer. I thought you said purple.'

Something nipped Julia's leg. She pushed back the bedclothes to find a flea on her leg. Her legs were covered in bites. There were some half a dozen fleas on the sheets. Giving a yelp of horror, she jumped from the bed and began slapping at herself and shuddering.

'Is there something wrong, Mrs Spencer?'

'Yes, you damned fool. The bed is full of fleas and they've bitten me. Fetch me some salve.'

Was that a smirk on the girl's face as she turned away? Julia strode across the room and jerked her round to face her. 'Do you know how they got into my bed?'

The maid avoided her eyes. 'No, Mrs Spencer.'

'You're lying, girl.'

'I'm not lying.' The maid's eyes met hers. 'How would I know how they got there? Perhaps the earl's dog came up here and made himself comfortable on the bed.'

'Don't you answer me back, you lazy little slattern.' Her hand whipped back and forth across the girl's face and she shoved her back against the wall. 'Get the bedding changed, and if I find one flea afterwards, I'll give you a good thrashing.'

Tears tumbled down the girl's face and she muttered, 'You always blame me. You've got no right to beat me.'

'Haven't I?' Losing her temper, Julia picked up her cane and set about the girl.

Her yowls brought Roxanne running in. 'Stop it this minute, Julia, before you bring the whole household down on us. For God's sake, Talbot is bleeding from the nose.'

Breathing heavily, Julia paused in her punishment. 'She's a lazy, good-for-nothing trollop, and a liar.'

'I'm a good girl,' Emily said defiantly. 'I don't know anything about any fleas, and I'm not working for you any more, Mrs

Spencer.'

'You're not? May I remind you that you're required to give a month's notice if you wish to leave my service, or you'll not receive any salary. And don't expect me to furnish you with a reference. See how far you'll get without one. You'll probably end up in a house of ill-repute.'

'It can't be worse than working for you. The way you carry on with men is indecent, I wouldn't be surprised if you ended up in one of them places yourself, that I wouldn't.'

Julia lashed out with her stick, catching the girl a blow on the shoulder with the silver knob. Emily fell as she tried to dodge out of the way.

The maid's face drained of colour as she stared at her, then she staggered to her feet, turned and walked unsteadily away, holding her shoulder with the other hand, her nose dripping blood.

Roxanne said, 'I think you went a little too far, Julia. What's wrong with you?'

'Everything. It's this place. It's so boring, and Kynan insists on playing lord of the manor. What's more, he's neglecting me shamefully.'

'He has work to do, and he *is* lord of the manor.'

'I've a good mind to ask Peter to take me back to London.'

'He's enjoying it here. It will only be for a

few more weeks.'

'When I marry Kynan I'm not going to live here for most of the year. I'll stay in London and have some fun.'

'Kynan has proposed, then.'

'Not yet. But he didn't invite me down here without reason, and when he does I've decided to accept. He was hinting at marriage in London. Men have no qualms about taking you into their beds, but they take a damned sight longer to make up their minds to marry.'

'Perhaps the house party tomorrow will cheer you up. I'm looking forward to it.'

'Being polite to the locals is not my idea of fun.'

'At least it will give you a chance to practise your airs and graces for when you become a countess. All you need to do is make sure you look like a countess, as well. It's inconvenient your maid going off like that. I'll have to arrange my own hair, I suppose.'

'Oh, Talbot will return. She has no money and nowhere to go.'

Her attention was caught by something dark moving out from under the bed. What was it? It had spines and looked ferocious.

Her heart began to thump as she stared at it with fear in her eyes. 'What's that animal?'

As Roxanne headed for the corridor as fast as her legs could carry her, Julia jumped back on to the bed, where her legs were immediately covered by bloodsucking fleas. Her breath came in short, harsh gasps as hysteria overtook her. Then she swooped in a long breath and began to give loud, piercing screams, which were partly fear and partly rage.

'It was a hedgehog, and it dropped fleas everywhere. Julia seems to think her maid put it there deliberately. I've moved Julia into another room while that one is being cleaned.'

'What happened to the hedgehog?' Weatherby said casually.

'It curled up in a ball and nearly died of fright when Julia started screaming. James has taken it to the woods to release it. I imagine the poor creature will find its way back home, eventually.'

Haining helped himself to some sausages and eggs from the buffet. 'I doubt if the creature could have managed to find its way upstairs by itself. Has the maid been questioned?'

Kynan shrugged. 'She's packed her bag and left. The housekeeper said Talbot was trembling, and upset, and seemed to be favouring her arm. I wonder if she realized the seriousness of what she'd done. Julia's overwrought, of course. She's covered in flea bites. My housekeeper has bathed the wounds with witch hazel and treated them with soothing salve. I've advised her to stay in bed and rest.'

Weatherby grinned. 'A hedgehog ... I'll be damned. How delicious.'

'It's not in the least bit funny.'

'So why are you trying not to laugh, my Lord? You're surely not inclined to take such a prank seriously. It's quite possible that the dastardly deed was perpetrated by someone other than the maid – someone who played an innocent trick, and gave little thought to the consequence.'

Haining chuckled. 'You haven't got an innocent bone in your body, Weatherby, so it can't be you.'

'I wouldn't deliberately evoke the fair Julia's wrath.'

It didn't take much to evoke that, these days, Kynan thought soberly, remembering the savage manner in which Julia had treated her maid on arrival. He felt uneasy about the incident. He wondered where she'd gone. He thought he might take a ride after breakfast. There was only one road in and out of the estate, so Talbot couldn't have got very far.

The Patterson girls had just finished breakfast, and were about to commence their lessons under Mrs Mortimer's gimlet gaze.

Alexis was clearing up the kitchen and

232

preparing vegetables for the evening meal, when somebody rapped at the door to the back garden.

She opened it to find James Mitchell, standing there. He was supporting a young woman, who had a bruised face. One arm was tucked inside the bib of her apron.

'Goodness,' she said, her hand flying to her throat. 'Has there been an accident, James? Bring the poor girl inside and lay her on the sofa in the drawing room. She's shaking. Go and fetch a blanket and a pillow, Lally.'

When they'd reached the drawing room she turned to James. 'Who is she, d'you know?'

'It's Emily Talbot, Mrs Spencer's maid. I found her up in the woods. I think her arm might be broken. Can I leave her here while I go and fetch the doctor out from Dorchester?'

'You won't have to go to Dorchester. Dr Chivers usually comes to the village on Fridays to visit Ada Brown's mother, who has the wasting disease, and should be in the infirmary. He usually visits about now, and remains for about fifteen minutes, though sometimes he stops off to see Reverend Curruthers. If you're quick, you should be able to catch him.'

He nodded, and was gone.

Lally came back with a pillow and blanket. Alexis sent her for a bowl of water and a cloth, and while she waited for that, she made the girl more comfortable.

Her face was pinched and pale, and she moaned when Alexis moved her. 'I'm sorry, Emily. I didn't mean to hurt you. James has gone to fetch the doctor.'

She took the cloth and bowl from Lally. 'You'd better tell Mrs Mortimer I need to see her as soon as possible.'

Emily opened her eyes when Alexis began to gently bathe her face, and whispered, 'I'm sorry to be so much trouble, miss.'

'Hush, my dear. You're no trouble, at all.' She turned when Cordelia came in. 'There has been an accident.'

Cordelia said, 'Do you have anyone we can inform, Talbot?'

Tears squeezed from under Emily's eyelids and she whispered, 'Please don't make me go back to Mrs Spencer.'

'Mrs Spencer did this to you?' Cordelia heaved a big sigh. 'Hardly an accident then. All right, you may stay here until you've recovered.'

Emily's nod was followed by a groan. 'Thank you, ma'am. Please don't tell anyone. They wouldn't believe it anyway, with her being so fine.'

Cordelia's lips tightened as she nodded and turned to Lally. 'Prepare a room in the servants' quarters for her. Talbot may remain here until she's recovered.'

When Lally had gone, Mrs Mortimer said, 'Can you manage alone, Alexis? I'm about to give my pupils a spelling examination, to see how much of my teaching is being absorbed.'

'Yes, I can manage. When Lally comes back down we'll help her up the stairs between us, then the doctor can examine her in private.'

With the move upstairs achieved, Alexis left Emily sitting on the edge of the bed and went to find a spare nightgown and two pairs of scissors.

When she came back, she said, 'I've got to get you out of that bodice and skirt. I know it will hurt, my dear, but I'll be as gentle as possible. As you can't lift that arm over your head I'll unpick the seam at the back. Lally, you can do the same to the nightgown. It will save trying to get it over her head.'

Emily hardly gave a murmur, though she caught her breath on a couple of occasions as Alexis eased the garment down her arms and over her hands. Her shoulder was misshapen and she was covered in welts and bruises. Alexis bit her lip. How could Julia Spencer be so cruel?

They'd hardly finished easing the nightdress on to her when Dr Chivers arrived with James, who told her, 'I left Emily's bag in the woods. I'll go and fetch it.'

There was no nonsense about Dr Chivers.

The man took one look at her and said, 'That shoulder is dislocated. I'll have to manipulate. It will hurt like hell, but there's nothing I can do about that.'

Emily gave a little mew of terror.

'Aye, I know, lass,' he said kindly. 'But it's got to be done. I'll give you some laudanum in advance to help ease the pain.'

Dr Chivers gave Emily a measured dose, then indicated the door. When they were outside, he lowered his voice. 'I'll need another man to hold the girl down.'

Just then, someone banged loudly at the door. When Lally opened it, she heard Kynan's voice. 'I saw the doctor's rig outside. Is someone unwell?'

'There's been an accident, my Lord.'

'Ah, just the person,' Chivers said, and boomed down the stairs. 'Get yourself up here, my Lord. I need a hand.'

Kynan's long legs carried him up the stairs two at a time. His eyes lit on Alexis at the top, and relief filled them. 'Thank God it's not you,' he said under his breath and turned to the doctor. 'How can I be of assistance?'

'It's a dislocated shoulder so I'm going to hurt the girl. I can realign the bones easily enough if she's still, but I need someone strong enough to hold her firmly, otherwise the result could be permanent disability.'

'I can do that. Is this one of your sisters, Lexi?'

'It's a maid,' she said shortly. Let him find out for himself who the maid worked for, and how cruel a mistress that person was, she thought.

His gaze questioned her sharpness for a moment before Dr Chivers broke in. 'It would be reassuring for my patient if there was another woman present. Are you up to it, Miss Patterson? I don't want your services if you're the fainting type.'

She didn't know whether she was or not, but nodded. Someone had to do it.

When they all crowded into the room, Emily whimpered, but her eyes were dulled from the laudanum.

'It's all right, Emily, I'm here with you,' she said.

Her glance went to Kynan who seemed slightly shocked by seeing someone from his household in such a bad way.

'Have you seen this procedure carried out before?' Chivers asked. Without waiting for an answer he divested the bed of its sheet and folded it. Wrapping the fabric around Emily's torso, he handed the ends to Kynan. The nightdress was slipped from her arm and shoulder, exposing her bruises.

Breath hissed between Kynan's teeth when he saw the extent of Emily's injuries.

'Come closer to the bed, man. Press your thighs against it. This is no time to be delicate. I want you to keep the sheet taut.

The object is to act as a counterweight to me. I'm going to apply sustained pressure to this arm. I'm going to hurt the girl, but it's got to be done. It will be less painful if the desired result is achieved at the first attempt. Understand?'

Kynan nodded.

'Then let me know when you're ready, my Lord.'

Kynan pulled the sheet ends tight and held them firmly with both hands as he said calmly. 'Ready.'

Chivers grasped Emily's upper arm with one hand, and the lower arm with the other. He leaned back and applied a gentle pressure. Emily began to whimper, then as more pressure was applied, her eyes flew open and she screeched in pain.

Alexis stroked the girl's hair, but tears sprang to her eyes. She watched through a blur of tears as the doctor, his face a study of concentration, manoeuvred the shoulder. There was a muffled clunk.

Chivers grunted and smiled in satisfaction. Emily fainted dead away.

Alexis looked across at Kynan, who wore a sheen of perspiration on his forehead. His eyes were as troubled as a stormy sea and she wondered what his thoughts were now.

'You can release the sheet now,' Chivers said, and modestly covered the girl's shoulder. 'There's no need to bind the shoulder, but the girl will need to rest that arm in a sling for several week while it heals. Maid or not, that means she won't be able to work. Is that a problem?'

'No,' Kynan and Alexis said together.

Emily's eyes fluttered open, and she sought out those of the doctor, saying faintly, 'Thank you, sir. It feels much better now.'

'Aye girl, it would do. You were a brave lass. You're to stay in bed for the rest of the day so the laudanum can wear off. Others can wait on you for a change.'

Alexis stroked Emily's hair back from her forehead. 'I'll send Lally up with some tea for you to drink, then you can sleep for a while.'

She followed Chivers and the doctor out. 'Send the bill to me,' Kynan said as they went down the stairs.

Chivers nodded as he picked up his hat. 'I'll drop in on the girl next week to see how she's getting along.'

After the doctor had left, the tears she'd been trying to hold back threatened to choke Alexis. She gave a sob as she sucked in a desperate breath.

Kynan's fingers closed loosely around her wrist. 'Would you mind telling me what's going on?'

'I would have thought that was obvious,' she said in an angry whisper. 'Let go of my wrist at once. I refuse to be fettered.'

'Fettered?' He gazed down at the loose connection between them, gave a faint smile, then opened his fingers. 'Away you go, butterfly. Are you annoyed with me?'

'Yes.' Tears scalded her eyes.

Gently, he applied his handkerchief to them, then when she gave a sob, pulled her gently against his shoulder. 'Why? I didn't do that to the girl, you know.'

'I know. I just need to be angry with someone, however illogical it seems.'

How sweet it was to be in his arms like this, his skin warm, and, lingering about him, the smell of cinnamon. Each time he exhaled, his breath caressed warmly against her scalp.

Mrs Mortimer's voice blew through the hall like a blast of winter air. 'My Lord, I will expect you to explain your extraordinary behaviour!'

Kynan sprang backwards and nearly went sprawling as his heel caught on the edge of the hall rug. He regained his balance quickly. 'Miss Patterson was upset. I was comforting her.'

'You should have called me to comfort her.' She sniffed. 'This sort of behaviour might be common amongst your circle of friends in London. But here, and especially for a man in your position, it's scandalous, to say the least. If observed, such an intimate gesture of friendship could be misconstrued, and Miss Patterson's reputation could be tarnished beyond repair.'

Kynan looked decidedly uncomfortable. 'My pardon, Mrs Mortimer. Please rest assured that the familiarity arose entirely from concern for Miss Patterson's well-being. She was upset by the treatment required to relieve the unfortunate maid of her pain.' He turned to her. 'Miss Patterson, it was unforgivable of me to cross the bounds of propriety. Please forgive me.'

'Your apology is accepted.' She mourned that fact that it might never happen again and turned to Cordelia in an effort to relieve him of some of the blame. 'It was just as much my fault.'

'Only a hussy would admit to something so blatant,' Cordelia said calmly. 'My Lord, did Miss Patterson encourage you in any way?'

Alexis gasped.

'Certainly not, Mrs Mortimer. The incident was one entirely of my instigation. If anyone is to be chastised, it should be me.'

Something Cordelia had already done. She was a truly formidable woman when pushed to it, Alexis thought.

Cordelia bestowed a smile on her. 'Good, then we shall not mention it again. Come into the drawing room, the pair of you. Your manservant is waiting for you there. I want to know everything there is to know about this wretched affair.'

Alexis's face was warm with embarrassment, and she couldn't meet anyone's eyes. All she wanted to do was escape. 'Where are my sisters?'

'They're too unsettled to concentrate on their work, as anyone would be from hearing that poor girl scream. They're waiting in the drawing room, where we all can discuss the situation sensibly.'

They trooped into the drawing room, where Kynan immediately joined his man-servant.

Cordelia gazed round at them all. 'Well, who's going to tell me what started this affair?'

'I will,' said Kynan. 'It started with a hedgehog. Somebody put one in Mrs Spencer's room and she was badly bitten by its fleas. The appearance of the creature frightened her because she'd never seen one before. I understand she accused her maid of placing it there. The maid decided to leave her employ.'

He'd omitted to tell them that the Spencer woman had beaten the poor maid half to death, Alexis thought. Or perhaps he didn't know. It wasn't something Julia Spencer would have admitted too, after all. Alexis wished the fleas had carried her off.

Blythe made a little whimpering noise in her throat. 'Is the maid all right?'

Alexis nodded. 'Her shoulder was dislocated. The scream you heard was when the doctor pushed the bone back into position. It was painful. But she's a lot better now.'

'How did her shoulder get ... discoluted, Lexi?' Esmé asked, which brought a chuckle from Kynan.

'I'm unable to tell you. Emily asked me to keep the information confidential.'

Cordelia looked affronted. 'Am I to take it that I must ask her for the details, myself?'

Gently, Alexis answered, 'If you feel it's important for you to know ... yes, I suppose you must.'

'Are you being impertinent, Miss Patterson?'

She'd had enough and her anger rose. Anyone would think she'd ill-treated the girl herself. 'That's not my intention. But I'm not in the habit of breaking confidences. While I respect your right to expect certain behaviours of me, the manner of the questioning I'm being subjected to is taking on the appearance of an inquisition.' She stood. 'Perhaps you'll excuse me.'

'Lexi, calm down,' Kynan said.

She ignored him and, storming out of the room, picked up her skirts and headed down the garden. There, she climbed the wall, and fled towards the quiet safety of the woods. Her gown ripped as the skirt caught on a bramble, and her heart pounded.

Reaching the nearest clearing she sat on a fallen log and yelled with frustration. Above her, several rooks squawked in alarm and rose to circle about the pines.

A flash of blue in the corner of her eye caught her attention. It was Blythe, pale-faced, her cheeks streaked with tears and her eyes wide with fear. Her sister must have followed her. 'Blythe ... whatever is it? I'm sorry, I upset you.'

Blythe took several steps into the clearing. 'You didn't do anything. It's me. I was the cause of everything.'

'You? How can it be? I don't understand.'

Advancing towards her, Blythe said, 'I put the hedgehog in that woman's room. It was the one I found in the woods yesterday. I rolled it into the picnic basket, and brought it home. I took it to the manor when I knew they'd be at dinner and everyone would be busy. She was so horrible to you, and I hated her for what she'd said to you at church. I only wanted to give her a scare. I didn't intend to cause so much trouble. I swear.'

'Oh, Blythe,' she whispered.

'What shall I do, Lexi? It's so horrible when everything I do turns out to be the wrong thing. Everyone thinks I'm such a nuisance, or they laugh at me behind my back. And Lexi ... I just hate myself, some-times. I'm so clumsy.'

Alexis held out her arms and her sister came into them. 'Oh, Blythe, I love you so much. You have such a wonderful innocence and independence to you. You're very precious to us all. Your awkwardness will go away eventually, I promise. People only laugh when you laugh at yourself. They're not being unkind.'

'You always make me feel better,' Blythe said, but still a trifle glumly.

'As for the rest of it, I'm afraid we must go and tell the earl of your involvement in this affair. Emily Talbot sustained a serious injury because of it. We must spend the rest of the week apologizing to just about everyone.'

'Even that detestable Mrs Spencer? She's so horrid.'

'Especially her. You gave her a fright, and being bitten by fleas is uncomfortable. She was obviously irritated beyond reason. Although that doesn't condone, or excuse her cruelty towards her maid – it does explain why she lost her temper.'

'Do you think the earl will forgive you, Lexi? After today, he might not want to see either of us again.'

'One thing I'm sure of, Lord Trent has a good heart and a generous mind.'

'You really *are* in love with him, aren't you, Lexi?'

'Yes,' she said with a sigh, 'but this must remain a secret between us. It would be embarrassing for him and unbearable for me if it were to become common knowledge, since he loves another woman. I must respect that. My fervent wish is that he'll always be happy.'

Blythe frowned. 'Only a fool could be happy with her.'

'Mrs Spencer is very lovely to look at ... it's no wonder the earl is in love with her.'

'She looks like a snake with her cold, mean eyes. I should have put a rat in her room instead of the hedgehog. She'd probably have swallowed it whole for breakfast.'

Alexis only just managed not to smile. 'Enough Blythe. You know what we have to do. Let's go and get it over with.'

Arms about each other's waists they headed back towards the house.

After a while, Blythe asked, 'What do you think of Mr Weatherby? He's such good fun to talk to. He owns several gentlemen's clubs, where they fight with swords and wrestle. I wonder if he knows anything about cannons...'

'Cannons?' Weatherby said the next afternoon, his eyebrow arching in surprise. 'If I were you I'd start with a pistol, Miss Blythe. They're much easier to load.'

She gave him a broad smile. 'Oh, I know how to shoot a pistol. Lord Trent has surprised me. He offered me a pair of his pistols to shoot, and I'm entered for the ladies' match.'

'You have surprising talents for one so young, m'dear. By the way, I'm sorry you didn't get away with the hedgehog prank. I wouldn't have told anyone about the beastie.'

'Oh, not for a moment did I think you would. I've been chastised by everyone since my sister told me to confess to the earl. He was very stern. I've been ordered to apologize to Mrs Spencer today. In public, he said.'

'A thousand commiserations, m'dear. I hope Julia's in a good mood. She doesn't react lightly to being made a fool of. If it's any consolation, the screech she gave dislodged half the tiles from the roof.'

He gave a dry chuckle when she laughed. 'Ah, I notice that your remorse is of the fleeting variety, Miss Blythe. A woman of my own heart. The poor hedgehog nearly died of fright from the commotion she made, you know. Would you like me to talk to the earl, ask him to allow you to deliver your apology in private?'

Relief filled her. 'Thank you, Mr Weatherby. You're so kind and thoughtful.'

'Yes, I suppose I am,' he said with some surprise.

'About cannons?'

'Ah, yes, the cannon ... what exactly did you want to know about such weapons?'

'How do you make them fire?'

Fourteen

'Miss Blythe is only a girl, Kynan. Don't be too hard on her.'

His host looked puzzled. 'Did she ask you to champion her cause, Weatherby?'

'Certainly not, but I do feel partly responsible for her predicament, since I carried the hedgehog back from the woods for her.' He chuckled. 'It was in the picnic basket. Miss Blythe was quite open about it. She told me it contained a hedgehog and I was to be careful not to catch its fleas. But I didn't believe her.'

Kynan grinned. 'The devil, you did! You knew who'd planted it there right from the beginning, then.'

His friend shrugged. 'It didn't take much to deduce who the culprit was. Well, are you going to allow the girl to make her apology in private, or not?'

'Julia has requested otherwise. So give me a good reason why I should, Weatherby?'

'Because at this moment I'm asking you to as a favour to me. She's an engaging little puss, and I like her ... I like her a lot. Julia wants to draw blood. Think on, friend. Miss Blythe is a local, and you're a newcomer. Humiliating her will reflect badly upon you.'

'Blythe is provocative and unpredictable. She needs taking to task.'

'A public flogging won't change her nature. I'll tell you this, Kynan, if you attempt to go ahead with a public apology, I'll intervene.'

Kynan stared hard at him. 'You feel that strongly about her welfare?'

Weatherby grinned. 'Never fear, my Lord. Miss Blythe still needs the safety of her family around her. I'll wait for her to properly bloom before I pluck her from the vine. Just expect me to visit now and again while she does.'

'You're serious about this, Weatherby, aren't you?'

'Of course. I've never met anyone I liked so much at such short acquaintance.'

Would wonders never cease? Kynan thought, and he nodded. 'I'll be lenient on this occasion just for you, my friend. You may tell Miss Blythe to present herself in my study at three o'clock to make her apology in private, which is just before the ladies' shooting contest begins. And I'll caution Julia to keep control of herself. It might be better if Miss Patterson comes with her sister, since I'll also be in attendance.'

* * *

The apology did not go well. It was obvious that Julia Spencer was not the type of person to forgive and forget, Alexis thought.

She was arranged on the leather sofa in a flimsy gown of dark red with gold trim. Kynan stood behind her, grave of demeanour, his slim hand resting on the back of the sofa, and looking every inch the earl. His eyes were bland, his thoughts hidden from her.

Blythe's voice trembled as she made her apology. Beneath her nervousness, Alexis could detect the disdain Blythe felt for this woman, who accepted the apology grudgingly, with a sneer on her face. She understood Blythe's feelings, and shared them.

'Miss Patterson,' Mrs Spencer said, as Alexis turned to lead her sister away. 'I believe my maid is residing with you at the moment.'

'Yes, she is. My understanding is that Miss Talbot has left your employ.'

'A silly misunderstanding. Talbot is temperamental.'

'The doctor has said she must rest for several weeks.' And so the woman would know she knew how Emily's condition had come about, she added harshly, 'She's suffered serious injury, and she needs to heal.'

Julia's tawny eyes were half-hooded, the expression in them malicious as she purred, 'The girl was clumsy, she must have fallen

250

over in the woods. Typical of her to blame her accident on me. She has always lied to draw attention to herself. Send her back, would you? She can rest here.'

'Florence House is the residence of Mrs Mortimer. I'm not in the position to dictate to those who find shelter under her roof.'

The silence was fraught for a moment as their eyes met and held. Then Julia gave a thin smile. 'Ah yes, you're reliant on the earl's largesse, aren't you? I'd forgotten.'

'So had I, for the earl never reminds me of the fact.' Alexis turned to him, and continued softly, 'You're already aware of how grateful I am.'

'You've nothing to be grateful for. Julia is ignorant of our business arrangement.'

'What sort of business arrangement?' Julia said suspiciously.

Alexis didn't give her an inch. 'It's a private matter between myself and the earl.'

'Kynan?' Julia's eyes shifted sideways, and she moved her elegant arm across her body. Her bejewelled hand landed possessively on Kynan's, and closed around it.

He didn't move his hand away, but she saw it tense. He didn't like being manipulated in such a manner. 'It's nothing for you to worry about, really, Julia.'

Alexis's eyes met Kynan's, and she didn't bother hiding the scorn she felt. He was no better than his ancestors. How could she have fallen in love with such a man? Because he was the most intriguing, handsome man she'd ever met, and he brought her body alive every time she saw him. When she was with him her blood sang inside her and her mind could think of nothing else. And Kynan must feel exactly the same – but not when he was with her, when he was with Julia Spencer.

As for herself, she'd probably end up married to someone like the Reverend David Hill, or one of the other two men who wished to call on her.

Just to annoy Kynan, she curtsied. His lips tightened, because he knew she was mocking him. She wanted to kiss the softness back into them. She also wanted to kick him because he allowed this woman to hold his hand with such familiarity.

'Excuse me, my Lord,' she said, her emotions so mixed up she thought she might be turned inside-out if she stayed any longer. She turned her back on them.

Alexis and her sister both let out a long, wobbly breath when they got outside.

Weatherby stepped forward from the shadows. 'I've been appointed to load your pistols for the contest, Miss Blythe.'

'I know how to load a pistol. Who appointed you?'

'I did. Having me do it will save time. You look flushed, Miss Blythe.'

'I'm upset. But not with you, Weatherby. I would have hated to have gone through that in public. She made me feel as low as a worm.'

'Ah, I see. Well, you have reason to be upset, I imagine? Do try and calm yourself before the competition. Anger and guns are not a good combination.' He escorted them outside to where the targets were set up. 'Where are your pistols?'

'There, on the table.'

One of Weatherby's eyebrows arched. 'The Queen Anne breech loaders? Good grief!'

'There's nothing wrong with them. I've used them before. They're quite safe.'

He picked one up, tossing it from one hand to the other, muttering, 'Good balance.' Holding the weapon at eye level he squinted along the short barrel, humming approvingly in his throat when he finished. 'It's in good condition for an old gun.'

'It's French.'

'No m'dear. The gun is English. It was manufactured by Thomas Stanton.'

'But the old earl said he took it from a French sea captain who sailed his ship into the cove and tried to blow Longmore Hall to pieces with his cannons. He said they were pirates. How exciting that would have been. Though I do suppose it was one of the old earl's tall tales, since he told some wonderful stories and liked to fill our heads with them.

All the same, I wish it were true, and I'd been here to witness something like that.'

Weatherby's lips twitched. 'It was brave of the former earl to engage a ship load of plundering pirates. And there's no reason why a French sea captain couldn't have had an English gun in his possession, especially beauties like these.'

'The old earl taught me to shoot with them. He said I was the best shot he'd ever seen, and it was a pity I hadn't been born a boy.'

Alexis smiled. Philip Weatherby handled Blythe's exaggerations well, and seemed genuinely interested. She wondered when her sister would grow out of these stories. Never, probably, for Cordelia was encouraging Blythe to write them all down and they would become legend, like the damned Welsh heir had.

'It will provide a record for the history of Longmore,' Cordelia had told Blythe, and Alexis could only think it would be a rather colourful one.

In answer to Blythe's statement, Weatherby said, 'If the old earl thought you were a good shot, I'll take his word for it and place a wager on you. As for being born a boy, that would have been a tragedy to my mind.'

'Why would it?'

'My dear Miss Blythe, don't you realize that you're a quite delightful creature as you are? What about you, Miss Patterson? Are you competing?'

Alexis shook her head. 'I'd rather be a spectator, but I'm going to wager a shilling on Blythe.'

'A whole shilling?' Blythe said, her cheeks pink. Though from Weatherby's compliment, or just sheer excitement, Alexis couldn't tell. 'Can we afford it?'

'Allow me to provide you with a stake.' Weatherby took a florin from his pocket and handed it to her. 'Also place a shilling on your sister's shooting prowess on my behalf, Miss Patterson. And since the match starts in ten minutes, you'd best go and find the earl's servant, who is keeping the book.'

As Alexis walked off she heard Weatherby say, 'I believe the earl has provided a five guinea prize for the winners of each section. And another five for the last man standing.'

'Or woman,' Blythe challenged.

Kynan watched Alexis making her way toward James. She looked exquisite in a simple blue gown with an overskirt of embroidered muslin. The rise of her breasts was covered in lace. The thought of uncovering the tempting delights was attractive. Her ankle-length skirt fluttered against her slim ankles.

In stark contrast, red and gold material clung to Julia's superb figure. She was too sure of herself, of him. Marriage was out of the question, he could see that now. She simply would not fit into his life here, and her constant carping annoyed him. He'd been shocked by the damage she'd inflicted on her maid – and even more shocked that she'd attempted to discredit the girl in an attempt to exonerate herself. Julia had tripped herself up with those remarks, since the maid hadn't laid the blame anywhere.

Only Lexi knew the truth and he admired the way she'd respected the maid's wishes not to tell Cordelia the details. Having battled too long in an effort to raise and protect her sisters, Alexis wasn't going to allow Cordelia to dictate to her.

Her sisters were gathered around her now. At her request, they had all joined his mother on the terrace, where they'd have a good view of the proceedings. They waved when Blythe turned to look for them. What was it Weatherby had said? That Blythe wasn't ready to leave the safety of her family yet. Alexis had done a good job in keeping them together. But one day her sisters would marry and leave home, and she'd be left alone to face a life of spinsterhood.

Kynan smiled when Blythe's glance fell on him. She gave him a tentative smile, one that became a beam when she turned back to Weatherby, who placed a pistol in her hands. Kynan saw in Blythe then, what Weatherby had noticed, her sheer vulnerability.

There were four other women in the match: Julia, Roxanne, Mrs Clark and Cordelia.

James had told him that most of the wagers had been placed on Julia or Roxanne. Since Weatherby had taught both of them to shoot, and his reputation had gone before him, he wasn't surprised.

Peter Haining called for quiet and the simple rules were read out. Five shots each. The one with the most points won. If there were tied points, another three shots would be fired to determine the winner, and so on.

Kynan joined his mother and the Patterson girls on the terrace. Even his mother's eyes were sparkling with excitement.

Haining lifted his hand and a hush fell over the spectators.

Julia made the first shot. Her aim was too high, the recoil saw it clip the top edge of the target. A groan went up. Roxanne's first shot hit the target just outside the bull's eye. Everyone cheered and clapped. She turned and bowed. Mrs Mortimer and Mrs Clark scored solidly in the outer ring.

Then it was Blythe's turn. As steady as a rock, she held the gun out at arms' length. In one smooth motion she lowered it slightly then fired. It struck just inside the outer edge of the centre.

'Good shot!' Kynan heard Weatherby

exclaim with some surprise, and Kynan grinned when a buzz went through the crowd. A fluke, someone said loudly, to which remark Blythe directed a black look.

Julia took an age to line up her next shot. It went wide. So did Roxanne's. The two older women scored well.

Just as Blythe was about to fire, Julia gave a little scream, 'A wasp.' When Weatherby whispered something to her, Blythe then lowered her pistol and waited quietly, while Julia slapped at the air around her. When a spectator hissed at her Julia fell quiet, looking sulky.

Her face a study of concentration, Blythe lifted her gun and fired her shot in one movement. When it hit the centre, everyone erupted into cheers. The locals were solidly behind her now.

Weatherby glanced over at Blythe, a delighted look on his face. If he hadn't been smitten with Blythe before, he certainly was now.

'It looks as though Blythe is going to win the purse,' Kynan said to Alexis.

'I never doubted it.'

'I placed my money on her.'

Alexis laughed as she mocked, 'I wouldn't call that a sound business decision, my Lord.'

'Sometimes I prefer to act on my instincts.'

'Yes ... I know.' As soon as the words left

her mouth, she coloured.

He grinned. 'Unfortunately my instincts seem to get the better of me when I'm around you.'

Her gaze wandered to Florence Trent, who was occupied with something Daria was saying. She turned back to him and, lowering her voice, said, 'I warn you. I won't appreciate another lecture on my shortcomings.'

'You have no shortcomings. You're just perfect. Your mouth is trembling to be kissed, and I have an urge to kiss you, right here and now.'

'Oh ... you and your London ways.' She rose, in case he carried out his threat in this public place for everyone to see. When she casually moved a pace or two away from him, he chuckled.

Blythe won the ladies' section outright. Roxanne kissed her cheek and Cordelia and Mrs Clark congratulated her. Only Julia threw her gun aside and walked away without a word, her bad sportsmanship plain for all to see.

Escorted by Weatherby, Blythe came to where they sat, her face glowing with pride.

'You said I'd be surprised, and I am,' Weatherby drawled as Blythe was hugged by her sisters. 'I've never seen better shooting from a woman.'

Alexis noticed there was a touch of hero worship in the glance Blythe sent after

Weatherby when he went to take his place in the men's line-up.

Weatherby won the men's section easily. In the shoot-out between Blythe and himself, he won by a whisker, in a taut finish in which the pair reached tied points, twice.

'Well done, Mr Weatherby,' Blythe said when she was returned to the family group.

Weatherby told her, 'I'm stronger than you are, and that pistol you're using is heavy for a girl of your weight. I imagine your shoulder is aching.'

Blythe nodded.

Generously, Weatherby said, 'You'd probably have won if your arm hadn't been tired. Since we've provided entertainment for the guests, we'll share the purse, shall we?'

How nice a young man Philip Weatherby was, Alexis thought. Apart from the detestable Julia, she liked all of Kynan's friends.

After an early supper served in the hall, the evening entertainment took place.

Julia's singing voice was superb. She gazed soulfully at Kynan, who accompanied her on the piano. A knife twisted in Alexis's heart.

Roxanne was the most popular entertainment of the evening. Kynan's threat to engage Alexis in a duet never came about. He must have forgotten about it. She was relieved. Her piano playing was mediocre compared to his.

The dancing started, though some of the men began to drift towards the card tables.

Outside, lanterns had been lit and a purple dusk was falling softly over the landscape. Soon the moon would rise to lay a pathway of rippling silver across the sea.

Alexis sat alone on the terrace wall, sipping a glass of punch and enjoying a moment of solitude.

'May I join you?' Kynan seated himself beside her when she nodded. As they gazed into the gloaming light, Alexis felt at one with him. She didn't resist when he took the punch from her hand and drew her head against his shoulder. 'I wonder what Mrs Mortimer would say,' he murmured.

'She'd tell me I was a hussy.'

He chuckled. 'I wonder what she'd say if she knew I have every intention of kissing you.'

Even knowing it was provocative, she turned her face up to his. 'Do you have every intention?'

'What man wouldn't?' His lips were a scant inch away from his. He found the niche under her chin with his finger, and his mouth settled over hers as if it belonged there. It was a proper kiss this time, a delicious, lingering caress, one that made everything inside her crumble and melt.

'We should put a stop to this, Florence,'

Cordelia whispered, turning to her cousin.

'Of course we must. Let them enjoy it for a few seconds longer. I want Kynan to realize there's someone better than Julia Spencer he can pursue.'

'I think he's noticed that already. What if he seduces Alexis? She'll be ruined.'

Despite the earl being her own beloved son, Florence was aware that such a possibility existed. 'We won't give him the chance to be alone with her for any length of time, just enough to whet his appetite. I'm going to invite her back to London with me.'

'I doubt if Alexis will leave her sisters. She has suitors, too, three of them. All of them would make her a worthy husband.'

'Then encourage them to call. We'll arrange events between us.'

Florence raised her voice. 'Look at that moon, Cordelia. It's superb. Shall we go out on the terrace to get some air?'

There was hurried whisper and a scuffle. When they emerged through the French widow, Alexis was alone, sipping her punch.

'Ah, Alexis, dear. There you are, all alone.'

Looking flustered, Alexis rose. 'I just came out to watch the moon rise. I must go and look for my sisters. They'll be tired.'

'We'll come in with you. I do hope you've enjoyed yourself.'

'Thank you, Cordelia, it's been a most wonderful day,' Alexis said dreamily. 'The earl has been most kind.'

'My son is generous in bestowing his favours. He can be an absolute saint, at times.'

From the shrubbery came a strangled noise.

'What on earth was that?' Cordelia said.

'I didn't hear anything,' Alexis answered, 'though I did see a rat on the terrace, earlier.'

'A rat?'

'A large, black one with gleaming eyes ... and menacing teeth.'

'Menacing teeth?' the two women said in unison and headed for the French doors, ushering her before them.

Alexis thought she heard Kynan burst into laughter.

Fifteen

The following Monday Alexis was called to the drawing room.

Lessons were over for the day, it was Cordelia's turn to help with the cooking, and she was just about to accompany her sisters to the cove.

Reverend Hill rose from his seat when she entered and Mrs Mortimer nodded at her. 'You have a visitor, Miss Patterson.'

Dismay filled her. 'I was about to go to the cove with my sisters.'

'Your sisters must go without you. I'll go and tell them.'

She seated herself and glanced over at Reverend Hill, feeling trapped. 'It's been a warm day for early in July,' she said.

'Yes it has. But my dear Miss Patterson, I'm not here to discuss the weather. I'm here to advise you of my circumstances.'

Her chin lifted a fraction. 'When you approached me after the church I thought I made it clear that I did not wish you to call on me.'

'And the reasons you gave were that you

have your sisters to care for, Miss Patterson. I consulted Mrs Mortimer on this matter. She assures me they're adequately cared for here, by herself. I have two young children of my own who need a mother. Can you not find it in your heart to consider their welfare?'

Although he had pleasant features, Alexis didn't like his shrewd eyes. They contained no softness, and, as he examined her it was clear from his expression that he felt she possessed bodily attributes he could exploit for his own pleasure.

And when he muttered, 'You're fair, and you look as though you might bear children easily,' she felt like the commodity he regarded her as.

She pulled her shawl up around her shoulders in an attempt to hide her upper body from his probing glance. 'You already have two delightful, well-behaved children, Reverend Hill. I grew up without the love and guidance of either parent, so I know they'd benefit enormously from the love of a mother, but—'

'Had they lived, no doubt your parents would have expected you to wed the man they chose for you,' he said smoothly. 'Unfortunately, their demise means that you're lacking in the duty and obedience you'd have learned from their teaching.'

'I am? No doubt your intention is to teach

me those virtues.'

'It's a reasonable assumption. I'm prepared to overlook those flaws in your personality, and your poverty. Although, I'm assured you have a portion of land of your own – one that the Earl of Longmore would surely be willing to purchase.'

Had he consulted Kynan on this, as well as Cordelia? 'Did the earl tell you he'd purchase my land?'

'Not directly. Again. It's a reasonable assumption.'

'Is it?'

He managed an indulgent chuckle. 'My dear, women rarely have a head on them for business, so don't expect me to explain. God created women to become wives and bear children. Under my paternal guidance you'd soon learn to be accepting of your wifely duties and responsibilities. You'd live a useful life, and become a helpmeet to me within the boundaries of my parish, as my former wife did. God rest her soul.'

Pompous ass! Her ears began to burn with temper.

He fell to one knee. 'I have stated my case, therefore, I present my petition for your hand with due respect. Miss Patterson, will you do me the honour of becoming my wife?'

'With the respect due to your position, I refuse it, Reverend Hill. I cannot accept such

266

an honour. I'm neither humble nor obedient, nor am I pious or biddable. As I have no interest in acquiring *any* of those qualities, sir, it's obvious to me that I'd not make a suitable wife for a man in your position. As for your paternal *guidance,* I'm afraid it would be wasted, since your wisdom would fall on deaf ears.'

His mouth pursed as he rose to his feet. 'You mock me, Miss Patterson, and you are, I fear, too outspoken.'

'Not as outspoken as my nature dictates I should be, Reverend Hill, but it's entirely possible you could goad me beyond the edge of my endurance, for you make too many assumptions.'

He bristled with affront and his voice took on a condemning pulpit thunder. 'I can see I misjudged you. You're correct, Miss Patterson. You would not make me a suitable wife, at all. Never have I been spoken to thus. I'd be obliged too, if you'd keep your own counsel about my petition, since it was a momentary lapse of good sense on my part. I'll not bother you again.'

She felt like snatching up the fire irons and beating him to a pulp. However, she knew Cordelia wouldn't approve. Through gritted teeth her words escaped like wasps with their tails on fire. 'Please, do allow me to show you to the door, Reverend Hill. You might consider Mrs Mortimer a more suitable candidate. She's experienced with children, is wealthy, and could probably meet your exacting standards.'

'Hmmm, yes, Mrs Mortimer might be worth consideration.'

Closing the door rather forcibly behind him, Alexis picked up her bonnet from the hall stand and jammed it on her head.

Cordelia came down the stairs. 'Well?'

Alexis turned, still managing to keep her control intact. 'I've told the reverend he might like to present his petition to you, since you seem to possess all the qualities he requires of a wife. They are ones he considers that I lack, I daresay. He said you might be worth his consideration.'

Cordelia's eyes widened so much they were in danger of escaping from their sockets. 'How dare you suggest such a thing to him?'

Alexis held her gaze as she opened the door. 'I see no reason why you should object, do you? I'm simply returning the favour you did me. After all, you are a widow. It stands to reason that you must be looking for a husband to manage your affairs.'

Cordelia's glance wavered, then strengthened. 'Oh, my dear, it was so wrong of me. I'm sorry.'

Alexis couldn't forgive her that easily. 'Excuse me, Cordelia; I need to catch up with my sisters.'

Cordelia's voice firmed. 'We must discuss

this before you go, Alexis.'

'There's no must about it, and it's better if we don't,' she said gently. 'I'm too angry, and frightened of what I might say.'

'Alexis...'

Ignoring her, she closed the door behind her and drew in a deep, shuddering breath.

Down the twisting hill, Reverend Hill had just brought his rig to a stop outside the church. Perhaps he intended to pray for her soul.

Alexis didn't take the short route to the cove. Instead, she headed for the site of her childhood home, seeking comfort there, perhaps. It was the first time she'd been there since the day it was demolished. The workmen had been thorough. The site had been picked clean and long grass and trees marked the spot. How nice that the trees had been left to provide shade, and a home for the birds that had always lived there.

She stared at the site, trying to connect with some long lost incident of her childhood. The memories wouldn't come. It was hard to believe that here, her mother had suffered in childbirth to bring herself and her sisters into the world – that she'd stayed long enough to set them on their way into life, then departed, taking the men of the family with her. She wished her mother was here for her to talk to.

Choking back a sob, Alexis plucked up her

skirt and began to run, heading for the cliff top, where a winding path would lead her along the coast to the cove. She felt as though her insides had been shredded. As she neared the sea the wind freshened, bringing with it a smell of salt and seaweed. Here, the tough cover of vegetation came to an abrupt end. The cliff face fell away in a pale slide on to rocks, over which the sea crashed and churned.

She fell to her knees, gasping for breath. The racing rhythm of her heart began to slow. When it was back to normal, she stood. Throwing her arms wide, she inhaled the biggest breath she could, then expended it in a long-drawn-out yell of frustration.

Seagulls were startled out of their nests in the cliff face. They wheeled upwards on a current of air to assess the source of the intrusion, their wings silver-tipped as they hovered, screaming and wheeling.

She hardly heard the bark of a dog over the noise.

The cliff curved round to her right, where the Isle of Portland towered into the sky. To the distant left, the columns of rock known as Old Harry stood.

Feeling better, she turned towards the cliff path, only to find Kynan standing there, blocking the way, Jasper at his heels.

They gazed at each other for a few seconds. His dark hair ruffled by the wind, his eyes were intimate against hers. 'What's the matter, Lexi?'

Everything! she wanted to scream, and remembered the incident on the terrace, his mouth on hers and the heat of him reaching out to her. That kiss had stripped the innocence from her eyes. It had been the kiss of a man who'd wanted to love her in the carnal sense. It had revealed her own desire, told her what she was capable of. She felt naked before him, but he'd made her feel desirable rather than lusted after.

Alexis observed him now in the same way, seeing the strength of his thighs, his lean and muscular body. Hidden by her lashes, her glance travelled downwards to the divide of his well-cut trousers. She wanted to see his nakedness uncovered, wanted to lie with him, open to his gaze, to his loving. She wanted to run her tongue over his smooth olive skin, to inhale the cinnamon smell of him and accept his maleness into her body. She wanted exactly what he wanted.

Kynan was promised to another, she thought, and hated him for it. She'd be obliged to wed someone she didn't want to give herself to, body and soul. Reverend Hill had also looked at her in the way a man did. His examination of her breasts and measure of her hips had been furtive and lustful. His remarks had shamed her.

She burst out, 'Cordelia Mortimer has

gone too far. She has taken it upon herself to find me a husband.'

'The devil she has!'

'Reverend David Hill called upon me today with a proposal of marriage, after I had told him not to. He made me angry.'

'Men are persistent when they are in pursuit of a woman. You didn't accept him, surely?'

'When he took great pains to point out my shortcomings, and indicated I would benefit from his guidance? Certainly not.'

Kynan's lips twitched. 'Tell me of your shortcomings, sweet Lexi?'

'I appear to be lacking in all the skills the wife of a reverend needs to be endowed with. He seemed to think he was bestowing a favour on me.'

'And how did you answer him?'

'I told him Cordelia had all the qualities he desired and he should propose to her, instead. Cordelia wasn't amused when I told her.'

He gave a little grin, then he gave a chuckle, then he began to roar with laughter.

'I do not find the situation at all amusing,' she said, and, feeling miffed, she turned and stalked off.

If anything, he laughed harder.

The funny side of the situation began to dawn on her. She grinned when she remembered the look on Cordelia's face, and flung over her shoulder at him, 'Damn you, Kynan Trent!' She began to run.

When he reached her, he caught her up, and swung her round. She was breathless when he set her down on her feet.

She clung to him. When the world steadied she gazed up at him, laughing, her arms circling his neck. She moved them down against his chest. Her smile slowly faded. So did his.

His hands moved lower, smoothing slowly down over her buttocks. He pulled her gently against him, leaving her in no doubt that he was built exactly as she imagined.

'I'd enjoy so much to make love to you, Lexi Patterson.'

Mouth dry, words tumbled out of her as she pushed her hands against his chest, her thoughts a contradiction to what she was saying. 'You mustn't ... You have a woman, position, obligations ... Do you seek to ruin me?'

'Ah, Lexi, my love,' he said, and he ran a finger over her lips. 'You're like wine in my blood. Yes, I'd ruin you given the opportunity, and I'm certain that one day I'll tumble you like a strumpet in my bed and drive you out of your mind with need. And when you think that need is satisfied, I'll have you crying out for more.'

She gave a small gasp at the thought of such a sensual experience, but it was more vicarious pleasure than shock. Her knees weak, she whispered, 'What sort of man are you to speak to me thus, Kynan?'

'A sensual one. But you're right. I do have a position to maintain, and I have obligations. As you rightly pointed out, I'm doing Julia a disservice, for she has expectations and I've been neglecting her. Were I still in London, no doubt we'd be preparing for our nuptials. But then, you and I would never have met, and I would not be in the awkward position I now find myself in.'

Her emotions churned at the thought and she gazed wordlessly at him.

'Have you nothing more to say for yourself, Lexi Patterson?' he mocked.

'You've rendered me speechless,' she whispered. 'I can have no respect for a man who professes to love one woman while he attempts to seduce another.'

'While Julia's here as my guest, I must pay her the attention due to her. And to my other guests, of course. And I must do what is right for myself, and for the estate.'

'But I'm expendable ... a female to be pursued for your personal pleasure.'

'Neither, Lexi. You're an exquisite and intelligent woman who was born to be loved. There's nothing wrong in delighting in the touch of a man. Be honest. You know you welcome my attention, as you did on the terrace last night. How sweet a kiss that one was.'

'You took me entirely by surprise.'

And he took her by surprise again, for he leaned forward to casually claim her mouth, leaving her free to run or respond. To her shame, she allowed him to prove his point, and he took his time, leaving everything in her on fire when he stepped back.

The imprint of his kiss still stinging her lips, she thrust at him, 'The old earl would have killed you for that.'

'No doubt he would have, since he had plans to wed you himself as soon as you came of age. His intention was to have you provide him with an heir.'

She felt the blood drain from her face. 'Who told you such a wicked lie?'

'Reverend Curruthers. The old boy told him.'

She shuddered at the thought of the old man harbouring such unwholesome thoughts about her. Her hands covered her cheeks and she felt ashamed that she'd been the object of such a sordid intention.

She told him, 'The conversation is at an end. I've had enough of the company of men. I'll go and find my sisters.'

'I'll walk with you.'

'No. *You will not!*' she said in a flash of temper. 'I don't want you to. You're unfit company, my Lord, and I never want to see you again.'

'You don't mean that, Lexi.'

No, she didn't. How could she mean it?

'I do mean it.'

'We're neighbours. You can't avoid me, Lexi.'

'I can try. I beg you to stay here until I am out of sight.'

Kynan watched her go, hating himself for what he'd done to her. She was right. He'd treated her with disrespect, and he'd shocked her.

She hurried along the path, seeking the safety of her sisters' company, her back stiff.

He willed her to look back at him.

He seated himself on a mound and gazed out over the glittering sea, Jasper pressing against his side. Kynan scratched the dog's ear. He'd never wanted a dog, but the old fellow was perfect company when he was alone.

On the horizon two ships were under way, sails spread. He pondered on their destination.

He was in love with Alexis Patterson.

He shook the thought away. He was expecting one of the company ships with cargo of wine from his warehouses any day, spices, cooking utensils. Various other goods. He hoped it would arrive soon.

He was in love with Alexis Patterson.

She was not his type. Lexi amused him.

She was too unworldly and bruised too easily. Her eyes looked like crushed cornflowers when they gathered hurt into them, and made him feel guilty. Her lips were soft and giving, and what he awakened in her was all too obvious. She made him feel like a conqueror, and he thought of the legend. Had his rogue Welsh ancestor felt like this about the woman he'd stolen from his brother?

His mother had told him Alexis had suitors. What if she married Reverend Hill? He scowled. He would pluck her from the altar and carry her off.

'I'm in love with Alexis Patterson,' he said out loud, and finally he allowed himself to believe it. A smile spread across his face.

Jasper gave an approving huff.

This was nothing to do with having her in his bed, and taking his pleasure of her, he rationalized – an easy thing to achieve. First and foremost, it was a sense of wanting to spend the rest of his life with her and devoting himself to making her happy.

As if she'd read his thoughts, she began to dance as she moved away, her feet taking dainty steps over the ground, seemingly oblivious to anything but the music in the wind and the pain in her heart. But there was a womanly awareness in her, for it was a small feminine display, as if she knew his eyes were on her.

'If you look back I'll know you care for me,' he whispered into the wind.

She turned at the last moment, walking backwards a few steps.

He blew her a kiss so she'd remember the tenderness that had passed between them, rather than the affront she'd suffered. But she didn't smile or acknowledge him, and his heart sank. She'd reached the highest point now, a place where the ground sloped down. A few steps and she was gone, disappearing into the hill as if it had swallowed her up. The depth of his feelings for her were so profound that Kynan knew that he had no choice but to pursue her to the inevitable end.

But what he'd said to Lexi earlier was true. He did have an obligation to his guests. A two year association with Julia meant he couldn't insult her by discarding her out of hand, unless he was pushed to it. She'd never tolerate being made a public fool of.

Julia must reach her own conclusion, and unless her behaviour became totally intolerable, she had to voluntarily leave his home before he could properly pursue the relationship he desired with Alexis.

'But I'd rather celebrate my birthday here, with my sisters.'

'The earl has arranged a supper in your honour. It's your coming of age, after all. To refuse him now the invitations have been sent out would be a dreadful snub.'

'You don't understand, Cordelia.'

'Then tell me, so I will, my dear.'

Alexis shook her head. Her feelings were too private, too raw be discussed with anyone. Her moods fluctuated between elation and despair. 'I simply cannot accept.'

They had been doing the household accounts, something they did on a weekly basis. Though, out of habit, Alexis had spent hardly anything of their allowance.

Placing her pen on the ink stand, Cordelia said gently, 'Very well. Let us discuss this. You have been avoiding the earl of late, have you not? You declined to attend church last Sunday, and refused the invitation to take tea with Mrs Trent at the hall. She was hurt by your refusal, you know.'

'It was not my intention to upset her. As I told you, I was not feeling well on those occasions. I had a headache.'

Cordelia sighed. 'It was a pleasant day. The earl and his guests joined us. It was kind of him to enquire after your welfare, I thought.'

Alexis couldn't imagine Julia Spencer being pleasant company. 'What did the earl say?'

'That he hoped it was nothing serious and you'd recover in time to attend the supper he'd arranged for you. When he visits me today, we will assure him that you're well enough, since you will join us in the drawing room.'

'The earl is coming here, today?'

'Didn't I just say so? In about an hour. Mrs Spencer will be with him. She wishes to offer her felicitations and is willing to let bygones be bygones.' Blandly, she said, 'The maid is to be given her job back.'

'But I've already promised to accompany Emily into Dorchester. She does not wish to return to Mrs Spencer's employ. Her intention is to register her name with an employment agency.'

'That might not be necessary.'

'Perhaps Emily should be asked which she would prefer to do.'

'Talbot *will* be asked by her former mistress. What is the girl to you, pray? We've taken her in and have done our best for her. Now she's recovered, she must return to her employment for she cannot live indefinitely on our goodwill.'

'But, Cordelia—'

'Oh ... why must you argue so, Alexis? This is a case of one person's word against the other. From what I can gather – since you saw fit not to discuss the matter with me in the first place – it's a trivial incident that got out of hand.'

'You consider Emily Talbot's injuries to be trivial?'

'You know very well I do not.' She sighed.

'You cannot rescue all the unfortunates in the world, my dear.'

Alexis bit down on her lip, knowing the girl would be given no choice, but to go back to her former mistress.

Then a solution came swiftly into her mind. She closed her accounting book and placed it tidily in the drawer. No doubt her action would cause a stir, but she was in a reckless mood for once, and didn't care.

'I'll shall go and make sure the drawing room is tidy before they arrive,' she said swiftly.

Alexis had capitulated too easily, Cordelia thought. Her eyes narrowed. She guessed the girl was up to something.

She just couldn't think what.

Sixteen

Mrs Trent accompanied Kynan and Mrs Spencer.

Julia took a seat on one of the sofas. Cordelia instantly seated herself beside her on the outside. The chair on the other side of Julia was claimed by Mrs Trent, trapping Julia behind the table on which the tea tray resided.

Exquisitely gowned in grey silk and dark pink roses, Julia Spencer had a faintly sour look on her face as she glanced from one woman to the other.

For the first time in a fortnight, Alexis's glance fell on Kynan. His expression was pleasant, but there was an edge of strain to it. 'Please be seated, Miss Patterson.'

When Alexis took her seat on the sofa, Kynan took the only seat left, next to her.

She was too aware of him, of the faint cinnamon smell that lingered about him. She fussed unnecessarily with her skirt, edging along the seat, so she could move as far away from him as possible.

His eyes glittered behind his lashes. 'You

seem restless, Miss Patterson.'

She stopped fidgeting immediately. 'Yes, it's been a trying morning. I cancelled my plans when I heard you were visiting.'

'Ah, I thought it might be because I was sitting too close to you for comfort. I feel honoured that you cancelled your arrangement on my behalf, and sorry that the result tried your patience.'

He was in fine form this morning, and she doubted if he felt in the least bit honoured. 'My Lord, a lesser mortal simply does not place their own wishes before the visit of an earl.'

He chuckled. 'I'll be sure to write that down in my journal. How shall I word it? Allow me to think for a moment ... ah yes. My word is Miss Patterson's command.'

'It is no such thing,' she spluttered.

'But you just said—'

'You know very well that I was referring to good manners.'

'So was I, Miss Patterson. What else could it have been when I'm reminded of them at every turn?'

Julia twittered with laughter. 'You'll never get the better of the earl, Miss Patterson. He's such a wit.'

'Without a doubt,' she said drily.

The atmosphere was drawn so tight it resonated with the tension. Florence and Cordelia attempted to fill the spaces with conversation.

They consumed the tea and scones, exchanged meaningless remarks about the weather and the latest fashions, of which Alexis knew nothing, and cared less.

Kynan turned to her with a smile. 'I was wondering if you'd advise me on a gift to buy to commemorate Barnaby Hardin's christening on Sunday week.'

'I've bought him a silver spoon. Perhaps a silver cup, a bible, or a cross to hang on the wall next to his crib would be appropriate.'

He nodded. 'I've never been a godparent before.'

'Neither have I. But it won't be the last time for you, I imagine. As the incumbent earl, you'll be expected to be fully immersed in the affairs of the community.'

'I've already been invited to open the county fair, and have more demands on my time than I expected. Reverend Curruthers wants me to read the lesson on the day of Barnaby's christening.'

Julia released a sour note into the conversation. 'My dear, Kynan. If you move back to London the locals will not be able to monopolize your time in this manner. You do pay an agent to run the place, after all. Why stay here, when you can simply take a profit from the place?'

Alexis pointed out, 'Absent landlords do not gain any respect from their workers.'

Julia shrugged. 'He doesn't need their respect.'

'He does if he wants his crops to grow, since it's their labour which provides the estate with an income.'

'Workers should do as they're bid.' Julia came to the point of the visit. 'I understand that my maid is fully recovered, so she'll be returning with me to Longmore Hall. I'd be obliged if someone would acquaint her with that fact.'

Drawing in a breath, Alexis's stomach began to twist and cramp as she told the woman, 'That's not her wish.'

Cordelia leaned forward, and said sharply, 'Miss Patterson, please go and inform Talbot that she must return to Longmore Hall with her mistress.'

'I *am* her mistress,' she said calmly.

Beside her, Kynan made a small choking noise.

All eyes turned her way.

Cordelia gazed at her with a reluctant sort of dread. 'Please explain that remark.'

'Certainly, Mrs Mortimer. I've engaged Emily Talbot to act as ladies' maid to myself and Blythe ... and yourself if that's your wish.'

Cordelia leaned back in horror. 'This is the first I've heard of such an arrangement.'

'My pardon. It's so recent that I haven't had time to acquaint you with the fact.'

'How recent?'

Alexis gazed at the mantle clock, then sat back and waited for the storm to begin. 'About an hour ago.'

Julia glared at her. 'What are you saying?'

Alexis offered her a smile. Indeed, she saw no reason to be frightened of this woman, and was beginning to enjoy herself. Slowly, she began to repeat herself. 'I – have – engaged—'

Julia screeched. 'Did you hear what this odious creature said, Kynan? She's stolen my maid. Do something!'

'Do calm down, Julia. I'm not deaf. Of course I heard Miss Patterson. If the maid prefers to work here, then she's free to do so.'

There came a huffy and exaggerated sigh from Julia. 'I demand to hear that from Talbot's own lips. She has blackened my name and I intend to confront her with her lies.'

What a stroke of luck, Alexis thought. Julia had unwittingly played right into her hands. 'By all means. Shall I go and fetch her, Mrs Mortimer?'

But Mrs Mortimer's full attention was on Julia, and she was frowning. 'I'd prefer it if you didn't insult Miss Patterson by calling her an odious creature. I think an apology is called for.'

'So do I,' Florence echoed.

Looking decidedly uncomfortable, Kynan

rose to his feet. Alexis could almost see his patience draining away when he made the request, 'Ladies, can we please resolve this matter amicably.'

'There's nothing to be resolved,' Florence told him. 'Mrs Spencer's maid has left her employ and is now working for Miss Patterson. What could be simpler?'

'Oh, you would side with *her* since you've made it very clear I'm not welcome in your son's house. Yes, do bring Talbot down – we shall see who she wants to work for.'

'That was an uncalled for and *spiteful* remark, Mrs Spencer.'

As Alexis slipped out there was a babble of quarrelsome voices. She was halfway up the stairs when Kynan's voice rose firmly above the noise.

'Oh, do be quiet, all of you! You sound like a flock of gabbling geese.'

The voices ceased, replaced by a seething silence.

Emily was waiting for her on the landing, a worried look on her face. 'I didn't think it would cause such a stir.'

'Don't worry, most of them are on your side. You do understand that, at the moment, I can only afford to employ you for six months. If you want to return to Mrs Spencer's employ I won't think any the less of you for it.'

'Yes, I understand, Miss Patterson. But, at

least I can earn myself a reference with you. What did Mrs Mortimer say about it?'

'She was surprised. I know she'll accept the situation, though. No doubt, I shall be a recipient of a lecture for causing such a furore. I must warn you before we go down, Mrs Spencer seems to be in a somewhat volatile mood. Try not to become upset if you are questioned, and speak the truth quietly. Remember, Mrs Spencer won't dare to set about you, because there will be witnesses.'

'Yes, Miss Patterson. I'll try.'

The drawing room was quiet when they entered. Kynan was standing by the fireplace, his forehead creased in a frown. As she placed an imaginary kiss there to soothe it, he said sternly, 'You may resume your seat, Miss Patterson.'

'But—'

'*Sit!* I will conduct this interview with Talbot.'

Woof! she thought, and sat.

He turned to Emily. 'A dispute has arisen over who you are to work for. Are you willing to be questioned? You are at liberty to decline.'

'I don't mind, my Lord.'

'Good. Mrs Patterson says she has recently engaged you as her maid. Mrs Spencer, who has been your mistress for the past four years, wishes you to remain in her employ.

288

What are your thoughts?'

'I would prefer to work in the household of Miss Patterson and Mrs Mortimer. They took me in and nursed me back to health after Mrs Spencer had accused me of placing a hedgehog in her room, and set about me with her stick.'

Cordelia folded her arms across her chest and nodded.

'You're a liar,' Julia hissed. 'I picked you up from the gutter and trained you into a position in my household, and this is all the loyalty I get.' She gazed around the room and cried out, 'Surely nobody believes this girl. Her mother was a fallen woman.'

'Her parentage has no relevance to the matter we are discussing.' There was silence for a moment, then Kynan asked Emily, 'Were there any witnesses to this beating?'

'Yes, sir. Miss Roxanne Dupré saw it. She tried to prevent Mrs Spencer from beating me further because my nose was bleeding. It's not the first time Mrs Spencer has beaten me. I couldn't stand it any longer and I told her I was leaving her employ. In return, she told me I was a slattern and a trollop who would end up in a house of ... *ill repute*. Mrs Spencer said I was required to give her a month's notice, and if I left her employ, it would be without reference or wages.'

'Ungrateful girl. You didn't deserve any.'

Tears began to trickle down Emily's face. 'I asked her who she thought she was, to call me wicked names like that, when she entertains—'

'Be quiet this instant, or I'll have you arrested and charged with slander.'

Emily bit her lip when Julia glared at her, then said shakily, 'That was when Mrs Spencer really took to me. And all that over a few flea bites from a hedgehog, that I didn't even put there in the first place.'

'I think that's enough, Emily,' Alexis said, and she rose and placed an arm around the girl's shaking shoulders. 'The earl has finished his questioning.'

Emily gazed around at them. 'I would like to say one thing more.'

Alexis looked at Kynan, who nodded wearily, 'Go ahead.'

'I'd rather die than go back to work for Mrs Spencer.'

'And if I get my hands on you, that's what will happen, you ungrateful little cur,' the seething Julia screeched, and she picked up the teapot and threw it at her.

Luckily for Emily, it was empty, and Julia's aim was too high.

Unluckily for Kynan, the silver teapot hit the wall over the fireplace. As the dented utensil bounced back, he instinctively caught it. The lid flipped open and he was splattered with the dregs.

The succinctly delicious oath he uttered was unfit for human ears, but Alexis grinned anyway. The attention was all focussed on Julia now, as she tried to get to Emily.

'I apologize,' Kynan said to nobody in particular, as the tea tray went crashing to the floor.

The cat abandoned his sleep in the sun on the windowsill. Giving a yowl he slunk off toward the door, skittering through it and nearly tripping Emily up as she made her escape.

Cordelia rushed to the door. Closing it, she leaned against it, one arm outspread, the hand of the other splayed dramatically against her heaving bosom, like a heroine in a drama.

Meanwhile, Florence tried to calm Julia's hysterical invective.

Kynan placed the teapot carefully on the mantelpiece, where it leaned drunkenly against the chimney-piece. Taking up a napkin, Alexis crossed to where he stood and began to gently brush the dregs from his previously immaculate jacket.

When he gave an impatient little grunt, she gazed up at him and said drily, 'Between us, I think we sorted the matter out satisfactorily.'

If she caught a flicker of amusement in his eyes, it was quickly masked when he muttered, 'I hold you entirely responsible for what has happened here today, Miss Patterson.'

'I've never known you to be unfair.'

'There's a first time for everything. You placed me in the distasteful position of needing to insult one of my guests while I defended her former servant.'

'The interrogation of Emily was entirely your idea, so I dispute that statement.'

'There is enough dispute going on at the moment. You knew what the result of hiring the girl was likely to be. You cannot defend every waif and stray that crosses your path, you know.'

'I can but try.'

His eyes narrowed. 'If your intention is to manipulate me into recognizing the ridiculousness of this situation – and, believe me, if you succeed on that count then retribution will be swift – I will turn you over my knee and spank your backside so hard you won't be able to sit on it for a month.'

'You wouldn't,' she said, giving a tiny gasp at the thought of such an indignity.

His eyes were as dark as woodland moss, enigmatic rather than threatening, but his voice held a menacing purr. 'I warn you, I'm hanging on to my temper by a cobweb.'

His expression told her this was no idle threat. She would err on the side of caution, she thought, immediately trying to squash an image of him dangling like a spider from a web in the corner. Lest she laugh, she decided she must retreat rather quickly. Before she did, she had one last word for him.

'Hah!' she whispered, and, dashing the napkin against his chest, she moved towards the table. Stooping, she began to pick up the shattered china from the rug.

She spared a glance for Julia, who now reclined limply back against the cushions, feigning a swoon. Alexis had the feeling she'd missed nothing.

Julia's eyes glittered like winter ice through her dark lashes. Her voice laced with pathos, she said, 'I'm sorry I lost my temper. I was wrong, accusing her of putting the hedgehog there. The girl did lie about the beating, and that horrible thing she said about my behaviour is entirely untrue. There is nothing improper about the gentlemen guests I entertain in my house.'

Kynan's eyes narrowed slightly and a nerve in his jaw twitched.

Julia's eyelashes fluttered. 'You do believe me, don't you, Kynan? You may ask Roxanne what happened, if you wish.'

'It will not be necessary, and the affair need not be alluded to again. No doubt my mother's maid will continue attending you while you remain in my home.'

An aggrieved note entered Julia's voice. 'I'll never take that girl back now. She doesn't deserve a reference. I'll make sure her wages are paid up to date, though. It's only one guinea, after all.'

Kynan did what was expected of him. Taking the money from his pocket he handed it to Cordelia, then kissed her cheek to reassure her that he blamed her not at all. 'See that Emily Talbot gets it, would you? I'll take my mother and Julia home.'

'I think I shall stay a little longer,' his mother said.

'Do stay and have dinner with us. I would enjoy your company. Stay the night if you wish.'

'Thank you Cordelia. I will. Where are your sisters, Alexis?'

'They've gone to Prosser's farm to inspect the new litter of puppies. They'll not be long.'

Tears had thickened her voice. The argument had buffeted Alexis. She felt soiled, even though she felt she was in the right.

Had she gone too far in the need to have her own way? The reprimand from Kynan had been hard to take. His assessment of her had been brutal. The manoeuvre he'd accused her of had been more transparent to him than it had been to herself.

She hadn't considered the amusement the scene had generated might seem petty. Now, she questioned whether she'd acted out of genuine concern for the maid, or from the need to trounce Julia Spencer because of what she felt for Kynan.

Julia was clinging to him now, all helpless and feminine wiles, as he helped her to the door. How devious she was. Why couldn't he see that she was as slippery and venomous as an adder?

Kynan glanced back at her, looking troubled. He seemed about to say something. Then he gave a slight shrug and changed his mind, following after Cordelia with his lady love clinging possessively to his arm.

As Alexis bent to her task, she tried to fight off her tears.

'That was rather an unpleasant scene. I hope you are not too upset, my dear?' Mrs Trent said kindly.

Alexis gulped as she sat back on her heels. 'It was all my fault.'

'Let the servants do that.' Florence held out her hands and helped her up. 'It was certainly not your fault. You acted only on behalf of the maid. We all know that Talbot told the truth, even Kynan. And the girl received the wage she was entitled to.'

'But the earl said he believed Mrs Spencer.'

'No, he didn't. He simply said the affair need never be raised again. It was difficult for him. The questions he put to the maid encouraged the truth to emerge. Julia's actions affirmed it. As her host, my son cannot be less than courteous or gentlemanly towards her. Come my, dear. You must not be so hard on yourself.'

Drawn into Mrs Trent's arms, the hug Alexis received healed her hurt, for it evoked a memory, that of a comforting hug from a mother she could hardly remember.

The woman held her at arms' length afterwards. 'I was thinking, my dear. Perhaps you'd like to come back to London with me when I return next month.'

Alexis's eyes snapped open. 'I couldn't possibly leave my sisters!'

'Not even for a few weeks? Come, dear, Cordelia is more than capable of looking after them. You know they'll be well cared for. You should consider doing something for yourself now. I have many friends with sons of marriageable age. You'll be invited to the theatre and social evenings. You do want to marry and have children of your own, don't you?'

Alexis did, but not to just *any* man. All the same, she was torn between the exciting thought of visiting London, and the thought of not being able to see Kynan.

'May I think about it for a while?' she said.

'Of course, my dear, and you might like to discuss it with your sisters, perhaps. Come now. Let's go and find Cordelia. I'm sure she'll be wanting a word with you.'

So did Alexis. They found her in the garden running a critical eye over the rose bed.

She turned and smiled at them as they crunched across the gravel path. 'What a disagreeable women Mrs Spencer is. I feel quite relieved now she's gone.'

Alexis thought she'd better get her apology over with. 'Cordelia, I'm so sorry—'

'Don't you dare apologize. Talbot was terrified of the woman. I can't understand why I didn't think of offering the girl employment, myself. We have need of an experienced ladies maid. How much did you offer her, pray?'

'Three guineas.'

'Three guineas a month!'

'For six months. I know it isn't as much as she should earn, but that's all I can afford. In the meantime Emily will have a roof over her head and will be able to earn a reference.'

Surprisingly, Cordelia embraced her. 'You have a kind heart, Alexis, even though it's a little misplaced sometimes. But since we're to entertain more, we must try and look our best at all times. Talbot will be your maid, but I'll make her salary up, and if you will allow, prevail upon her services when I wish to make an impression.'

'Of course I will allow her. I'm so relieved this business is over and done with, except I doubt if the earl will speak to me again.'

'Nonsense, dear. Kynan doesn't possess a petty bone in his body.'

There was a clatter of a horse outside the

gate and Blythe brought Weatherby's horse to a halt. Riding astride, she was showing a great deal of calf and grinning all over her face.

Both ladies gasped out loud. Cordelia said faintly, 'Blythe Patterson!'

Leaning forward, Blythe patted the mount's neck. 'Isn't he the most wonderful horse in the entire world? His name is Doddles.'

'I have no doubt that Doddles is a wonderful horse, but the person riding it is a disgrace. A lady does not ride astride like a man. Dismount from that beast, at once.'

Blythe's smile faded. 'I have always ridden like this. The old earl taught me.'

'Then the old earl should have known better.' She lowered her voice. 'My dear, you could ruin yourself for marriage, riding like that.'

Cordelia's smile faded when the rest of them came into view. Lord Haining was leading his horse with Celeste and Daria perched astride.

Weatherby had Esmé clinging to his back like a monkey.

They all smiled and waved.

'Hello, dear ladies,' Weatherby drawled, and bending from the knees allowed Esmé to slide off his back. He turned to swing Blythe down from his horse. 'You have a good seat on a horse, Miss Blythe. I've never seen anything like it.'

'And will not see it again if I have my way, Mr Weatherby. Go inside you girls. Wait for me in the drawing room.'

Her sisters trooped indoors, looking decidedly down in the mouth.

'As for you, Lord Haining. You should know better than to encourage such hoydenish behaviour in impressionable young women.'

'My pardon, Mrs Mortimer. I saw no harm in it since many of the country girls here ride astride.'

'The Patterson girls are not ordinary young girls. They are young ladies of good birth, Lord Haining. They are under the Earl of Longmore's protection, and I am charged with turning them into educated and socially acceptable young women who can take their rightful place in society.'

'I assure you, it will not happen again.'

'Thank you, Lord Haining. Mr Weatherby? Do I have your assurance too?'

Weatherby, who'd finished lengthening his stirrups, looked up at her and cleared his throat. 'As you say, Mrs Mortimer. Apologies, of course. Miss Blythe is an engaging scrap, and hard to resist when she sets her mind on doing something. She's a good little rider, too. Doddles is as gentle as a lamb with her, and easy to handle despite his size, you know. He understands perfectly how to behave with a young lady.'

'Enlightening as that may be, I do not credit any horse with the intelligence you describe. I require your assurance, Mr Weatherby.'

With alacrity he said, 'You have it. I will not allow Miss Blythe to ride my horse again.'

'Thank you, Mr Weatherby, and also to you Lord Haining. I'll trust you to keep your word. You may both leave now.'

Both men bowed slightly, then mounted their horses and rode off.

Cordelia sighed. 'What a day this has been, so far. I feel quite the ogre. Alexis, my dear, I shall leave you to point out to your sisters the error of their ways, and the need to remain modest while in the company of members of the opposite gender. They might listen to you.

'Oh, and before I forget, again, a Mr Stephen Fosset left his card yesterday. He said he hopes you'll allow him to approach you after church on Sunday. He seemed a nice young man, said you'd been introduced at Sibyl Clark's assembly.'

She remembered him, a rather serious young man who worked as a clerk in his father's law office. Panic rose in her. 'What did you tell him?'

'That you would make up your own mind to that.' She threaded her arm through that of Florence. 'Let's find ourselves a shady spot in the garden where we can gossip to our heart's content.'

'Would you ask Lally to bring us out some more refreshment, please, Alexis? I take it we have a second best teapot somewhere. And some scones and jam with some lemonade for the girls. They are bound to want to greet Mrs Trent, and will also be hungry.'

Her sisters were relieved when Alexis said, 'You've been spared one of Mrs Mortimer's lectures, since it has fallen on me to deliver it, instead. We all must be more careful, since how we conduct ourselves in public reflects on all of us. Blythe, you were showing your knees and you allowed your enthusiasm to get the better of you. Mrs Mortimer and Mrs Trent were quite shocked to see you riding astride.'

'It was so exciting.' Blythe sighed. 'I wish I had a horse of my own.'

'The Prosser's cockerel flapped his wings and chased me away from the hens,' Celeste said. 'I had to run to get away from him. Mr Weatherby and Lord Haining came across us as we were on our way home and decided to walk with us. We were going to invite them in for refreshment, until Mrs Mortimer gave them a wigging.'

'I wish Mr Weatherby was my brother,' Esmé chimed in. 'We've had so much fun since the damned Welsh heir arrived, and his friends came, too. I love living here at Florence House. There are always so many interesting things to do, now.'

Daria gave her a big smile. 'You should have come with us, Lexi. The puppies were so sweet. You must have been so bored staying home with Mrs Mortimer.'

Bored! Remembering the events of the day, Alexis shook her head, bemused. She suddenly remembered she was to ask Lally to take some refreshment out.

'You may visit Mrs Mortimer and Mrs Trent in the garden if you wish. No doubt they'll be interested in your farm visit, once you've apologized to them for your behaviour. Go and ask Emily to tidy you up a bit first. You'll be pleased to know she's to remain in our household as personal maid to Blythe and myself.'

'Me?' Blythe said. 'What do I need a maid for?'

'Because we are being invited to more and more social evenings, and we need to be well groomed. You're a young lady now, aren't you?'

A charming blush of pink seeped into Blythe's cheeks as she thought about it. 'Yes, I suppose I must be.'

Seventeen

It was a beautiful gown, a gift from Cordelia.

The overdress of fine, ivory lace, high-necked and scalloped at the edges slid over Alexis's head and arms to settle over a hyacinth blue gown underneath. Under the high waist a narrow belt was secured by a buckle of pearls. It was a gown of provocation, a mixture of innocence and sensuality.

Emily gently removed the silk scarf protecting Alexis's hairstyle. Her hair was fashioned in a high knot decorated with silk flowers. A single, spiralling tendril fell from the side of her forehead, brushed against one side of her face and ended at the curve of her chin.

Emily turned her towards the mirror, the pride of a job well done in her eyes. 'There, Miss Patterson.'

'Excellent, Emily. I hear the carriage. Go and tell the girls to assemble in the hall.'

When Emily had gone, Cordelia handed her a jewellery case. 'The earl has sent over his birthday gift to you, and requests that you do him the honour of wearing it.'

Alexis hadn't seen Kynan since the episode with the teapot. She gazed at the case with both curiosity and anticipation. 'What's in it?'

'Open it and see.'

Her hands trembled as they revealed a single strand of creamy pearls, so flawless and pure that they stole her breath. 'I've never seen anything so exquisite. The earl shouldn't have, it's too much.'

Cordelia smiled. 'It's exactly right. A fine gift and a measure of his esteem. Lord Trent has impeccable taste.'

'He's forgiven me, then.'

'There's nothing for him to forgive, my dear.' She handed Alexis her gloves, followed by a long stole, the same colour as her gown and silk evening pumps.

They went down to where the family waited in the hall. Blythe looked self-conscious in her grown-up hairstyle. One thing Alexis had learned of late. Her sisters revelled in dressing up and attending social occasions. She supposed it was because they'd been deprived of it up until now.

They had set to learning social graces with a will. Celeste, with her natural dainty elegance proved to be an apt pupil, and was a good role model for Daria and Esmé. Even Blythe did her best, though her sense of drama often got the better her.

Their sense of excitement had floated up

to her as she descended the stairs behind Cordelia. A critical eye was cast over them in a last minute inspection. There was a collective holding of breath until Cordelia announced, 'How beautiful you all are. I'm so proud of you. Remember your manners and try not to fidget in the carriage on the way there.'

The earl had sent his carriage. It was a little crowded, but they arranged themselves without too much fuss, and in a manner to create a minimum of creasing. Jude carried them gently back to Longmore Hall.

It was a fine evening, the gloaming light was a soft, misty gold. The layered cloud bands were gilt-edged as the sun moved down into the sea.

It was a cinnamon sky and it seemed as though Kynan had created it especially for her birthday as they breasted the ridge and saw Longmore Hall.

She felt a strange sense of dreaming, as if the landscape had faded. An elusive drift of perfume came to her – a fleeting caress against her cheek which made her smile. Tiny goosebumps quivered along her neck. Thank you for loving me, she thought, as her mother came instantly to mind.

Cordelia chose that moment to reach across Daria's lap and take her hand. 'Your parents would have been so proud to have seen you all looking so splendid tonight.'

Had her mother's spirit sent the kiss as her sign of approval for Cordelia? The tiny flicker of resentment Alexis had always harboured towards Cordelia was faced for what it was – then discarded. Cordelia was not trying to steal the love of her sisters, or usurp her authority over them. In fact, Alexis now knew that she probably needed her sisters more than they needed her.

She gently squeezed Cordelia's hand and they smiled at each other.

Peter Haining said, 'Will you look at that eldest Patterson girl, Weatherby?'

'Gad! What a beauty, she is.' Weatherby's gaze fell on Blythe. 'Personally I'm waiting for Miss Blythe.'

'Do you think our host will ever make an honest woman out of Julia?'

Weatherby laughed. 'Would *you* be inclined to when there are woman as fair and innocent as Miss Patterson? Observe the blush on the young lady's cheek when he teases her. I heard that Mrs Mortimer gave him a good dressing down after she caught him comforting her.'

Haining grinned. 'There is comfort, and there is *comfort*. Sometimes, one leads into the other. We have both learned how formidable Mrs Mortimer is. My ears are still burning from our encounter with her. All the same, I think I'll give Kynan a run for his money tonight. It will be worth another wigging from Mrs Mortimer.'

'Just don't challenge him to a duel, dear boy. I gave him a practice session this morning and he could have killed me on two occasions. He's been practising with his servant, I believe. Perhaps we should arrange a fencing tournament. Nothing attracts ladies like two men fighting.'

'A good idea. Look, Mrs Mortimer has taken the younger children and has gone off to gossip with Florence. Kynan is heading for the Patterson girl. Come on.' Detaching himself from the mantelpiece, Haining made his way rapidly across the drawing room.

Weatherby followed.

Alexis watched their progress. Haining got to her first, took her hand in his and bore it to his lips. 'You grow more beautiful by the minute, Miss Patterson.'

'Thank you, Lord Haining. You're most kind.'

'Not a bit of it. I'm merely being truthful.'

Weatherby kissed her other hand. 'He couldn't have said a truer word, m'dear.' Sliding his hand into his waistcoat pocket he whipped out an ivory and lace fan and presented it to her. 'For your birthday. And for you, Miss Blythe...' Another fan appeared from his sleeve. 'Doddles begged me to have his portrait painted on it for you.'

Spreading the fan, Blythe said, 'What

nonsense, Weatherby. How can this be Doddles, when he's a chestnut? The horse on the fan is a dark bay.'

Gazing at it, Weatherby seemed genuinely surprised by what he saw. 'Doddles must harbour pretensions of grandeur. I must speak to him about it.'

Blythe grinned as she handed the fan back to him. 'Do show me how you make the fan appear from your sleeve so quickly, Weatherby.'

He repeated the manoeuvre, faster than the eye could see. 'I was a sharpshooter in a travelling show when I was fourteen, and a magician showed me some tricks.'

Blythe's eyes widened. 'A sharpshooter!'

'A clown would be nearer the truth,' Haining murmured, and offered Alexis his arm. 'Come with me, my dear. While Weatherby is being a bad influence on your sister, I'll find you a glass of punch to drink.'

'I've just brought her one,' Kynan said from behind them, and indeed, he had a cup in each hand.

Weatherby relieved him of one for Blythe, and Haining took the other from him. 'Nice of you to act as manservant, but you're the host and you have guests arriving. It would be wrong of you to neglect them,' Haining said smoothly. 'I insist on taking this delectable creature off your hands.'

'Must you, Haining? I've hardly had time

to exchange a word with her myself.'

Laughter filled her and she turned to Kynan, who shrugged, and smiled ruefully. 'Later, then, Miss Patterson. You can trust Lord Haining to look after you. He has a son who is almost your age.'

Lord Haining winced. 'Ignore him. How would you like to come out on the terrace and watch the moon come up with me?'

She laughed. 'Only if you'll tell me about yourself. You said you attended the same university as my father?'

Haining winked at Kynan. 'Hear that, my Lord? This is a woman who wants to listen to me talk about myself. I adore her, already.'

'Nevertheless, I expect her back in time to escort in to dinner,' he said.

The second gong had been struck for dinner. Roxanne had made her entrance down the staircase half an hour earlier and had been conducting an animated conversation with Blythe and Weatherby on the terrace. She strolled arm in arm with Blythe, and greeted Alexis warmly. 'How lovely you look. Dear Julia will turn green with envy.'

There was no lack of admirers to take Roxanne into dinner. She laughingly bestowed the favour on a tall military gentleman, telling him her bronze gown contrasted well with his uniform, and their eyes matched.

'We will not wait for Julia any longer and

allow the food to cool,' Kynan said quietly.

They filed into the dining room, where the long table was set with gleaming silver, and crystal that picked up the light from the flickering candles in the sconces.

Kynan took his seat at the head of the table, with Alexis seated on his right side, and his mother on his left. The empty chair at the other end of the table was conspicuous by its lack of occupancy. Alexis though it odd that Julia would be seated so far away from the earl.

As the servants filed in with the food, to set the dishes on the warmers, Kynan tapped a fork against his glass. 'Ladies and gentlemen, may I introduce my guest of honour, Miss Alexis Patterson, who today celebrates her birthday amongst her friends.'

The door crashed open and Julia stood there, obviously in a pose. She was dressed in a black gown of sheer, clinging fabric. Pink silk pantaloons, tied at the ankle with black ribbons, could plainly be seen though it. Her pale bosoms were bolstered high, and swelled over a low cut bodice, where a single diamond nestled into her cleavage, winking fire in the light. If she took a deep breath she would have to be careful not to spill over the top, Alexis thought. A diamond clip in Julia's hair sprouted three tall pink feathers.

Roxanne gave a husky laugh as all heads turned Julia's way. 'You seem to have forgotten your gown, Mrs Spencer.'

There were murmurs from the men and outraged gasps from some of the women.

Julia's smile was aimed directly at Kynan. 'I'm sorry, I'm late, Kynan, dearest. I lost all track of the time.'

He didn't look pleased by Julia's appearance, or her familiarity towards him in company. It was obvious that his position was beginning to sit more comfortably on his shoulders, for he was much more in command of himself.

A laconic comment came from Weatherby as he left Blythe's side. He walked to the end of the table, helped Julia into her seat and said in his usual bantering voice, 'You're not at all sorry, dear one. I'd say you timed your entrance to the split second. Bad form, Julia. The earl was just about to raise a toast to the guest of honour.'

'Oh yes, I'd forgotten there was a guest of honour. Congratulations on your birthday, *Miss* Patterson. When I was your age I'd already been married for several years.' Her glance went to Kynan, narrowing like those of a cat as she purred, 'I'm seriously considering embarking on the state of matrimony for a second time,' and her smile spoke of the intimacy between herself and the earl.

Kynan's jaw tightened as a speculative buzz went around the table.

'Oh, be sure, Miss Patterson does not lack

for suitors,' Cordelia said.

Hastily, Alexis interrupted with as much dignity as she could muster, even though her heart had just been kicked into her shoes at the confirmation that Kynan must have proposed to Julia. 'I'm sure that's of no interest to the company, Mrs Mortimer. Thank you for your congratulations, Mrs Spencer. It was kind of you.'

'Well done,' somebody said.

Deep down Alexis felt pity for Julia, who, by Mrs Mortimer's account, had been married off to an old man at a very young age. In exchange, she'd been left a fortune when he'd died. She wondered what Julia's wedding night had been like. Probably a nightmare.

That fate could have been hers if the old earl had been determined enough, for she wouldn't have had anyone else to turn to, or anywhere else to go if he'd turned them out. She understood now that the autocratic old man had been eccentric in the extreme. His influence over them had been quite damaging.

She basked in the smile Kynan bestowed on her, even knowing he was only being friendly when he raised his glass. 'I ask you all to join me now in offering Miss Patterson our sincerest felicitations and a long and happy life.'

After everyone raised their glasses and

drank to her, she briefly thanked him, her voice trembling because she was shy of this attention that was being showered over her.

From the other end of the table, Julia glowered at her.

Despite that, it was a wonderful evening. She managed to snatch a few moments alone with Kynan. 'Thank you for the pearls. I've never owned anything so fine before.'

'It was my pleasure. I do hope you enjoyed yourself. I thought you'd prefer a small dinner.'

'It was kind of you to think of me at all.'

'I think of you constantly,' he said, his voice grave. 'Let's go through to the drawing room, shall we? Roxanne and Weatherby have arranged some entertainment between them, and it will probably be outrageous.'

It was. The pair had swapped clothing, and they sung a duet in their new roles. It was ridiculous, but clever, especially when Weatherby got so mixed up he forgot he was supposed to be the female, then remembered too late, and began to sing the male part in falsetto. Alexis giggled all the way through and there was great deal of applause when they finished.

While they changed, Julia played the piano and sang, her voice ringing out like a silver bell. She was very accomplished and Kynan was enthusiastic in his applause.

Weatherby and Roxanne returned, suitably

dressed again. Roxanne took her seat at the piano while Weatherby assisted Blythe from her seat and stuck an old tricorn hat on her head. 'Now, for a special treat. May I present Admiral Blythe Patterson, who will relate a story of great adventure, one she composed especially for our entertainment tonight. It is titled *The Ship of Souls*.'

He clicked his fingers and all candles except one were snuffed. That one illuminated Blythe's face most dramatically.

A murmur of unease ran through the room when thunderous crashing chords came from the piano.

When it faded there was a moment of pause, then Blythe said in a dramatic voice, 'It was a dark and stormy night at sea. Captain Slain's crew had been washed overboard, and carried off by a whale. The good captain was struggling to keep the ship on course single-handed, when from the depths of King Neptune's realm, rose a host of drowned Welsh seaman. They'd once been raiders and plunderers, who'd been in the pay of the damned Welsh usurper. But their leader had carried off the beloved of the true earl, and they had been banned from Longmore Cove.'

There came a gasp from Mrs Mortimer, who was seated behind them.

'Save me, save me!' Roxanne yelped in an over-theatrical voice.

Blythe resumed her tale, her voice low and menacing now she'd gained confidence. 'The ghostly crew rose, wailing, crying and dripping gore, so the decks ran red with it.'

Various ghostly wails, moans and cries came from the darkness and some of the audience joined in. Roxanne's fingers ran up and down the piano keys.

When the noise abated, Esmé's voice piped up. 'Stop it, Blythe, you're scaring me.'

Blythe said, 'Stick your fingers in your ears, then, Es,' and returned to her story with enthusiasm. 'The valiant Captain Slain took out his cutlass and set about the ghouls, but they had no substance and the weapon sliced right through them without doing damage.'

Behind Blythe, it sounded as though knives and forks were being inexpertly juggled. Alexis began to shake with laughter.

'Captain Slain's brave fight was to no avail, for twenty daggers pierced his heart.'

Clutching a knife to his chest, Weatherby staggered into the candle glow and fell at her feet, accidentally banging his head on the table leg as he went down, and lying very still.

Blythe poked her toe in his ribs, and gazed down at him, uncertain. 'Are you all right, Weatherby?'

'Yes, I'm acting dead. Go ahead,' he hissed out of the side of his mouth.

When Alexis giggled, beside her, Kynan rumbled with laughter and his hand folded around hers in the darkness, making her feel rather wicked.

With great enthusiasm, Blythe said, 'Overcome by the force of the evil spirits, Captain Slain became one of the ghostly crew. They set sail for Longmore Cove, their ship tattered and torn from the storm. Sometimes they appear in the mist and step ashore to search for the secret treasure, which was hidden hereabouts by their evil cousins, who were smugglers.'

She grinned at them all. 'And that's the end of my story. It's a true one, so everyone beware if you see a ghost ship in the cove.'

When a servant lit a taper and began to apply it to the candle wicks, Kynan tickled her palm and slid his hand from hers.

Laughter, cheers and deafening applause filled the room. Weatherby rose from the floor. Roxanne joined them and they all bowed low. Blythe, whose hat was in danger of falling down over her eyes, and whose hairstyle was in ruins, was grinning from ear to ear.

Julia was standing near the door with Lord Haining, a slightly sneering smile on her face. 'How droll,' she said languidly.

'I do hope that girl doesn't get ideas in her head about going on the stage,' Cordelia said to Florence.

'Oh, I hope for exactly the opposite, Cordelia. She was quite wonderful, I thought. I have not enjoyed myself so much for a long time. Blythe, my dear, how did you manage to stop yourself from laughing?'

'Weatherby threatened to throw me over the cliff if I did,' she said cheerfully.

'But when did you rehearse?'

'We didn't rehearse. Weatherby and Miss Dupré told me what to do when we were on the terrace, didn't you Weatherby? I just had to narrate the story, and he told me where I should pause, so he and Miss Dupré could put in the dramatic sounds. It was great fun, and I wasn't a bit nervous.'

Blythe's eyes came her way, shining with excitement, and seeking her approval.

'You were quite wonderful. You all were.' Alexis gave Blythe a hug. 'I laughed so much I nearly fell off the chair. I enjoyed your reading enormously.'

'So did I,' Kynan said. 'It was most entertaining.'

The evening ended shortly after that, for the guests wanted to get home while the moon was still bright enough to light their way.

'Thank you for a most wonderful evening, my Lord,' she said.

'Your pleasure is mine, Miss Patterson. I'll see you in church next Sunday for the christening party, no doubt. There are some birthday gifts for you. Jude has them with him.'

Kynan assisted them into the carriage and stood back, but his eyes came up to hers for a moment and they stared at each other. Alexis felt that, somehow, their friendship had reached a new stage.

Her sisters began to giggle, and were firmly hushed by Cordelia.

Kynan took a step back. 'Goodnight ladies, and thank you for coming.'

'Goodnight, my Lord,' they all said. 'We had such a grand time.'

The pleasure they'd displayed warmed Kynan. They were charming girls.

Alexis had charmed him even more. Her shyness had been a delight. She was obviously not used to being the focus of attention, as she'd been tonight. As he'd walked amongst his guests he'd heard nothing but good spoken of her.

His smile faded. Julia had gone too far tonight. Her dress and behaviour had shocked people. Against Alexis, who'd been totally desirable in a modest, but tantalizing covering of lace, Julia had simply looked vulgar.

His glance swept over the landscape and he had a new sense of pride. The people here were curious about him, but generally they were good-hearted folk, and friendly, who made the best of any opportunity to enjoy themselves. Even Mrs Clark had improved on further acquaintance.

He smiled as he remembered Blythe poking her toe into Weatherby, vulnerable in her youthfulness for a moment as she'd enquired after his health. She felt safe with Weatherby, and the bond between them was obvious. Cordelia had noticed it too, and, no doubt, would be vigilant.

Julia did not fit into the environment at all – nor his future. He'd been very tempted to send her packing. But his manners overrode his good sense.

The change their relationship had undergone must be obvious to her now. If not, it soon would be. When she left his house to return to London, any remaining attachment between them would be completely severed.

Kynan went inside. The servants were scurrying about, snuffing candles and clearing away the dishes.

He wasn't ready to retire for the night. Going to his study he poured himself a night-cap.

From the wall over the fireplace, the old earl, white-whiskered and fierce-eyed, bristled at him from his gilt frame.

The blood tie was well diluted, they were nothing alike.

Kynan raised his glass to him.

Eighteen

It was barely dawn and they were still in their nightgowns. Alexis's sisters were piled on to her bed.

Yawning hugely, for she'd hardly slept a wink, Blythe was brushing the tangles from her hair. The others were unwrapping her birthday gifts.

'Be careful to keep note of who gave me what, so I can write them all a letter of appreciation. Celeste, you can make the list. There's a pencil and paper on the dressing table.'

A minuet tinkled. 'Oh, look ... a silver musical box from Lord Haining. How pretty it is with that blue enamelling.'

'How thoughtful of him. It's lovely.'

'He paid you a lot of attention last night, Lexi. I think he's enamoured by you.'

'Nonsense. It was because of my birthday. He's very nice to talk to. He was friends with our father, you know, and he attended our parents' wedding.'

'Silk gloves from Mrs Clark. And here are some lace handkerchiefs from Roxanne

Dupré.'

'She's such fun,' Blythe said wistfully. 'I wonder if she'll marry Weatherby.'

'Of course not, silly,' Celeste said. 'She's too old for him; at least thirty. She should marry Lord Haining. I saw him kiss her on the forehead and they are very close friends.'

'That doesn't mean to say they love each other. I saw Mrs Spencer kiss the earl on the mouth once. I think everyone must kiss each other a lot in London.'

Alexis's stomach tensed. 'You mustn't gossip in such a wicked manner, Daria.' Nevertheless, she asked, 'What did the earl do?'

'Oh, he smiled a little bit, the sort of smile he uses when he's not really smiling.' Esmé's giggle earned her a black look from Daria. 'But even that faded when she walked away. He took out his handkerchief and wiped the kiss off.'

Alexis's heart lightened at the thought of him doing that. 'What's in the tissue-wrapped package?'

A little bag embroidered in silk roses slid out. 'That's from Mrs Curruthers. Isn't it beautiful? She does very fine work.'

A figurine of Punchinello was uncovered, short and fat, and funny in his clown hat. Unexpectedly, it was a gift from the staff of Longmore Hall. 'How sweet of them all,' she exclaimed, touched by the gesture. A silver

321

framed dressing table mirror from Mrs Trent was next.

Alexis had never owned so many lovely things – and she'd never expected, when the old earl had died, that her life, and those of her beloved sisters would have improved so much.

Rising, she went to gaze out of the window. She was pleased to see the sky was clear. Next month the wheat and barley would be harvested. A storm at this time of year would ruin the crop. Not that Longmore had any corn crops to ruin this year. Still, they'd pray for good weather at church on Sunday.

She turned to her sisters and said, 'Mrs Trent has invited me to accompany her to London when she returns home.'

'And will you go?' Celeste asked her.

'I've not yet decided. It would be exciting because I've never visited the capital and there must be so many interesting things to see. But my inclination is to stay here with you.'

'You don't have to worry about us,' Blythe said staunchly.

'I know I don't, now you have Mrs Mortimer to turn to. I'm just not sure I want to go.' She made a face. 'Mrs Trent wants me to meet young men of marriageable age. It seems to me that everyone wants to marry me off to some man or another.'

'When it's plain as the nose on your face

that you're in love with the earl.'

'Daria Patterson, how dare you suggest such a thing?'

'Oh, you don't have to pretend. We've all noticed that you love him, even Mrs Mortimer and Mrs Trent, because they watch you all the time when he's around and are happy when the earl pays you attention. And we're sure he likes you a lot.'

Alexis pressed her hands against her burning cheeks. 'Do be quiet. The earl loves another.'

'But Mrs Spencer doesn't like living here so she'll go back to London soon.'

'If he has promised himself to her, that won't make any difference.'

Daria shrugged. 'Perhaps we could find another hedgehog and put it in her room.'

'Or a snake,' Celeste suggested.

Esmé said enthusiastically, 'What about a pot full of spiders? There are lots of them living in the attic. We could collect some and empty them in her wardrobe so they go in her clothes.'

Celeste shuddered. 'Ugh! I'm not going to catch spiders. We could hide a fish under her bed, so it would rot and attract flies.'

It was the best idea yet, but Alexis hid her grin. 'You'll do no such thing.'

And Blythe added quietly, 'The innocent might be blamed, like they were with the hedgehog.'

There was a moment of silence, then Alexis told them, 'Go and get dressed now, would you, then I'll braid your hair.'

Celeste grimaced. 'Can't we have ringlets like we did at the earl's dinner? Mrs Trent said we looked so pretty.'

'They're for special occasions. Perhaps next Sunday for the christening.'

Kynan woke early with the sound of the sea in his ears, almost before the servants were up. His first thought was happy: being that today was Sunday, he'd see Alexis Patterson at church.

Pulling on his robe, he padded over to the window, stretched and breathed the bracing sea air deeply. He gazed out over his domain with some satisfaction. He'd never felt so well.

He'd received mail during the week, reassuring him that the family business was operating as it should, and informing him that the goods he'd ordered would shortly be consigned to him.

They were mostly household goods, furnishings for the main bedrooms and the drawing room, for he disliked sleeping in a dead man's bed, and felt the old earl's disapproval of him most strongly.

He didn't disturb James, who would be up before he got back, but pulled on his riding habit, ran his fingers through his hair and went downstairs.

In the dining room he found a pot of hot coffee waiting for him. Haining arrived shortly afterwards, followed by Weatherby. He savoured the company of his friends on these early rides and they exchanged greetings before heading for the stable and saddling their mounts.

The ride always set him up for the day. They enjoyed a leisurely canter along the cliff top. The tide had just turned and was beginning its surging, energetic churn. The day was going to be a warm one.

'I fancy a swim,' Weatherby grunted.

They raced each other back to the cove, where they threw off their clothes and ran naked into the water in a flurry of foam. Diving into the incoming waves, they gasped at the water's coldness, and ducked and splashed each other before indulging in an impromptu race.

'What's in the folly?' Weatherby asked, when they were trying to pull their clothes on over their wet bodies.

'I've never been in there. The door was locked the last time I tried it. I believe the Patterson girls used to spend a lot of time in the folly. Miss Blythe used to keep a look out for the ghost ship. On the day I arrived she would have blown my head off if I'd have admitted to being the damned Welsh heir. I persuaded her to blow the top off a hitching post, instead.'

Weatherby chuckled. 'There's not much difference, if you ask me.

Kynan punched him on the shoulder and grinned. The next minute Weatherby wrestled him to the sand and the pair rolled around, pitting their muscles against each other.

'Tide!' Haining shouted, and, picking up his boots, headed rapidly for the path. The next moment a wave rolled over the top of his hapless companions.

They spluttered up out of it and headed after Haining, who was laughing uproariously as they waded through the thigh-deep water. Exchanging a glance, Kynan and Weatherby picked him up and threw him into the next wave.

James didn't comment on the state Kynan was in, even though he was obliged to rinse the sand from his hair and vigorously rub it dry. As usual, his manservant chatted all the way through, giving his observations on this and that.

Usually, James's gossip washed over Kynan, but today his ears pricked up at one snippet of information. 'Miss Patterson has been invited back to London by my mother?' Without success, he tried to hide his dismay. 'I had no idea mother needed a companion. She has many friends and seems to lead such a busy life there.'

James expertly arranged Kynan's cravat. 'I'm sure she does, my Lord. I understand that she feels that Miss Patterson's opportunities of finding a suitable husband here are limited, even thought Mrs Mortimer encourages suitors to call on her.'

Kynan was miffed by the thought that his mother hadn't told him. 'And what does Miss Patterson make of this?'

'I believe she finds the *interest* in her personal life quite irksome, but by all accounts she's beginning to bow to the pressure.' James picked up a clothes brush and set about grooming his master.

Giving him a suspicious look, Kynan said, 'How did you learn this, James?'

'Oh, everyone's business soon becomes public knowledge hereabouts. And everything the Earl of Longmore does, automatically causes speculation, of course.'

'The devil, it does!'

James shrugged, saying blandly, 'You're a newcomer to the district, the damned Welsh heir. They're bound to talk.'

Kynan shrugged. 'Then you'll know that Weatherby is of the mind we should hold a fencing tournament.'

James's eyes widened. 'I hadn't heard that. And the purse?'

'That's up to Weatherby. How much did you make out of the shooting tournament, by the way?'

'I profited nicely from Miss Blythe's win. I'm starting to think about taking a wife for myself. I like it here. I'm of a mind to marry and get myself some children to comfort me in my old age.'

Kynan laughed. 'There must be something in the Dorset air. Haining seems to have taken an interest in Roxanne, and Weatherby intends to pursue Miss Blythe when she matures a little. Who have you set your sights on, may I ask?'

'I'm still thinking about it, sir, but I have my eye on Miss Emily Talbot.'

'Julia's maid?'

'I believe she's Miss Patterson's maid now.'

'Ah yes, so she is.' Lexi had certainly displayed her mettle over that when put to the test. The recollection of the young woman's bruises and her cry of pain when her shoulder had been doctored, made him shudder. She'd been slightly built. 'I thought a more buxom wench suited you, James.'

His servant grinned as he stood back to admire his handiwork. 'Emily needs someone to look after her. I might as well tell you now, my Lord, if she accepts me I'll be looking to start my own business. I've always wanted to be my own man. If my plans come about, I'll be setting up an establishment as a barber if I can find suitable premises.'

'I'll be sorry to lose you when the time comes, James. But I wish you luck, in all ways. Are my guests going to the service, d'you know?'

'I believe so. Shall I order the carriage, or should the phaeton be harnessed?'

He didn't want to travel with Julia. 'The phaeton, I think. The younger women can drive it and I'll go by horseback.'

He didn't want to sit next to Julia in church either, since it would encourage the kind of speculation he was trying to discourage. When they reached the church he lingered in the doorway chattering to various people until his guests were settled. Then, rather obviously, he seated himself at the end of the pew next to Haining, who grinned.

Kynan looked across the aisle to where Lexi sat, her head bowed in prayer. What did young ladies of her age pray for? he wondered, as he grinned at her sisters. Probably, that some handsome young man would carry them off to the altar.

He'd not expected to fall in love so fully – to feel so needful of someone. It was more than just physical attraction. Even so, he sighed as he remembered the way Lexi's lace overdress had covered the rise of her breasts. She'd seemed unaware of how provocative that gown had been.

Today, she looked lovely in spotted lilac, with matching ribbons on her hat. Unlike

the London ladies who would have dampened their petticoats to emphasize their figures,
Lexi made sure hers was modestly covered.
He'd never seen her hair up before the night
of her dinner. It flowed to her waist in a dark
torrent and would smell deliciously of the
lavender on her hat if he buried his nose in
it.

He should not be thinking these wicked
thoughts. God, save me from debauchery,
but thank you for sending me Lexi Patterson. And thank you for creating me as a
man, so, at least, I can imagine her with
some anticipation, he thought irreverently.

Daria elbowed Alexis in the ribs and her
eyes opened. His breath caught in his throat,
for they were full of dreams. She started
when she caught sight of him. Her smile
dawned slowly, then disappeared, only to
reappear in the midst of a delicate blush.
Her lips had a ripe lushness to them, the
bottom was shaped into a natural pout,
which he would kiss the very next time he
got the opportunity.

'Good morning, Miss Patterson,' he said,
then remembered the others. 'And all of you,
of course.'

Cordelia inclined her head. Kynan was not
surprised to see his mother sitting next to
her, since she'd already stated her intention
to spend the day with her cousin at Florence

House, something that was happening more and more.

'Good morning, Lord Trent,' they all said together, then giggled, until Cordelia gently coughed.

Reverend Curruthers appeared, to smile benignly upon his congregation. 'Let us pray.'

Kynan thought he'd prayed enough for one morning and went back to his daydreams, until he was called to read the lesson. Later, he and Alexis took their places at the font. Barnaby, his hair aflame, and dressed in a long white gown, snuggled in Alexis's arms and went to sleep as the promises were made. Kynan couldn't take his gaze off her. Her eyes were filled with such tenderness as she gazed down at the infant. But although she smiled, there was a slight glitter of tears in her eyes.

He wondered if she was still thinking of the baby brother who'd perished with her parents?

'Will you be responsible for seeing that the child you present is brought up in the Christian faith and life?'

Softly, she said, 'I will, with God's help.'

Kynan followed suit. He must keep his mind on his responses. How lovely the light was, slanting through the stained glass window. It shone on to a tablet on the floor. *Edwyn Godfrey Trent, the 3rd Earl of Long-*

more. The earl from whose loins the feuding families had sprung, he thought, but there was a sudden surge of pride in his heritage.

'Will you by your prayers and witness help this child to grow into the full stature of Christ?'

They said together, 'I will, with God's help.' Alexis gently kissed the babe and handed him over to the reverend for naming.

If she'd have him for her husband, one day she'd hold his child in her arms, he thought.

Reverend Curruthers poured water on the infant's head three times and named him, Barnaby Joshua Hardin.

'I baptize you in the name of the Father, Son and the Holy Spirit.'

When the boy opened his mouth and gave an almighty roar of disapproval, Kynan exchanged a grin with his agent.

'That do mean the devil is cast from the infant's body,' Mrs Dawson said loudly and knowledgeably from the back of the church. 'You won't have no trouble with him now, Mr Hardin, I can tell you that, right enough.'

When Barnaby's sister Kate frowned, then poked her tongue out at the minister, who'd dared to pat her gently on the head, Kynan glanced at Alexis, and chuckled.

Obviously, Mrs Dawson didn't know much about boys, Kynan thought.

Intercepting the exchange between Kynan and Alexis Patterson, Julia's eyes narrowed.

'Kynan's trying to make me jealous,' she said to Roxanne when they were on the way back to Longmore Hall. 'He can't possibly like that pasty little virgin. The whole pack of Pattersons are clodhoppers.'

'On the contrary, Julia, Miss Patterson is a very nice young woman. And even though she acts a little young for her age, Blythe is a lot of fun and a good sport. She has Philip wrapped around her little finger.'

Julia's smile was contemptuous. 'Weatherby has always been an idiot.'

'For an idiot he's done very well for himself, considering he started out with nothing.'

'How dare those girls try and make a fool of me,' Julia snarled. 'First it was the maid, now it's Kynan. He's mine, and has been for nearly two years. He was going to propose marriage, I was sure of it.'

'It seems as though he's thought better of it. I don't think he liked the way you treated your maid.'

'I paid out her wages.'

'So you did. But he's never seen that side of you before, Julia, and it's making him think twice. Also, as I recall you couldn't make up your mind whether you'd accept a proposal from him, or not. Besides, you wouldn't fit into his life here. You said so yourself. You don't even like the place. Let him be.'

'I can change my mind about marriage, can't I? I don't have to live here. I'd really enjoy being a countess, you know. There are those in London who look down their noses at me, and I'd enjoy being able to put them in their place.'

'I wonder if Kynan—' Roxanne bit her lip.

'Go on,' Julia said.

'Perhaps he's heard rumours.'

'About what, pray?'

'About *whom*, would be more appropriate. I'm talking about your affairs, Julia.'

Julia shrugged. 'I was discreet. How could he possibly learn about them, unless you told him?'

'Kynan is not stupid, Julia. He also wants an heir. You could almost read his mind when he was looking at Miss Patterson holding that infant.'

Julia thought about that for a moment, then she gave a thin smile. 'No ... he's not stupid, is he? How very annoying of him. But then, neither am I. You know, Roxanne, just because I didn't give my husband a child, it doesn't mean it was my fault.'

'But you said the doctor told you you'd be unable to conceive an infant.'

Julia shrugged. 'He was only guessing. I wasn't going to say anything yet, but...'

'You're carrying my child?' Kynan said three hours later, and his heart fell as he gazed across his desk at Julia. 'How can you be?'

'Don't tell me you've forgotten the few nights we spent together.'

Kynan only wished he could.

Nineteen

Kynan's first thought was that he wanted the infant, but not Julia.

Sensing his reluctance, Julia said, 'I thought there was an understanding between us.'

'Yes, at one time I thought there was, too. But you see, Julia, my heart has been engaged by another. I've been waiting for an opportunity to tell you.'

'As I have noticed, Kynan dear,' she purred, and her eyes glittered. 'I'm sure Miss Milksop will not be able to resist your considerable charm, and will come to your bed if you apply yourself to the art of her seduction. You'll need someone to satisfy your appetites, which seem somewhat dampened of late. I wouldn't want to live here when we are wed, anyway. I much prefer London.'

'You don't understand, Julia. I have every intention of asking Miss Patterson to become my wife. And I believe she has *certain feelings* towards me.'

Julia smiled. 'Are you talking about love? At such short acquaintance, and the girl with

336

no dowry to her name. How drearily provincial you've become. We're used to each other, my dear, and I understand that you'd need more than I can offer you. Think what you'd be giving up, full access to my fortune, your infant—'

'Be certain, I'd support the infant.'

'Without you, there cannot be one, Kynan. There are ways and means that only women know about ... and I'll not bring a bastard into the world. It would ruin my reputation completely. I've a mind to marry, and you're the logical choice, since it's expected of us, even by me. Can you deny that you intended to offer me marriage before that girl came into your life?'

'To be truthful, I cannot refute what you say.'

'Then I'll hold you to that. The title is a bonus, of course. I daresay I shall quite like calling myself the Countess of Longmore.'

Fury rose to scorch his chest. He asked himself: Why now, after all this time? He wished he'd never met Julia, let alone touched her. But he had, and now there was to be an infant. Somebody had to bear responsibility for that. 'Damn you, Julia. If you don't want to keep the child you can give birth to it here at Longmore Hall, and I'll bring it up. Nobody will be any of the wiser.'

'And how would you explain an infant to

Miss Alexis Patterson?'

'I'd tell her the truth. She'd understand.'

Julia began to laugh. 'You'd expect her to accept the result of your passion with another woman? Do you seek to shame her, Kynan? Believe me, Miss Patterson would grow up in a hurry, despite those *certain feelings* of hers!'

Julia stood. 'Beware, Kynan, women don't think or act in the simplistic way men do about matters of the heart. Deceive one and she will seek retribution in any way she can. Your abandonment of me in my time of need would certainly give rise to thoughts as to the suitability of your character. As sure as the locals would pity Miss Patterson and scorn the infant, they would both come to despise you – and so would any offspring of your marriage.'

He wanted to wrap his hands about Julia's beautiful throat and strangle the life from her. But she was right. Lexi would come to despise him, as surely as he now despised Julia Spencer.

'I'll allow you to think this over before you come to a decision about the fate of your off-spring, and to save you further embarrassment I'll not tell anybody of what has been said here.'

That said, she left the room, gently closing the door behind her.

At least Julia hadn't demanded an answer

straight away. She'd given him time to think things through. Feeling like a rat in a trap, Kynan rested his head in his hands. Julia's lack of feeling for the child was all too apparent. She had been, in fact, far too controlled about the whole thing ... the conversation had sounded rehearsed. *Women don't think in the simplistic way men do in matters of the heart*, she'd warned. Was she bluffing about the child, in an attempt to force his hand?

After changing, he went to the stable, where the new stable boy saddled his horse while he passed the time of day with Jude. It was time to ride out with Joshua Hardin. Today, they'd visit the Antelope Hotel in Dorchester to meet with some of the local farmers and businessmen. It was a regular meeting, a mixture of business and social. They discussed the weather, predicted the price that the harvest would bring in and supped freely of the ale. Kynan was there to learn, but his position in the district brought with it, its own restrictions.

The atmosphere was smoky and the conversation of the farmers rolled rich and throatily out of their mouths. Sometimes he found it hard to understand, but his ears were attuning to it and he was beginning to understand some of the local dialect.

He also intended to drop in on Richard Hough, the lawyer, and ask his advice. He needed someone to talk to about the situation, someone with an older and wiser head, who he knew would be discreet.

Hough greeted him with a smile and shook his hand. 'Nice to see you again, my Lord. Your presence enhances my humble establishment enormously.'

'I'm sure it doesn't need enhancing, since most people around here seem to judge a man by the way he conducts himself and his business, rather than his status in life.'

Hough fetched a decanter of porter, and poured them a glass apiece. 'How can I be of assistance to you then, my Lord?'

'The advice I need is more personal than legal.'

Hough nodded. 'One of my sons is your age, the other a little younger. You may present your problem, and I'll do my best to advise you. I just wish they would do the same sometimes.'

Kynan drew in a breath. 'A young woman of my acquaintance has recently advised me that she is in a delicate condition.'

Hough started. 'Not Miss Patterson, surely? It was noticed that you paid her attention at the dinner.'

'Of course I did. So did everyone else. It was in honour of her birthday, after all.' He shrugged, then sighed. 'I'll be honest with you. I have fallen completely and utterly in love with Miss Patterson.'

'Then you must do your duty towards her

and wed her as soon as possible, before she is ruined completely.'

Kynan stared at him. 'You don't understand. It's not Miss Patterson who says she is with child. How could she be when I have taken precautions by furnishing the Patterson girls with a chaperone – one who will guard them against men like me?'

'Or any man.' Hough's mouth twitched. 'Ah ... my pardon, my Lord. Of course Miss Patterson would not be so free with her favours. May one enquire...?'

Kynan quickly outlined the problem.

'A man in your position must be careful, for he can be brought down by a clever woman who covets a title. The fact is, this woman was a wife for several years, yet did not produce an infant. She has also been your *close friend, and confidante* for almost two years, with the same result. But at the very moment when you acquire a title, and withdraw your favours from her, she becomes fecund. That is highly suspicious.'

Kynan had fleetingly considered this himself.

'From my experience, and I have five children of my own, it takes a little while before a woman can know for certain she is with child. May I be so bold as to say she's found your Achilles heel and is about to exploit it. Call her bluff, my dear sir. And do make enquiries. If she's with child, it's quite possible it may not be yours.'

Thanking Hough for his advice, Kynan left the lawyer's office feeling greatly relieved, and knowing he wouldn't marry Julia under any circumstances. It would be Alexis Patterson or no one.

Alexis had not expected to receive a visit, especially from Julia Spencer. She'd arrived in the phaeton, and was alone.

Her sisters were in the garden. Sitting under the shade of a horse chestnut tree, they were reading out loud to Cordelia. Alexis was darning a hole in one of Blythe's gloves, the cat was asleep on the rug at her feet, when Agnes showed Julia into the drawing room. She set her sewing aside. She'd rather not have taken refreshment with Mrs Spencer, but couldn't be impolite.

'I feel I owe you an apology for my behaviour the last time I was here, Miss Patterson,' Julia said with a smile as brilliant and as brittle as crystal.

Alexis didn't want her apology. 'Perhaps you should offer it to Mrs Mortimer instead. I can send a maid to fetch her from the garden if you wish.'

Julia's eyes glittered with annoyance. 'Oh, do get off your high horse and sit down, Miss Patterson. I sent the woman a note just a few days ago, and it's you I came to see. I just feel that we got off on the wrong foot.

Kynan was quite annoyed over the incident. He thinks very highly of you, you know.'

Alexis smiled at the thought.

'And your sisters, of course.' Julia looked at her hair. 'One of Emily's better styles. It makes you look grown up.'

'I am grown up, Mrs Spencer.'

'Of course you are. You've certainly blossomed since I first came here. Even Kynan has noticed it. You have a natural elegance and style.'

'Thank you, Mrs Spencer.' Nevertheless, Alexis was suspicious of the compliment.

'Unlike your sister, Blythe, of course. She's so gauche and ungainly, and her antics give all of us at Longmore Hall endless hours of amusement.'

They fell quiet while the refreshment was set on the table, waiting for Agnes to depart. Not by the flicker of an eyelid did Alexis show how annoyed she was about the slur on her sister. Amusement indeed! How small-minded the woman was. Picking up the teapot, she looked Julia in the eyes. 'How would you prefer your tea, Mrs Spencer?'

Julia frowned at the implied threat, but she also appeared amused by it. 'Weak, and with a small amount of milk added.'

When will this woman get to the point of her visit? Alexis thought, wishing the milk was poisoned as she dribbled it on Julia's tea and handed over the cup and saucer. She had no intention of encouraging her with meaningless conversation, so simply waited, even though it was wearing on the nerves.

The tension in the room tightened as the two women sipped the liquid and gazed at each other. Alexis's heart beat noisily against her bodice. The clock on the mantelpiece ticked time away steadily and dust danced in a shaft of sunlight coming through the window.

The cat stood up, arched its back, yawned, then began to claw the carpet. 'Shoo,' Alexis said, nudging it gently with her toe, her voice sounding loud in the silence. It jumped on the window sill, where it began to groom itself. One velvety paw was licked then circled several times around each ear in turn. Suddenly it stopped, paw held in mid-air, looking intently at the door. It gave a little mew, then resumed its task.

Julia's cup clattered into her saucer. 'I despise cats.'

Alexis shrugged. Mrs Spencer's likes or dislikes were of no interest to her.

Julia's face tightened into a mask of annoyance. 'You're not making conversation between us easy, Miss Patterson.'

'My pardon.' She's not as composed as she appears, Alexis thought.

'Aren't you wondering why I'm really here?'

Alexis declared war. 'Since we seem to

detest each other, not for one moment did I believe you came here to apologize for your outrageous behaviour.'

'Oh, you're wrong. I embarrassed Kynan, and wanted to make amends.'

'I'm sure the earl will survive being embarrassed.'

'Which is the very thing I wished to talk to you about. I believe you harbour tender feelings towards Lord Trent.'

Alexis's heart began to pound. 'My feelings are nobody's business but mine.'

'Oh, but they are. You're making it obvious to everyone. In fact, you are becoming a laughing stock. Every time Kynan pays you attention you simper and smile, and make sheep's eyes at him. Your glance follows him everywhere. At first it was amusing, but now, my dear, you must stop, for neither of us wish you to continue your embarrassing display.'

'You're mistaken,' Alexis cried out, denying what she knew to be true. 'The earl and I are merely friends.'

'No, my dear. At first, Kynan was flattered by your adoration of him. Now it's become deeply embarrassing. He cannot marry you, since he's promised himself to me. And soon we are to be blessed with—!' Her eyes rounded. 'You must forget I uttered a word of that, since we must be wed as soon as possible, and privately, to avoid a scandal. I believe you have received marriage proposals. Perhaps you should accept one. Having a man of your own will help you forget any romantic notions you may have towards mine.'

The blood drained from Alexis's face and the world spun around her.

'Are you all right, Miss Patterson?' Julia cooed, all false concern. 'Shall I fetch *your* maid.'

Alexis told her bitterly, 'Since you've effectively delivered your message, Mrs Spencer, perhaps you'd oblige me by leaving me in peace now.'

'Oh, but first I must tell you, my dear. When I become the Countess of Longmore, I shall insist that you and your sisters be removed from this house.'

There came a knock at the door and Emily entered. Her glance went to Alexis's strained face, then back to Julia's triumphant one.

Julia smiled nastily at her. 'I do hope you were not up to your old tricks of listening at keyholes, Talbot.'

'Don't you accuse me of doing any such thing. I've just come down those stairs. You ask Miss Blythe if you don't believe me. She passed me on the way up.'

'It doesn't matter whether Mrs Spencer believes you or not,' Alexis said wearily. 'It's none of her business what you do.'

'Both of you will regret taking me on,' Julia

sneered. 'In fact, the whole pack of you will regret it.' She swaggered off, slamming the door behind her, causing the windows to rattle.

'Is everything all right, Miss Patterson?'

Making an effort, Alexis pulled herself together, even though she was filled with misery. 'Everything's fine. She made me angry, that's all. She intends to marry the earl, you know?'

'Lord Trent should know better now he's seen her nasty side,' Emily said. 'Though I daresay it's none of my business.'

Alexis bit down on her tongue. Her heart was aching so, but she was also furious, and she was filled to the brim with unshed tears. They pushed against her eyes, as though they filled her body almost to capacity and needed to escape.

'Your gentleman visitor has arrived. I've asked him to wait in the morning room.'

Alexis stared at Emily. Julia's visit had driven John Oliver from her mind. She recalled a pleasant, rather shy young man of average height, the son of a wine merchant. The sooner she got this over with the better.

He stood when she entered the morning room and handed her a bunch of roses.

'Thank you, Mr Oliver. That was thoughtful of you.'

He flushed, but said with great determination, 'Miss Patterson, would you kindly be seated. I wish to talk to you.'

'I understand that's why you are here, Mr Oliver. Please go ahead.'

And as John Oliver was stammering out his proposal she thought angrily, why not marry this man? He's personable, wealthy, and is heir to a flourishing business. He also owns his own home, of which you could be mistress. John Oliver would make her a decent husband and be a good father to their children.

But you don't love him.

She liked him though, and thought it possible she might learn to love him.

You love the earl.

Alexis knew she couldn't spend the rest of her life loving a man who was wed to another. She couldn't bear the thought that there would be a child born to Kynan and Julia, who would be a cruel mother if the behaviour she'd displayed so far was any indication.

And while she couldn't imagine bearing John Oliver's infants, she knew she would love them if she did. They'd all have his soulful brown eyes and look like puppies.

'Mr Oliver. Thank you for your consideration. I'm suffering from a headache at the moment, and would like time to properly consider your proposal, if I may.'

He looked pleasantly surprised by her answer, and she wanted to pat him on the head like a dog. 'Of course, Miss Patterson. How long would you need?'

'Four weeks.' It would give her time to see if she could get used to the idea of marriage to a stranger.

Not long after she'd closed the door on John Oliver, the earl arrived in a hurry. As Kynan dismounted, Alexis headed up the stairs, stopping to watch him from the landing window. She would not see this man, who had laughed about her most tender feelings with his London friends, and behave normally. How superficial they all were. He lopped up to the door as if he had a fire under his tail and she shrank back into the shadowy corner as he glanced up at the hall window, his eyes searching for her, as if he sensed her presence.

'If Lord Trent asks for me, tell him I'm indisposed,' she said to Lally as the maid came through to open the door to his knock. She ran the rest of the way upstairs. Once in the safety of her room she threw herself on the bed and allowed her tears to flow.

She didn't catch sight of her sister until Blythe rose from the chair. 'I heard everything that woman said,' Blythe said angrily. 'I hate her.'

'So do I. Oh, Blythe,' Alexis sobbed. 'What am I going to do? I feel so terrible. I didn't think being in love would hurt so much. All this time they have been mocking me.'

Blythe hugged her tight.

From the hall, they could hear Kynan's voice. 'It's imperative that I see Miss Patterson. Fetch Mrs Mortimer, as well, please.'

Alexis's tears wouldn't stop flowing and she began to sob, turning her face into the pillow to muffle the noise.

Mrs Mortimer's voice drifted up to them, calm and measured. 'How lovely to see you, my Lord. You look agitated.'

'I wish to see Miss Patterson, but the maid has told me she's indisposed.'

'Then she must be. I shall enquire.'

Blythe allowed Cordelia access, and hissed, 'The earl has broken Alexis's heart. Julia Spencer came to see Alexis. She is to marry the earl.'

'Alexis, my dearest.' Cordelia took one look at her tear-stained and tragic face, and her eyes softened. 'You might not think you'll recover from this, but you will in time. You have other suitors. How did Mr Oliver seem to you?'

Damn Mr Oliver! She blew her nose, trying to gather herself together. 'I liked him. I have promised to consider his offer and give him an answer in four weeks. But how can I marry one man when I love another?' She began to sob all over again.

'I must counsel you on this situation a little later. I'd not have you accept an offer in haste to spite the earl. It would not be fair to

John Oliver.' There was a soft kiss on her forehead, then Cordelia departed.

'I'm sorry, my Lord. Miss Patterson is indisposed.'

Kynan let his frustration show. *That* I've already been informed of. What's wrong with her, pray?'

'I'm unable to divulge that information. Miss Patterson will recover in time, I'm sure. Do you wish to leave her a message?'

'Yes, tell her ... No! What I need to say to her is best delivered in person. Tell Miss Patterson I'll come back tomorrow.'

'Very well, my Lord, but I cannot promise that her condition will have improved enough to see you. Please leave your card.'

'My card? You know full well who I am.'

'How am I to teach my charges etiquette if you will not behave like the gentleman you are?'

'Kindly remember I am not one of your charges. Oh, very well,' he grumbled. There was a moment of silence, followed by, 'To whom does this card belong? Who the devil is John Oliver?'

'The son of a wine merchant. A *mannerly* young man of pleasant disposition.'

'If that's designed to point out my own lack of manners, point taken. I apologize for my bluff manner, Cordelia. I admit my mood is less congenial than it should be. What was

351

the young man doing here?'

'Calling on Miss Patterson. He left a few moments before you arrived, I believe.'

'I think I passed him in the village. Was it John Oliver who upset her? If so, I'll have it out with him.'

'I did not say Miss Patterson was upset, merely indisposed. As for Mr Oliver, he's a fine young man who has offered Miss Patterson his hand in marriage. She's seriously considering it.'

'The devil she is? You must discourage this, Cordelia. Tell her to come down so we can discuss it.'

'I will not. You force me to be blunt, Kynan. Yes, Alexis is upset and she does not wish to see you. I'll also remind you that she is of age. How she conducts her life, and who she decides to wed is entirely her own affair.'

He thought that a fair statement, but there was more to this refusal to see him than that, and he thought he knew what it was. 'Julia Spencer has been here, hasn't she?'

Just then the door was opened and the dog came though. It was hardly more than a big puppy, with a friendly face and white socks. Its tail whipped around his legs like a rope. The three younger girls followed after it. Their smiles warmed him.

Celeste curtsied. 'We saw your horse and thought we'd come to greet you, my Lord. Are you well?'

'Yes, I am, thank you. And you likewise, I trust.'

'Are you staying for refreshment? Shall we tell Lally and fetch Alexis and Blythe down?'

Cordelia said firmly, 'Lord Trent only stepped in for a moment, and was just about to depart.'

'I'll be back tomorrow.'

'As you wish, my Lord.'

As the door closed behind him he became more and more certain that Julia was behind this.

When he arrived back at the hall he was tempted to tell Julia to come to his study. But he decided he'd rather lull her into a state of confidence. Since the damage seemed to have already been done with regards to Alexis, he would take the lawyer's advice and make enquiries into her activities. He would start by taking Peter Haining into his confidence. Peter had already advised him as to Julia's unsuitability. No man alive was more discreet than him.

Blythe, who had overheard most of the conversation between Julia and her sister, was as heartsick as Alexis. She thought her sister would never stop crying and brought their younger sisters up to date with the situation over the course of the day.

Later that evening, her glance fell on Emily. She must know more about Mrs Spencer than anyone else. 'Emily,' she said.

'I'm going to tell you what happened between my sister and Mrs Spencer. But it's a secret.'

Wide-eyed, Emily said, 'That woman's a bad lot.'

'She told Alexis that she's with child and is going to marry the earl.'

'She never is,' Emily scoffed. 'I was there when the doctor told her she'd never be able to carry an infant. He said that her female parts hadn't developed properly.'

'Would you tell the earl that?'

'I daren't. It would be too embarrassing. Besides, I never want to go near her again. She'd probably try and kill me if I went to the hall. She said she'd make me pay for what I did.'

'Then I'll go. I'll write down everything that was said on a piece of paper and slide it under the door of the earl's study.'

'What if they catch you?'

'They won't. I'll wait until it's nearly dusk. They'll be in the drawing room then.'

'What will Miss Mortimer say?'

'Nothing, since she won't know. I'll pretend I'm tired and go to bed early. She'll think I'm in bed. You'll have to sneak down and unlock the door so I can get back in. Now, what was the name of Mrs Spencer's doctor?'

The night was a cool one. Roxanne was

singing as Julia left the drawing room to fetch her shawl.

As she went up the stairs she saw Blythe Patterson crouching outside the study door. She gave a tight smile. All she had to do was shout. But first, a little fun. She crept along the corridor, reaching her just as she straightened up.

'What are you up to, you brat?' she said softly against her ear.

The girl spun round, her eyes wide and frightened. Then she turned and ran. Julia swiftly followed after her. Instead of turning in the direction where she lived, Blythe had headed down to the cove. She grinned; the girl was going to hide in the folly until she could make her escape.

The shadowy figure moved fast and disappeared around the small building. There came the sound of a key turning in the lock, a faint creak as the door was opened.

Julia said loudly. 'You come out of there, you pest. I'm taking you to the earl so you can explain to him why you're sneaking about his home.'

She heard a swift intake of breath and the door swung shut.

How silly of the creature to think she was going to hide from her? When Julia reached out for the doorknob, her hand encountered the key, and she smiled. It made a satisfying clunk when she turned it in the lock.

'Let me out,' Blythe said, her voice muffled by the sturdy door panel.

Julia laughed. 'It will serve you right if the ghost ship comes to carry you off. Sweet dreams.'

She turned and hurried back to the hall before she was missed, casting the key to the ground as she went.

Twenty

Alexis woke to Emily shaking her shoulder; she was bleary-eyed from crying and lack of sleep.

Although feeling miserable, her waking thought was that she'd cry no more over the damned Welsh heir.

It was early, still dark, at least two hours off rising. 'What is it, Emily? Has something happened?'

The candlelight revealed a frightened expression on the maid's face. 'It's Miss Blythe. Her bed hasn't been slept in.'

'Not slept in?' She sat up, and, swinging her legs over the edge of the bed, checked Blythe's room, then the rooms of her younger sisters, in case Blythe had slept with one of them.

Quietly, she asked the maid, 'Did my sister say she was going anywhere?'

'She stated her intention of going to Longmore Hall, miss. She said I was to sneak down and unlock the door after everyone was in bed, so she could get back in. I meant to wait up for her, but I fell asleep in the chair.'

Dear God. Surely Weatherby hadn't encouraged her – No! She must not think such dreadful things of her sister. 'Why did she go to the hall, Emily?'

Emily hung her head. 'I told Miss Blythe that Mrs Spencer couldn't possibly be with child, since I was there when the doctor told her that such an event was impossible.'

'Something which should have been kept confidential,' Alexis said severely. Nevertheless, her heart leapt at the news that the woman had lied.

'Yes, miss. Miss Blythe said she was going to sneak in and leave a note for the earl. Said she was going to slide it under the study door. Shall I rouse Mrs Mortimer?'

As if things weren't bad enough, her sister had involved her in the personal business of the earl and his woman! Alexis grimaced as it occurred to her that there was a faint possibility that this might need to be hushed up. 'No, we won't rouse her yet. Fetch my skirt and bodice. I'm going to the hall, right away.'

'By yourself, miss?'

'Since you're involved, you'd better come with me. We might come across her on the road. She may have twisted her ankle and fallen and be lying injured somewhere. Between us we should be able to bring her home. If not, I'll rouse the earl and he can instigate a search.'

'There's a thick mist out. We might not see her.'

'Blythe wouldn't have left the road, and the mist will clear as soon as the sun rises.'

Blythe had spent an uncomfortable night, every creak, crack and noise reminding her of the ghost ship.

Once, this had been her special place, where she could hide in times of trouble. She found the old blanket she kept here, and wrapped it around her shoulders.

There were candles, but groping in the dark didn't uncover them or the tinder box and tapers.

During the night the tide had come in, and the sea had beat against the cliff underneath. She could have sworn she'd heard the voices of drowned seamen, and the clash of cutlasses. Then she'd fallen asleep and dreamed of her mother and father, who'd perished with their baby son in the cove below. But when she reached out for them, she woke. How different life would have been if they'd lived, she thought. And if she and her sisters hadn't had their dearest Lexi to turn to, where would they have been now? She hated to see her, who she loved with all her heart, suffering so.

Now it was morning, for the window shutters allowed in a dim, grey light. Unfortunately, they were secured on the outside.

She clambered on to the barrel of the cannon to apply her eye to the beam of light coming through a knot hole near the top of the shutter. At first she could see nothing but greyness. She realized there was a sea mist.

Before she had time to look away, the swirling vapour parted for an instant. Her heart nearly stopped beating. There in the cove a ship was anchored.

She experienced panic. What had the old earl said? Don't bother opening the shutters. Just fire through them! But as soon as she got over her initial jolt of fright, she knew it couldn't possibly be a ghost ship – that was only a tale.

But if she fired the cannon, at least she'd draw attention to her plight, and if she blew the shutters out, she'd be able to escape and confront that woman with her lies before the damned Welsh earl made the biggest mistake of his life and married her, instead of Lexi. And she *would* confront her!

Her hands shook as she followed Weatherby's instructions, talking herself through them out loud. 'First make sure you have your flame lit, and keep it away from the powder.'

She found her implements easily now there was some light, and struck the flint vigorously against the charred cloth. Several attempts were made before the cloth began to glow and she was able to wrap it around a small amount of tinder. She blew gently on it, and, as the fire took hold, lit a small fire in a dish. From that she lit a taper and transferred it to the candle wick, before extinguishing the fire to preserve the charred cloth.

'Spoon the powder into the touch hole,' she said. But in the absence of a spoon, she was obliged to use a candle snuffer.

'Wadding,' she muttered, and tore a strip of fabric from her chemise.

'Shot.' There were two cannon balls, but she didn't have the strength to lift them. The canvas bag that held the grapeshot was beginning to rot, and some of the shot began to fall to the floor as she loaded it. Scraping it up, she once more used her chemise, fashioning the torn fabric into a bag and tying it with a piece of rag.

'Now for the really dangerous part,' she muttered, for according to Weatherby, one had to be exceedingly careful of this manoeuvre. Gingerly, she pushed it all against the powder charge with the rammer, heaving a sigh of relief when nothing untoward happened.

'Now what?' She must place the rest of the powder in the touch hole, light the taper and apply.

She picked up the taper, and hesitated, repeating everything in her mind, in case there was a step she'd forgotten. Ah, yes. She must remember to stay out of the way of the recoil.

She moved hastily to one side. As if she wasn't in enough trouble, she could just imagine the furore this would create if she blew herself up...

Kynan came running down the stairs, his hair tumbled from sleep, his shirt open at the neck. 'I apologize for my appearance. James said you urgently needed to see me. What is it, Lexi? Has something happened? Are you all right?'

She didn't waste time on preamble. 'Blythe came here last night to deliver a note to you. She didn't return home.'

'If she came here, I didn't see her. And neither have I received any note. She may have left it in my study.'

'That was her intention, I understand.'

Kynan turned to James, also in his shirt sleeves. 'Ask my mother's maid to check the ladies' rooms, without waking them if that's possible. If that's to no avail, rouse Weatherby and Lord Haining.'

He turned to her, all at once apologetic. 'James will be discreet if he finds her.'

She knew what Kynan was suggesting, and her face flamed. 'I'd prefer it if you didn't compare the morals of my sister to those of your ... *companion.*'

He looked taken aback. 'Of course. I'm

362

sorry, I didn't mean to infer—' He shrugged. 'Will you wait in the drawing room while I finish dressing?'

'I'd prefer the hall.'

'As you wish.' He disappeared up the stairs rapidly, taking them two at a time.

Seating herself, Alexis patted Jasper, who'd come down the stairs to greet her, his tail wagging. When he went to stand by the door and looked expectantly back at her, she opened it and let him out.

The mist was beginning to thin, and she could see a ship anchored in the cove. Had the damned Welsh marauders finally arrived? Despite her worry over Blythe, she smiled.

'Did you find the note Blythe sent you, my Lord?' she said, when he came back.

He nodded. 'I did.'

'What did she say in it?'

Soberly, he told her, 'I'd prefer not to disclose that, because it's of a personal nature regarding one of my guests. I'll deal with it as soon as I can. What matters most at this moment is finding your sister safe and sound.'

Five minutes later Weatherby and Haining came down, and they all moved outside to stand on the step.

'Is there anywhere special Miss Blythe might have gone?' Weatherby asked.

About to shake her head, Alexis suddenly said, 'We should try the folly. She always considered it her special place. The old earl told us all the story of the ghost ship there. He said Blythe must fire the cannon at it if it ever sailed into the cove. However, there's a ship anchored in the cove now, and it seems to be intact.'

'Let's hope she doesn't blow it out of the water, then. It carries a cargo of new furnishings from my warehouses, and wine to replenish the cellar with.'

Alexis offered Kynan a cool look. 'My sister does know the difference between a legend and a real ship. Besides, I doubt very much if she'd know how to fire a cannon.'

'Ah...' said Weatherby, and gazed around at them all. 'As a matter of fact, Miss Blythe did ask me to relate to her the steps needed to fire a cannon.'

'Good God!' Kynan said faintly. 'You didn't tell her, did you, Weatherby?'

Blythe peppered the last of the powder on the touch hole. Taking a deep breath she touched the lit taper against the powder. It began to make a little fizzing noise, sparking prettily as it disappeared down the hole, but leaving a stink in its wake.

Taking her blanket she hid behind a column and stuck her fingers in her ears.

For a moment everything went quiet and she thought the spark had gone out. Then there was a sudden and almighty bang that made her jump from her skin and cry out with fright.

The cannon jumped backwards, smashing into the wall, then it lurched forward. The windows and shutters cracked and shattered and everything exploded around her.

Giving a scream, she pulled the blanket over her head and cowered in a corner as dust and debris rained down on her.

'Obviously you *did* tell her,' Haining said. The three men leapt down the steps and began to run towards the folly.

They stopped abruptly when there was a loud rumble, just in time to see the cannon roll out through the french doors in a spectacular cloud of smoke. The weapon teetered on the edge of the cliff, then settled with one wheel askew and its smoking barrel, now split open, pointing skyward.

'Blythe,' Alexis screamed frantically, but she couldn't keep up with the men. Relief filled her when she saw her sister stagger, coughing, from the wreckage of the folly. She was covered in soot and the blanket she wore was in shreds.

Alexis pushed through the men to hold her sister tight. 'Oh, Blythe,' was all she could find to say.

Her sister tried to smile. 'I found the treasure. It's been there all the time. There's a chimney hidden in the wall the cannon was chained to. When the gun recoiled and the wall fell down, I swear I saw a treasure chest.'

'It doesn't matter about the treasure, my dearest. I'm just so relieved that you're safe and sound.'

Blythe's face screwed up. 'I feel funny inside, Lexi, like I'm made of jelly. And my ears are ringing and my head aches. I just want to go home.' Indeed, she was trembling from head to foot. Removing her shawl, Alexis wrapped it around her sister.

'Allow me,' said Weatherby and lifted Blythe into his arms so her face rested against his shoulder. Her tears were meandering through the dirt on her face. 'We'll take you home in the carriage. You could have killed yourself, Miss Blythe. Why did you do something so dangerous?'

'Because I wanted to get out of the folly, of course. Somebody locked me in.'

There was a dingy being rowed ashore. Men in it were shouting and waving.

'Would you remain behind and tell them the explosion was an accident and there is nothing to worry about, please, Haining.'

On the way back to the house, Kynan stooped to pick up a key from the grass.

He turned to Alexis. 'Is this the key to the folly?'

'Yes, my Lord,' she said stiffly.

'Lexi, please don't be angry with me,' he said softly.

'Give me one reason why not, when Blythe was almost killed today? It doesn't take much to guess who locked her in.'

'You don't understand—'

'Yes, my Lord, I most certainly do understand.' She moved off rapidly to join Weatherby and her sister.

He turned to James and Emily, who were lagging behind.

'James, go back and see if you can find the treasure Miss Blythe talked about. But first, make sure the folly is not going to fall down around your ears.'

'Yes, my Lord.'

'Emily, I'd like you to stay at the hall if you would. I received a note from Miss Blythe and would like to question you on the contents. Will you answer truthfully?'

'Yes, my Lord. But I'm frightened of what Mrs Spencer will do.'

'You needn't be frightened. You will not be mentioned, and James will stay with you the entire time, won't you, James?'

'Yes, my Lord,' James said with a smile.

The explosion had roused the Longmore household, and necks were being craned from various windows.

The horses were poled to the carriage and Blythe was restored to her family with a minimum of fuss. Alexis, her hair tumbling loose had not cast a glance his way in the carriage, but he could feel her seething like a pot of lava, so thought it prudent to remain quiet.

She walked indoors after Weatherby and his burden without saying a word; as if he didn't exist. The withdrawal of her favour cut him like a knife to the bone.

He didn't go in. Let Weatherby be the hero of the hour, he thought. Blythe would remember it when he began to seriously court her.

He heard Mrs Mortimer give a cry of distress, followed by a babble of female voices.

Weatherby strode back out a few minutes later. 'I think you might have cooked your goose as far as the delectable Alexis is concerned,' he remarked.

'Since when have my feelings towards Miss Patterson been public knowledge?'

'It's as plain as the sun in the sky every time you look at her, and the same when she looks at you. Why do you think Julia's been behaving like the spoilt brat she is? It was a mistake to bring the two together.'

'It was not deliberate, believe me. Did Miss Patterson say anything?'

He grinned. 'Oh yes. She was in a fine temper and she didn't mince words. She asked me to give you a message.'

'Which is?'

'That you might come from London, and you might be a peer, but to her you're every bit as despicable as your damned Welsh ancestors were. She said to tell you that she'll never willingly speak to you again, and she'll never waste another tear on your behalf.' Weatherby chuckled. 'The lady was so incensed that she stamped her foot. But she did waste a tear as she flounced off up the stairs, for her eyes were awash.'

'The Patterson girls cry easily,' Kynan murmured, the beginning of a grin lightening his features.

But Weatherby hadn't finished embroidering his tale. 'Then damn me, Kynan, if the younger three didn't stamp their feet as well, just like a trio of sprightly fillies. They tossed their heads and flounced off after her with their noses held in the air. I must say, those girls are certainly a lively bunch of beauties.'

'Lexi stamped her foot and cried?' Kynan's grin blossomed into a wide smile. 'Can it be that she loves me?'

'I think you could be right, my friend. She just needs to be convinced. So what are you going to do about it?'

'You'll see. I'll have her love back in a couple of days,' Kynan said confidently.

As soon as he arrived back at the hall he called Emily in. From her he learned of Julia's attempt to dupe him. He was about to dismiss Emily when she took in a deep breath. 'There's something else you should know, my Lord.' She gazed dubiously at

James, who nodded his head. 'She has gen-tlemen friends ... besides you, I mean. No disrespect meant, sir.'

'Do you have names?'

'Roger Brampton.'

'Isn't his wife one of Mrs Spencer's friends?'

'A lot she cares about her friends. Dominic Arguther is another. A fine upstanding magistrate *he* is, with a wife and five children waiting at home. There are others I can name.'

'Thank you, Emily, but I think I've heard enough.' He meant it, for what he'd already heard had filled him with disgust. His pride had been severely dented. 'James, make sure Emily gets home safely, would you? Come straight back, I have another task for you.'

'Yes, my Lord. About the treasure chest Miss Blythe thought she saw. I've placed it over there. It's locked, but it feels very light.'

'There's probably nothing in it. I'll investi-gate the contents, if any, later.'

After James and Emily had gone, he sent for his housekeeper. 'Mrs Elliot, I'd prefer my breakfast here in the study, please. Then ask Mrs Spencer to come and see me at ten a.m. sharp, if you please.'

'Yes, sir.'

'While Mrs Spencer is with me have her bags packed. Jude will have the carriage brought round about ten fifteen. Mrs Spencer will go straight from my study to the carriage, and without fuss.'

Mrs Elliot smiled brightly. 'Certainly, my Lord.'

Julia swept into the study in high dungeon.

'Nobody spoke to me at breakfast, not even Roxanne. It's not my fault that stupid girl blew herself up.'

Kynan spoke the names of the two men out loud. 'Roger Brampton and Dominic Arguther.'

Julia's face drained of colour and she blustered, 'What of them?'

'What indeed? You tell me.'

She shrugged. 'They were merely an amusement.'

'As was I, until I was handed a title.'

'Oh, don't be so damned stuffy, *my Lord.*'

'Your behaviour since you've been here has been reprehensible. First, you insult my neighbours, which they were kind enough to overlook. Then you cruelly beat your maid.'

'She lied.'

'No, Julia, it's you who's the liar. I don't appreciate being tricked into believing I've fathered an infant in an effort to force me to the altar. Also, I don't like being blackmailed. You're lucky I'm not bringing charges against you.'

She shrugged. 'Oh, you won't do that. You won't want the scandal that accompanies it.'

'Neither would you. Every door in London will be closed against you if it's rumoured you're having an affair with two married men. Arguther in particular would not welcome publicity. I warn you, some very shady people owe him favours. If I were you, I'd go and live abroad.'

She shuddered. 'You can't just can't throw me out after all we've meant to each other.'

'You will not remain in my house a second longer than you must. And you'll never be invited to step foot over my doorstep again.'

'How will I get back to London?'

'James will make sure you have a room at the Antelope until a seat on the stage is available.'

'You're going to propose to Miss Patterson, aren't you?'

'My future plans are none of your concern.' He rose when he heard a knock at the door. 'Goodbye, Mrs Spencer.'

'Kynan ... I—'

Striding to the door he held it open. 'I said *goodbye*, Mrs Spencer.'

Julia walked through it, her face flaming in anger, for there was no shame in her.

Kynan didn't feel in the least bit sorry for her, but he did feel responsible for the mischief she'd caused to the people he'd grown to love and respect.

Twenty-One

Alexis had not spoken to the earl for two weeks. She'd not glanced his way in church, or been available when he'd come to call.

In fact, she'd suffered agonies as she'd listened to his pleasant low-pitched voice as he and Weatherby had taken refreshment with her sisters and Cordelia in the drawing room beneath her.

Afterwards, her sisters had rushed upstairs to tell her everything that was said.

The big news was about the treasure from Blythe. 'Weatherby said the treasure chest in the wall was empty. He said it must have been there to put thieves off the scent – make them think somebody had already found it.'

'Perhaps they had.'

'No! Here's the exciting bit. Weatherby went to examine the folly because I told him that some of the grapeshot had fallen to the floor when I tried to load the cannon. He found just one piece, which was made gold, but painted with tar.' She held out her arm. From her wrist dangled a chain with a small gold ball attached. 'He had it cleaned and made into a bracelet for me. Wasn't that sweet of him? Weatherby thinks the treasure might have been the grapeshot, in disguise. But now it's lost for good, because when I fired the cannon off, most of it would have fallen into the deepest part of the cove. Imagine doing something so stupid,' she said gloomily.

Alexis smiled at that. 'Better the treasure, than pieces of you, my love.'

'That's exactly what Weatherby said.'

Celeste handed her Lord Trent's latest peace offering, a bunch of fragrant red roses. 'Lord Trent said he hopes you soon recover from your affliction.'

'I have no affliction,' she said, throwing the roses out of the open window, knowing she'd rescue them later. Except for him, of course, she thought darkly.

'Daria told him you had the bloat.'

'That's disgusting. I'm not a sheep.'

When she was forced to acknowledge Kynan in church, it was with a curt nod. She told herself she'd not allow him to charm her again. She was aware the whole district was talking about them, for Emily had told her.

Neither would she open his letter. It was sitting on her dressing table, addressed to Miss Alexis Patterson in an elegant hand.

After being captivated by his voice as he

opened the summer fair, she tried to avoid him, but he seemed to be everywhere she turned. 'Miss Patterson, perhaps you'd care to take refreshment with me.'

'I'm not thirsty, my Lord.'

'Walk with me, Lexi.'

'Esmé and Daria are waiting for me by the gypsy fortune-teller's caravan.'

'There is a tall, dark and handsome man of means who loves you,' the fortune teller told her, proving to Alexis that her own prediction that the gypsy would say exactly that was correct.

Hah! she thought, when Kynan, who was loitering outside, surreptitiously tossed a coin into the caravan and said, 'See, it's inevitable. Speak to me, Lexi.'

'You'll have to wait until she stops being stubborn, I'm afraid,' Celeste told him.

Alexis was already beginning to weaken.

Weatherby won the shooting match. He pocketed the prize money and presented the small silver cup that came with it to Blythe. 'Here, my dear, you can look after it for me.'

When Alexis arrived home, the letter on the mantlepiece drew her eyes. About it, lingered the exotic smell of cinnamon, which, when she inhaled it, brought to mind Kynan's fine features and faintly olive skin, of his mouth so firm, so soft to kiss. He did have elegant hands, she thought.

You're being stupidly stubborn. Like a mule.

'I know,' she said out loud, because curiosity had got the better of her.

She carefully inserted a thumbnail under the seal of the letter. If he mentioned Julia Spencer she'd stuff it in his mouth and make him eat it. She didn't want explanations.

Dear, dearest, Lexi,
I'm sorry I've hurt your feelings so badly.
I'm an insensitive fool...

She smiled and shook her head. Maybe she'd been insensitive too. Did she have the right to question his former life ... especially now?

...I live only to see you smile at me again.
Kynan

Alexis smiled. It was stupid not to speak to him. Besides, it was disagreeable pretending to be vexed with him all the time, when her feelings were exactly the opposite.

On the earl's next visit, she decided to capitulate. She'd made him suffer enough. She donned her prettiest gown and Emily put her hair up for the occasion.

When she entered the drawing room there was an intake of breath from Kynan. She smiled at him – one that quickly faltered when her glance fell on John Oliver, so obviously awed in the presence of an earl.

She felt sorry for him. 'Perhaps we should talk in the morning room, Mr Oliver.'

When Kynan's brows gathered into a frown, she gave him a cool glance. He'd not yet earned the right to dictate to her.

She'd just finished gently turning down John Oliver's marriage proposal when the door opened and Kynan strode in.

Eyes widening, she gazed at him. 'How dare you burst in here when I'm engaged in a private conversation with Mr Oliver? What are you about, my Lord?'

'Excuse me, Miss Patterson,' John stuttered. 'My Lord.' He practically ran from the room.

'He probably won't stop running until he gets to Dorchester,' Kynan said with great satisfaction. 'Which will save me the trouble of hunting him down and challenging him.'

Alexis found it hard not to laugh, when faced with this delicious and unconventional man, who she quite adored. 'Your behaviour is appalling.'

'Yes, I know it is,' he said. 'You're driving me insane, and I refuse to be ignored any longer. I adore you, Lexi Patterson and you're making me suffer. I pace up and down all day, live for your smile, toss and turn all night and think of nothing but you.'

'Oh ... how very uncomfortable for you.'

'Don't mock me. I'm serious.' He fell to his

knees. 'Will you marry me, my dearest Lexi?'

'I'd like to think about it.'

He stood, pulling her to her feet and against him. The depths of his eyes gleamed. 'Woman, you have exactly one minute in which to decide that your answer will be in the affirmative,' he growled. 'In the meantime...'

His mouth closed over hers as if he owned it, and she willingly allowed him to plunder it.

Behind them, she heard her sisters giggling. Then they were shushed, and a door gently closed. After a moment, those elegant hands of Kynan's smoothed down over her buttocks and pulled her closer. He is irresistible she thought, and he made her feel as wicked as sin, and weak from wanting him. Her body heated all over.

When he was done kissing her, Alexis gazed up at him. She wondered if the expression of love she saw in his face was mirrored in her own.

'I do love you, Kynan,' she said softly, and suddenly she was filled with shyness. 'I really do. I was so miserable at the thought that you might—'

He gently placed a finger over her mouth. 'I was going to abduct you if you refused me ... carry you off.'

'Like your damned Welsh ancestor did?' She began to laugh. 'I always thought that was such a romantic tale. I've never been to Wales.'

He placed a kiss against her ear. 'I was thinking more of Longmore Hall for a destination. It's closer, and more convenient. Come back with me now, so we can tell my mother. She'll be so pleased. Your family can join us by the by for a celebration dinner.'

Later, they watched the sun go down from the terrace. It was harvest time and the air was shimmering with dust from the wheat.

Inside the drawing room, Blythe was telling the story of her brush with death, and her sisters were teasing her, and giggling at the thought that she'd fired the treasure into the cove.

'Another legend to attach to Longmore Hall,' Alexis whispered. 'Do you suppose Weatherby made it up about the gold being the grapeshot?'

Kynan chuckled. 'Weatherby can be ingenious, but as long as it prevents Blythe from pulling Longmore Hall down around my ears to find it, I don't care if he made it up or not.'

'It's a good ending to the tale.'

He turned her against him as the sun began to slide into the sea, as the water became molten gold and the sky turned to glowing cinnamon. She could smell the spice of his skin.

'But this is a better one.'

But when his lips touched against hers, Alexis knew it wasn't an ending at all, just a very perfect beginning.